S'

HEAVENLY PEACE INN TWO

Malinda Martin

Other Books by Malinda Martin

Castle Clubhouse Romance Series

A Change of Plans
The Movie Star and the Mom
The Write One
Where There's Smoke

Christmas in Charity Series

Christmas Grace
Comfort and Joy
Merry Mary
Carol of the Bells

Beaumont Family Series

Heartthrob
Heart and Soul
Heart Attack
Heartbreak

The Biggest Part of Me

Christmas Dad

Sleep In Heavenly Peace Inn

Forgetting Christmas

Would you like a free love story? Just go to

www.malindamartin.com

and enter your name and email in the form.

Dedicated with love to my Granddaddy,
Edwin Johnson,
who's enjoying Christmas from heaven.
He always gave the best hugs and would have
made the perfect Santa Claus.

Chapter One

Mary Michaels felt an itch between her shoulder blades and not one that meant she needed a backscratcher. Something was coming, something that would change lives. But if there was anything that the Sleep In Heavenly Peace Inn excelled in, it was in changing lives.

She'd long ago decided to stop questioning the magic of the inn, knowing that Angela, the manager, would continue to mysteriously know things, the owner would continue to remain benevolent and secretive, and she, her husband Joe, and son Bradley would continue to live and work there with a great deal of happiness.

Pausing from her chore of dusting and glancing out the window, she took a moment to appreciate the beautiful countryside of Vermont, covered with a blanket of snow, the bright blue sky a deep contrast. The weather had been perfect for business this year and reports were that it would continue. Unlike the terrible blizzard they'd had two years ago. Much had changed in that time, and she couldn't be happier. Mary had everything she could ever want. She sighed.

A quick survey of the cozy parlor showed her all was in order, with plump couches and chairs, tables with puzzles at the ready, shelves full of interesting books, and a large hearth already cracking with a comforting fire, ready for the arrival of their guests, as was she. Just as soon as she finished dusting the small table next to the window.

"Mom? Where do you want me to put my shoe?"

It was an unusual question, even from her seven-year old son, who knew better than to be yelling in the inn. "Bradley, you know you aren't suppose to yell inside," she yelled.

Mary was glad Angela was out in the barn and Joe was on his way back from the airport to miss her hypocrisy.

The young boy appeared in the doorway clothed in his heavy coat, woolen hat, his cheeks pink from the cold weather. Holding a sneaker dripping in mud.

She gasped. "Bradley! You're making a mess all over the foyer!" She dropped her duster and ran to take the shoe from him, her eyes following the trail that disappeared down the hall to the kitchen door.

"It wasn't my fault. The mud puddle just came out of nowhere."

"Why didn't you have on your boots?" She handed the shoe back to him and took off her apron to use as a mop. As she cleaned, Bradley followed, carrying the offending shoe and unbeknownst to her, making another muddy trail.

"I forgot. I was in the kitchen getting a drink of water and when I looked out the window I saw the best dog in the world! He was big and hairy and he was smiling at me. Then he turned around and started running away. I couldn't let him get away before I met him." He paused and as if thinking to impress his mother with his manners, said, "That would be rude."

Mary snorted. "So you didn't take the time to put your boots on, got it."

"Yeah, he ran to the mud by the hot pool."

"Tub."

"Yeah, tub. So, where do you want me to put this shoe?"

"How about outside so we can hose it down. By the way, what happened to the—"

She opened the door to the kitchen and froze at the sight. A furry monster was currently making himself comfortable on her clean, polished floor, his body squirming and shaking, flinging mud everywhere. Mary heard a scream and a second later realized it was her.

The dog looked up, gave Bradley a doggy smile and then bolted over, his big body knocking the boy down on his bottom. After a loud bark, the dog pushed through the door and down the hall.

"Noooo!" Mary gathered her wits and tore off after the dog. He'd made it to the front parlor before she found him, making himself at home on one of the couches. She calmed her voice and said, "All right, dog. It's time you came with me. Okay? I have a treat for you in the kitchen. Don't you want a delicious treat?"

The dog cocked his head with an expression that seemed to show his amusement. She could almost hear him thinking, “You think I’m that stupid?” Mary walked carefully toward the couch, getting ready to grab the dog. There was no collar, nothing she could grab. Which meant she was going to have to wrap her arms around the dog and drag him out.

After another couple of steps, she quickly jumped onto the couch, just as the dog moved away, barking at the new game. Bradley joined into the fray, trying to corral the happy dog. Neither could grab hold and the dog slipped back into the foyer, lying on his back on the wood floor, emitting a contented moan as he wiggled back and forth. When Mary and Bradley caught up with him, the game began again. She was so engrossed in chasing the dog, she didn’t notice the front door opening.

She made a desperate last lunge and captured the dog against her body. “Aha, now I’ve got you.” Sensing they weren’t alone, she glanced at the door.

Their guests had arrived.

Two of the four guests appeared bewildered. The other two, a handsome couple, arm-in-arm, grinned. Mary let out a frustrated breath.

Before she could say anything, the back door opened and Angela came in, her eyes coming to rest on the dog. Mary watched in awe as the dog settled in her grasp, his tongue hanging from his mouth, panting, staring at the inn’s manager.

"Well, what do we have here?"

"I am so sorry, Angela. I'm afraid we had an unexpected guest drop in. We'll get the dog outside and the inn back in order immediately." Her face heated as she faced her guests and said, "Ah, welcome, everyone."

She stood just as her husband Joe, the inn's handyman, came in carrying luggage. When he grinned at the sight of the dog, Bradley, her, and a mud-splattered foyer, she wanted to slug him. His eyes went to the panting dog. "I don't believe I've met our new decorator." The one couple chuckled. Mary hoped they all didn't just turn around and head out the door.

She pushed back her dark hair, now sporting a speck or two of mud and walked forward. "I'm so sorry for the mess, folks." She glared at the dog, who seemed to smile at her. "Please come in and Angela will get you settled."

"Joe, perhaps you can take the dog outside," Angela said, not moving an inch. Joe immediately walked to the dog, picking him up and heading out the back door. Angela clapped her hands together, as if the last few minutes had not been chaos or the inn was not a mess of mud and dog slobber. "We are so glad to have you folks for the Christmas holidays. Please come over to the desk and I'll give you your keys.

"I am so sorry," Mary whispered as she walked past the woman to begin the cleanup.

In the kitchen, she found a remorseful Bradley waiting for her. "I put the shoe outside. Like you told me to."

She wanted to stay mad, wanted to scold and punish and lecture. But his big eyes, so like the father he had lost years ago, melted all anger away. With a slight grin, she said, "It *was* a cool dog." Walking to the mudroom, she pulled out all the cleaning supplies she'd need to set things to right.

Bradley followed. "Wasn't he? Can I keep him? Can I keep Fred?"

"Oh, hold on a minute. I think first—wait, Fred?"

"Yep. That's what I'm going to name him. Fred after Mr. Fred, the crossing guard at school."

Her interest peaked, she turned to him. "Ah, that's so nice. Very thoughtful that you'd name a pet after someone you admire."

"Huh? Nah, it's because Mr. Fred looks like a dog." Mary shook her head. "He has those droopy eyes and that big mustache and his hair—"

"Yes, I get it. But like I was saying, first we have to find out if the dog belongs to someone and return him. Even if he doesn't, we've already got one dog, one horse, three sheep, one cow, two chickens, and a duck out in the barn. I think that's plenty of animals, don't you?"

"But old rover is lonely for another dog. This one could be a playmate for him, don't you think?"

Her hands filled with rags and cleaners, she walked back to the kitchen. "Son, you know that the inn doesn't belong to us. We have to follow the owner's rules. He only takes in abused and homeless animals. Someone may be looking for this dog."

"But if they aren't?"

She sighed. "I'll see what Angela says." Bradley whooped and ran to the mudroom. "Hold on, just a minute." Her words had him sliding to a halt. "You helped make this mess by bringing that dog in so you're going to help clean it up." She threw a rag to him and said, "Let's get started."

Angela smiled warmly and then sat behind her desk, ready to receive the guests.

A tall statuesque couple approached. Angela already liked them for their amusement over the dog. "I'm Darren Matthews and this is my wife Tricia. I believe we have a suite?" he said with a slight southern drawl.

The couple was striking, each tall, with brown hair, although his was a lighter shade while hers was a deep mahogany. The man smiled easily as he looked around whereas the wife wrapped her arm around his, waiting for their key.

"Of course, Mr. Matthews. You and your wife have the 'It's a Wonderful Life Suite.' Here's your key. It's the last door on the right on the second floor. Joe will be right up with your luggage."

"Thank you." The couple started for the stairs and the wife turned to ask, "When is dinner?"

"Dinner is served each night at six-thirty."

The woman, Tricia, gave her husband a knowing smile. "Perfect. Come on, darlin.'" Darren gave a nod and followed his wife upstairs.

Angela watched them go, wondering when she'd seen a happier couple. Well, that was about to change. She'd have to be vigilant, compassionate, see that they both got the understanding they needed.

"Excuse, but we are waiting."

She turned back to the beautiful and irritated woman with the foreign accent standing before her. Her hair, which was styled in an elegant chignon at the back of her neck, was dark as midnight, her eyes wide and golden. Her face was beautiful, the makeup applied perfectly. Unfortunately, she was not smiling.

"I'm sorry. You are—"

"Natasha Safina. My manager made the reservations. I am performing in Stowe, Vermont."

"Yes, dear, I know."

The man behind her quickly inserted himself. "And I am Franklin Murray, pianist extraordinaire. Perhaps you have heard of mc." The man's intonation was precise, very proper British.

"Well, of course I've heard of you and Miss Safina. That's why we booked you two."

The twosome glanced at each other and then at Angela. "You mean we are performing . . . here? At little inn?" Natasha began muttering in Russian, explaining why she didn't think it was a good idea and her plans for her manager once she got a hold of him. Angela wondered if she should tell the woman that she spoke fluent Russian.

"I'm sorry, but I am a little confused. You mean our manager booked us to perform here?"

Franklin looked around. "At the Sleep In Heavenly Peace Inn? I don't understand."

"We decided to spice things up this year and have live entertainment. Now, we'll expect you nightly in the parlor—Mr. Murray, we have a small spinet there and Miss Safina . . . well, you have your own violin. Then from ten to eleven, in our small lounge. There we have a keyboard. We have a lovely music room down the hall with another piano. It's very quiet there. You two are welcome to practice there anytime you wish." She handed a key to each of them. "Miss Safina, you have 'The Grinch that Stole Christmas' room and Mr. Murray, the 'White Christmas' room. Second floor. Joe will have your bags up soon.

The woman became incensed. "I do not have suite? I must have suite to meditate. To practice. I cannot be my best if I have to live in little room."

"We only have one suite and it's been booked for months. But I'm sure you'll enjoy our Grinch room. It is quite charming."

"And what is Grinch?" Franklin was chuckling under his breath.

"It's a famous book from Dr. Seuss about a . . . well, there's a copy in your room. When you get the chance perhaps you'd like to read it. It really is a wonderful story."

"I do not want to read medical book by this doctor." Again, she began muttering in Russian about the ridiculousness of the situation and the ancestry of her despised manager. She turned away pulling out her phone, clearly to get said manager on the line.

Franklin watched her, shaking his head, then turned to Angela. "I'm sure the rooms will be satisfactory, Ms. . . ."

"Just call me Angela, Mr. Murray." Ignoring Natasha's rants, she added, "We are all very much looking forward to hearing you two perform. I'll see you at dinner tonight."

"Yes, thank you." Franklin walked to the stairs, also ignoring Natasha, who followed him, her rantings echoing through the inn.

She breathed deeply and looked heavenward, praying for strength. Glancing down at the reservation book, she smiled. They weren't finished receiving guests yet.

It was shaping up to be an interesting Christmas.

Chapter Two

Bradley loved the Christmas holidays. Not just because he was a kid and all kids loved Christmas, but because he got to spend it here at the inn, with his mother and stepfather. There were always new people checking in and sometimes there were other kids. He liked that best. Since Christmas was right around the corner, he had his fingers crossed that families with children would be checking in.

As he sat at the small desk in the kitchen, his mother busy making dinner, he worked on his Christmas list for Santa. After today, he added another item and put stars by it. "My very own dog." Surely Santa would know the one he meant.

After he'd finished cleaning with his mom, which seemed to take forever, he put his boots on and ran outside to find the dog. His papa had prepared a nice bath for the dog in the barn and was cleaning him off, or her, as Papa had informed him. That was after the mud puddle by the hot pool had been filled in. Why didn't grownups like mud puddles?

"Bradley, would you help me get the food out?"

"Sure." He folded up his list and stuck in the drawer to put in an envelope later, then grabbed two baskets with hot rolls to set on the dining room buffet for the guests. Eyeing one, he wondered if his mother would notice if he snuck one. Of course she would. One time she told him that mothers have eyes in the back of their heads, which was a pretty gross image but true as far as he was concerned.

As he was coming back to the kitchen to get more food, his papa walked in. Bradley watched as he went to his mother who was standing by the stove and wrapped his arms around her middle, kissing her on the neck. She chuckled and turned her head so she could kiss him on the mouth. Eww! Okay, he was glad they were married and that Joe was his stepdad, but really, they'd been married forever and were still kissing!

"Hey, Papa."

He turned and grinned. "Hey, partner. Helping your mom?"

"Yeah. Do you think you can mail my letter to Santa tomorrow?"

Papa grabbed a homemade French fry that had fallen on the counter and munched it, moaning. Bradley's mother playfully slapped his hand. After a quick kiss on her cheek, he said, "Be glad to. You sure you're finished?"

"Uh-huh. But it needs to go out soon so's Santa can get me everything I want." He heard his mother's sigh and hoped that didn't mean they were going to have a talk about the list. He purposefully did not want her to see it. It was a secret between him and Santa.

Papa smiled at him. Of course he understood. That's one of the many things he liked about the man. "Okay, buddy. Let's get the chow out so we can have our own dinner."

They were just finishing that task when they heard the front door open and Angela exclaim, "There you are. Am I glad to see you two."

Bradley went running to glimpse the new guests and when he spied them, let out a cheer. "Sam! Eldon! You're back!" He flew to Sam, the big man that was the spitting image of Santa Claus and threw his arms around him. "We haven't seen you in forever!"

Sam chuckled, not exactly a "ho, ho, ho" but very close. "Now it hasn't been that long." After a big hug, he held Bradley back and said, "My, just look at you. Why Bradley, I'll bet you've grown a foot since the last time I saw you."

Smiling, he said, "Yeah. And look?" He opened his mouth to show the man he was missing one of his two front teeth."

The short man accompanying Sam smirked as he approached Bradley. "Hey, kid. Don't tell me all you want for Christmas is your one front tooth." He looked just like an elf. That is, if an elf was a little taller than Bradley, and if an elf could have a sour disposition.

Bradley frowned at the man. "Why would I want teeth for Christmas?"

Sam laughed again. "He's got you there, Eldon. Angela, have you got our favorite room ready?"

"The 'Frosty the Snowman' room all ready to go."

"Wonderful."

"And you're just in time for dinner. I believe we're having macaroni and cheese, broiled broccoli, fruit salad, and homemade rolls."

"Yum, yum." Sam rubbed his hands together. "Mary makes the best rolls."

"What's for dessert?" Eldon asked.

Angela smiled. "Your favorite. Cherry pie."

The usually sullen Eldon actually sighed with satisfaction, causing the others to chuckle.

Everyone was introduced at dinner. As usual, Angela sat at the head of the table, making everyone feel at home. The Matthews sat on one side, Darren very cordial to the others, and Tricia, her attention completely on her husband.

Natasha sat next to Tricia and basically ignored the woman. Apparently, she was still fuming over her assignment and accommodations. Franklin sat on the other side of the table, at the other end from Natasha, quiet and keeping to himself. Eldon was next to him, too busy shoving in food to take the time to converse with anyone.

Sam was next to Angela, giving her looks throughout the meal. As the silence continued, she finally said, "Well, I hope everyone had a nice trip to Stowe." When no one volunteered an answer, she said, "Mr. and Mrs. Matthews, where did you travel from?"

He looked up and said, "Atlanta, Georgia."

"Wonderful. I've heard Atlanta is a very nice place to live. What do you do there?"

"I'm a dentist. My wife runs my business."

The sound of barking interrupted their conversation followed by Mary's voice. "Out! Out, you! Bradley, take that dog back to the barn."

Angela chuckled. "I assume one of our guests is not happy with her accommodations in the barn."

"No problem," Darren said, laughing. "I assume it's a newly acquired dog?"

"You could say that. Actually, the dog just showed up and unfortunately Bradley is ready to put a collar on her and name her 'Fred.'"

"Fred?" Tricia asked as Darren laughed.

"He didn't know the dog was female."

"Oh. Well, how about Frederica? I've always loved that name," Tricia said and Darren nodded.

"It is a nice name. I'll suggest it to Bradley." Angela cocked her head. "Do you have pets, Mrs. Matthews?"

"Yes, we do." She was at once bright-eyed, a smile covering her face. "We have two adorable Persian cats, Lucy and Ricky." She pulled a small wallet out of her purse and pulled out a picture, beaming at the photograph. "Here are my little sweethearts." The picture was passed to Angela who took the time to study it.

"My, my. Aren't they adorable? Now let me guess. Lucy is gray and Ricky is white."

Tricia giggled. "That's correct. Usually people think the opposite." She accepted the photo after it made it around the table. "They both are such darlings. Very affectionate. The best part of our coming home at the end of the day."

"I'm afraid we spoil them rotten," Darren said, putting his arm around his wife. "But as you can see, we love 'em."

"Understandable. We here at the inn love animals also."

Quiet resumed as everyone continued eating. Angela wiped her mouth and turned to Darren. "Do you two plan to do any skiing while you're here?"

"Sure." Darren turned to Tricia. "I've got to talk my wife into letting me teach her."

"Darlin,' I don't know if I should try. I don't want to get hurt. It might hurt our chances . . . you know." Her eyebrows lifted and lowered several times and Darren turned beet red. No one commented but seemed extremely interested in their dinner.

Tricia glanced at Angela and then back to Darren. "In fact, you may not see much of us during our stay. We'll be rather busy. Making a baby."

Angela dropped her fork, Eldon choked on his food, and Sam coughed loudly. Franklin grinned and Natasha did no more than lift a haughty brow.

Chancing a glance at the swinging kitchen door, hoping Bradley wasn't listening in, Angela cleared her throat. "Well, I've always believed that children are a gift from God."

She studied the couple, uneasy by their reactions. Darren patted his wife's hand, as if placating her, then dug into his mac and cheese. Tricia sighed dreamily and picked at her broccoli. They were clearly out of synch.

Angela turned slightly and said, "How about you, Miss Safina? Where are you from? You have a beautiful accent."

The woman looked up, as if surprised that anyone had addressed her. Her face bland, she said, "I am from Moscow. That is where I was born."

"I see. How long have you been in our country?"

A fearful look spread on her face as her cheeks grew pale. "I have green card. Everything is legal."

"Yes, dear, I'm sure it is. I was only asking—"

"You may call my manager and . . . what is word . . . verify. I have right to be here."

"For God's sake, Natasha, the woman's not from the I.C.E. She's just making conversation." Franklin didn't take the time to look up from his food.

Her breathing heavy, Natasha said, "I will play for you Ms. . . . Angela. But please, no questions."

"Of course. And I apologize for making you feel uncomfortable. As long as you're here, please feel at home."

Angela turned to Franklin. "That leaves you, Mr. Murray. Please tell us about yourself."

Evidently pleased to be the center of attention, the man sat straight and smiled. He cleared his throat and in a clear English accent said, "I am a concert pianist, Angela. Having played with the London Symphony Orchestra, the Vienna Philharmonic, and the Boston Symphony Orchestra for many years, I have settled down with the New York Philharmonic."

"What wonderful credentials. We are so delighted to have you here."

He nodded his head. "Thank you."

"Do you play often with Miss Safina?"

His cheerful expression immediately closed into what could only be called a sneer. "Miss Safina and I rarely perform together. Our manager made the arrangements. Without our consent, I will add. But it is what it is and I promise that *I* will give our performance the very best I have. Now if you would be so kind to pass the rolls?" Franklin took one, buttered it, and ate. Visibly finished with the conversation.

Before Angela could say anything, Franklin looked up and met the golden, furious eyes of Natasha. Emotions flared into a fevered pitch as they stared at one another, neither giving an inch. Tension filled the air, so thick she wondered how it didn't strangle them all.

The meal continued, in silence. Angela glanced at Sam, who lifted his eyebrows. She gave him a shrug.

It was going to be a long holiday season.

Following dinner, Sam helped Angela get the parlor ready. The spinet piano was set up near the bookcases. Next to it stood a music stand, ready for Natasha's music. Mary hurried in carrying a tray of cups, saucers, spoons, sugar, and cream. Joe followed with an urn of fresh coffee, set up by the fireplace.

Bradley came in and looked through the shelf of children's puzzles. After finding one, he plopped down at a table and dumped the pieces out. The boy worked with little interest, as if he wanted to be elsewhere so Sam walked over and sat with him.

"What's going on with you?"

"Huh? Nothing." Bradley sighed, reaching through the pieces. "Nothing at all."

Sam leaned forward to help him pick out the end pieces. "Are you ready for Christmas?"

He shrugged. "Yeah, I guess."

Frowning, Sam said, "You don't sound like a kid ten days out from Christmas. What gives?"

Bradley looked up. "I was just hoping for some kids to be staying here during Christmas. I wanted somebody to play with."

"Oh. I'm sure Eldon and I can make snowmen with you. Angela's planning the annual ice-skating party for the area. And Joe will play with you, when he can."

"That's just it. You adults all have stuff to do. And sometimes I just need another kid."

Sam smiled. "Don't give up hope. Maybe you'll get a new playmate."

Bradley brightened. "Well, I did meet someone today, and I'm thinking through my plan to get Mom to let me keep him. I mean, her."

His head spinning, Sam said, "I'm not sure I follow you."

"My dog. I met her today, in the backyard. I wanted to name him Fred but Papa said he was a girl so we'll call her Frederica. Papa and I cleaned her up and she's out in the barn now, meeting the other animals since Mom said she couldn't come inside."

"Ah, yes. I heard about your . . . mishap today."

Natasha and Franklin entered the room and begin warming up, Franklin on the piano and Natasha on her violin. Bradley watched. He leaned his head in his hand and sighed heavily. In a loud whisper he said, "Now I have to sit here and listen to fancy music. Mom said."

Sam hid a smile. "You never know, you might like the music. I'll bet they play some Christmas tunes, something you know."

"You think so? Think they'll play 'Jingle Bells' or something fun like that?"

"Possibly. Let's give them a chance."

The Matthews wandered in and sat together on a large couch, speaking in soft tones. Mary offered everyone coffee and sat at a table with Joe.

Franklin cleared his throat and standing, said, "We are pleased to bring to you tonight a series of holiday music to put you in a festive mood. Enjoy." After a flourishing bow, he sat to the applause of the group.

The first number was the march from The Nutcracker Suite. From there they played the Sussex Carol, The Holly and the Ivy, and Carol of the Bells. Sam knew them all. Bradley, however, looked bored, his eyes drooping.

After the next round of applause, Franklin again stood and said, "Thank you, thank you, ladies and gentlemen. We have one more song we'd like to play for you at this time, but if you'd like more, we'll be in the lounge at ten. He sat and seeing that Natasha was ready, he lifted his hands in preparation to play the first chord.

The front door opened and a voice called out, "Hello?" causing him his hands to jerk, landing on the incorrect notes. Natasha giggled and Franklin glared.

"Now, I wonder who that could be?" Angela stood and said, "Excuse me," walking into the hallway.

Franklin quickly regrouped and started playing the famous song, "White Christmas." Bradley muttered, "Finally, something I actually know."

As they were getting to the final few bars, Angela walked in with a young couple, the woman holding the hand of a small girl. Sam gauged the woman to be in her early to mid twenties. Her expression was tentative, but friendly as her blue eyes took in her surroundings, her short sunny hair and smile making him like her already.

The man was just as young. He had his cap in his hands, nervously fingering the edges, his sandy hair falling in his eyes.

And the little girl. His heart immediately clenched at her obvious injuries. Her hair was a white blonde, almost the color of snow. Her little face was a study of confusion and worry. And something was wrong with one of her eyes. It was a puffy and almost shut. Sam watched her with concern.

When the little girl saw him, her tiny face immediately brightened. He smiled back.

Once the twosome finished their song and everyone applauded, Angela announced that they had a few new guests.

"I'd like to introduce our new guests. Seeing Mary's confused expression, she said, "They've had a bit of car trouble. It was a good thing they saw our lights and headed down our driveway. Their car seemed to die just in front of our inn."

"Just up and died right in front of our inn, huh?" Mary whispered to Angela.

Angela cleared her throat. "This is Miss Stephanie Singer. She's a social worker from Burlington. And this is Mr. Tyler Buchanan. He's employed at the Orphanage in Newport. Sam, you remember that place. You did some work for them a while ago."

"I remember. It's a fine establishment. How are you, Tyler?"

The young man grinned, accepting Sam's hand. "Fine. Good to see you, sir. It's been a while."

Angela crouched down and put her arm around the little girl. "And this is Christy. Stephanie is escorting her to the orphanage." She turned to the little girl, smiling warmly. "But now it looks like she'll be staying a few days here with us. We're very glad to have you."

Bradley jumped up from the table and walked to the little girl. "Hi, I'm Bradley. You'll like it here. There's lots to do. I'll show you around on account of you don't know anything."

"Bradley," Mary said under her breath.

He turned and looked up at his mother. "Well, she don't."

Mary took Angela aside. "We only have one room available."

"That's fine. I gave Miss Singer and Christy the 'Miracle on Thirty-Fourth Street Room.' Mr. Buchanan can have the little room off the kitchen that Joe used to live in." She turned back to her guests and said, "Now you three must be starving. Why don't you come on in the dining room and I'll get some food for you."

"Thank you, ma'am."

"Yes, we really appreciate it. I don't know what we'd have done if Tyler hadn't seen your light." The woman turned to look at the man, whose eyes blinked a couple of times before he stepped backwards, tripping over the piano bench and falling into the keys, making a cacophony of sound.

"Careful there." Franklin helped him back up and subtly put the top down over the keys.

"If anyone else would like a little snack, or," she glanced at Eldon, "another piece of cherry pie, come on with me to the dining room."

As the group left the parlor, Angela turned to see Sam sitting on a couch, the little girl Christy in his lap. He smiled, patting her back as her tiny voice carried.

"A-a-and I'd like a b-baby doll with a bottle, a-and a Candyland game, and mama and d-d-daddy Barbie d-dolls."

Chapter Three

The Matthews opted to forgo the snack and retreated to their suite. Tricia was ready to be alone with her husband.

"That was fun." Darren stretched on the bed, closing his eyes. "But I'm exhausted. The trip up really tuckered me out."

She lay next to him and fingered a few locks of his hair. "Are you really that tired?"

"I am, yeah." He yawned and she tried not to take offense. "I'll need a good night's sleep if I'm going to hit the slopes in the morning." He snapped his fingers and said, "Oh, that's right. You don't know if you're going to ski. Since it might hurt our chances . . . you know." His eyes still closed, he moved his eyebrows up and down.

Something in his tone had her cocking her head and narrowing her eyes. "Darren. Is something wrong?

"What? No." He paused, then said, "Actually, yeah." He took her hand and turned to face her. "You know that I'm glad to be here with you, it was a great idea to come here for the holidays, away from everything at home, and be together."

"I know. Especially since the doctor said we may be more likely to conceive if we go someplace new."

A huff escaped his lips. "That's the thing." He rubbed the hand he held between both of his. "You know I want to have a baby." He hesitated. "But honey, you're telling everyone, strangers at dinnertime even, about our plans . . . it makes me uncomfortable."

"It does?"

"Not only that. The innuendos about us, implying that we're up here 'doing it' . . ." He shook his head. "I'm feeling . . . more like a prize stud than a husband."

"Aww." She kissed his jaw. "You're my prize stud." Her hands went to his shirt and started unbuttoning it, kissing the skin uncovered.

"Honey, you're not listening to me." Her hands continued their exploration until he finally grabbed them and pulled them away. "Tricia, no. I'm tired."

Now she was offended. "All right, why don't you take a shower and relax. It might give you a second wind."

He dropped her hands and stood up, pacing the room. "I don't want a second wind tonight, I just want to unwind. Can't we just enjoy this beautiful inn, not think about a baby, just enjoy being together?"

"Of course we enjoy being together. That's why we're going to make wonderful parents. We have a solid, loving relationship."

"True, but I'm getting a little tired of talking about becoming a parent."

His words felt like a slap in the face to Tricia. He had to know how important being a mother was to her. It was what she dreamed of, the fulfillment of their love. Without a child she somehow felt she was missing out. She wasn't let in on the magical element that gave purpose to living.

She knew Darren wanted children. However, as they got older, the ticking clock grew louder. It was the perfect time to get pregnant, they were at a romantic inn surrounded by the love of the season and he was tired?

"You know there are only so many days a month that I'm fertile."

"Yes, I know," he said, having the audacity to roll his eyes like he'd heard that many times before.

"Well, we're coming into that peak time. I don't want to miss our chance."

"Tricia, we're in the mountains in Stowe, Vermont for the holidays. How often do we get that chance? I want to enjoy the scenery, enjoy the skiing and whatever else we can find without any pressure."

"And I want to have a baby."

His expression hardened. Perhaps she was pushing too hard. The doctor had warned her about that.

He took a breath and grabbed his coat. "I need some air. I'm going out for a walk. Then to the lounge for a drink. Good night."

"Darren, don't go. Please."

"I need to cool off, Tricia. Go on to bed." Just before he left he added, "Oh, and I'm going skiing in the morning. You're welcome to join me. Or not."

The door closed firmly behind him, leaving Tricia sitting on the bed confused.

Sighing heavily, she stood and took a moment to tell herself it wasn't the end of the world if Darren wanted some time to think. He had always been a good husband, careful not to spew words in the heat of a discussion that would harm their relationship. They'd work this out, like they did with any other problem. There was nothing to worry about.

She looked around to truly appreciate the suite they were staying in. It was decorated in, of course, reds and greens. A lovely seating area faced a fireplace with a charming Christmas village on the mantel. A heavy oak dresser anchored the room, topped with framed pictures from the famous movie "It's a Wonderful Life." She picked up one that seemed to draw her. It showed George Bailey, his face glowing, his four children hanging on to him. Tricia's heart squeezed and she couldn't stop the tears that came to her eyes. She felt a sob bubble up and escape her throat.

No, she wouldn't cry. This was their time, their chance to be away from the pressures of life and make that baby that they wanted so desperately. She set the picture down and sniffed, blinking back the tears. She'd be positive, happy. That would help, wouldn't it? She'd be loving and caring with Darren, going with him skiing in the morning. They'd have the best time while here.

And surely they'd leave with a baby on the way.

The bitter cold temperatures helped him calm down. He didn't want to fight with Tricia. He loved his wife, as much as the day he'd said "I do," even more. But her obsession with having a baby was slowly driving him crazy.

He'd hoped that the intense desire for a child would lessen when they got away from all their nieces and nephews, all their friends' children and just concentrated on each other. He'd hoped for a second honeymoon but the pressure seemed to have followed them. How had they come to this?

He wanted a baby, sure, but more than that he wanted his wife back. For him that would be the best Christmas present of all.

Following his walk, he entered the lounge in the inn. It was small but warm and inviting with dark wood paneling and a fire blazing in the hearth.

Natasha and Franklin played softly and several tables were filled with people that Darren guessed were from the area, not staying at the inn.

"Mr. Matthews, what can I get you?" Joe stood behind the bar ready to serve.

After Darren gave him his order, he sat on one of the dark leather stools in front of him.

"You been outside?" Joe asked motioning to the flakes of snow on Darren's heavy coat.

"Went for a little walk." He removed the coat, laying it on the stool next to him. He rubbed his chilly hands together. "Nice piece of property you got here."

"That it is," Joe said placing his drink in front of him. "Got some nice cross country trails out back. The pond has frozen over nicely. It'll be ready for our big ice skating party next week. A few hills for sledding. Added a firepit and some chairs last summer. And . . ." Joe glanced around and lowered his voice. "We got a hot tub in the back that's really nice to take the missus to." He winked.

Darren tried not to flinch at the implied hint. Was he now going to get suggestions and winks from everyone at the inn?

About that time, the young man, Tyler, came in taking off his heavy coat, hat, and gloves, his eyes blinking and his shoulders drooped.

"Come on in, buddy," Joe said. "Let me treat you to a drink. Looks like you could use one."

Tyler cleared his throat. "Yeah." After glancing around, he said, "Nice crowd here tonight."

"It is. Since we've got Miss Safina and Mr. Murray, Angela spread the word through the surrounding area, inviting everyone over." He nodded at a middle-aged man sitting near Angela. "That's Tom. He owns the hardware store. Nice guy. And at the table next to him are Clara and Ann Thompson, sisters that have the quilting shop in Stowe."

Darren motioned to Sam and Eldon sitting with Angela. "What's the story with them?"

Joe smiled widely. "Sam and Eldon. They come through periodically. My understanding is they have a few businesses south of here. Never can seem to get a clear answer about where they come from. Best as I can tell, Sam's got a large spread north, probably in Canada."

"Oh yeah? He raise cattle?"

"Ah, no." A small smile came on his face when he said, "Reindeer."

Tyler nearly choked on his drink.

Darren said, "What? You've got to be kidding me." He turned to study Sam. "What does he do with reindeer."

"Again, he's really vague about that. I know he takes in injured or lost reindeer. We had one wander onto the property a couple of years ago. I understand he took him back home with him."

"You don't know?"

"It's a long story. Anyway, all that to say the man, along with his friend Eldon, is a little bit of a mystery." He frowned. "To be honest, so is Angela."

"How so?"

Joe glanced at the woman in question and leaned on the bar, lowering his voice to speak to the two men. "The woman just seems to know things. It's strange. I don't normally question it as it helps us all in the end. And don't get me started about the owner."

Getting into the discussion, Tyler asked, "What about the owner."

Shaking his head, Joe said, "That's just it. Don't know him. Don't know his name. Only that Angela speaks fondly and almost reverently about him. I know that he loves this inn. Gives us anything we ask for. Treats us real well. Adamant about our keeping the barn available to take in wounded animals."

"I wanted to ask you about that," Darren said. "Angela mentioned a barn at dinner." Joe nodded. "I'd love to see the animals sometime."

"Anytime. A few of them are skittish so just keep your voice down and treat them very gently."

"I'd like to hear more about the owner," Tyler said.

"Oh, yeah." Continuing with his story, Joe leaned down on the bar. "When Mary and I married several years ago, we told Angela we wanted to invite the owner to our wedding. It wasn't big, just a quiet ceremony here in the inn. She said she'd send an invitation to him. We didn't think anymore about it until we got back from our honeymoon. There was a package for us—a DVD of the ceremony. We hadn't hired anyone to do that, hadn't even noticed anyone filming at the wedding. Angela told us, the owner had taken it himself."

"He was there? You didn't notice him?" Darren asked.

"I suppose since it was my wedding I was thinking of other things, but no I didn't notice him. The strange thing was neither did Bradley. Or anyone else that had been there." Joe stood straight and took a breath. "I try not to figure it out any more."

The two men each took a sip, simultaneously thinking as Joe wiped the shining bar.

Joe let out a breath and said, "You get all settled in, Mr. Buchanan?"

"Oh, please call me Tyler. Mister makes me feel old." Darren and Joe shared a look. "Yeah, I'm good. I can't tell you how much I appreciate your taking us in on such short notice."

"No problem. Not too fancy being next to the kitchen, but seeing how it was my room before I married, I know it's comfortable."

Mary entered behind the bar and put clean dishtowels in drawers. "Hi, honey," Joe said, to which she grinned up at him. He turned back to Tyler. "Got any idea what's wrong with your car?"

Tyler shook his head. "It was fine when we set out from Burlington. When we were about a dozen miles from here I noticed it start to act up, shaking, making noises. Once I spotted your sign it started just shutting down. Lucky I was able to make it down the driveway.

Joe grinned and said, "Yeah. Lucky."

"Miss Singer and the little girl okay?" Darren asked.

He looked down at his drink and said, "I'm sure. Stephanie's really smart." A slight blush started on his face, causing Joe and Darren to share another look.

Joe asked, "So, she's traveling with you to take the little girl to the orphanage?" Tyler nodded. "She must be smart. And reliable to be responsible for the child." Another nod. "You known her long?"

"Three years." The tips of Tyler's ears were red as he took a sip of his beer.

Joe and Darren both grinned. Time to have some fun. Darren cleared his throat and leaned close to Tyler. "You kinda like her?"

"What? No! Of course not. I mean, yeah, we're . . . co-workers. It's our job to get Christy to the orphanage safely."

"You got a girlfriend, Tyler?" Joe asked.

"Me? No." He took another drink.

"Is Miss Singer involved with anyone?" Darren asked.

"No." His blush deepened. "I mean, she might have mentioned that she wasn't seeing anyone."

Darren raised a brow. "She's an attractive woman, Tyler. Intelligent, friendly. Might want to get to know her."

Tyler's eyes flew up, glancing at each man. "I . . ." His gaze dropped. "I don't think I'm her type."

"Why not? You seem like a nice guy. Never hurts to just ask for a date, just get to know each other."

"Yeah, what could it hurt?"

Tyler thought about it. "She could say no."

"Then you'd have an answer," Joe said. "And you wouldn't be turning red in a bar whenever the woman's name is mentioned." When he went beet red, Joe chuckled and Darren slapped him on the back.

"Women!" Franklin muttered and slammed his hand on the bar. "Mr. Puletti, would you please give me a double scotch, straight."

"Sure. Pull up a stool, Mr. Murray."

"I only have ten minutes before I have to get back to . . . hell," he muttered taking a fortifying gulp of the drink Joe put before him.

The men watched Natasha pull out a phone and leave the lounge. Franklin grunted. "Good luck, darling. You're just as stuck with me as I am with you."

Darren draped an arm around Franklin's shoulders. "Mr. Murray, you're in good company. Am I right, Tyler?"

"Amen, brother."

They all turned to Joe. He held his hands up. "Don't look at me, gentlemen. I have no trouble with my incredible wife," he said his voice raised.

Darren grinned. "She left the bar a few minutes ago, Joe."

Joe glanced behind him. "Never hurts to cover all bases."

Chapter Four

Classical music played in the dining room as Mary entered, ready to clean up after breakfast. She stopped midstep when she saw Bradley sitting patiently in one of the chairs. "What are you doing here?"

"Miss Singer said that I could show Christy the animals in the barn. I'm waiting for them."

"Oh, I see."

Stephanie entered the room holding Christy's hand and Mary crouched to speak to the little girl. "I hear you're going to see our animals this morning." The girl had her thumb in her mouth and nodded. "They'll be glad to have a visitor. How about I bring a few treats that we can give them?" The girl again nodded.

"This is so nice. Thank you for showing us," Stephanie said.

"You'll love our barn, Christy," Bradley said, hopping off his chair. "The animals all like little kids. I can show you my newest dog."

As Mary took the remaining dishes into the kitchen, Bradley continued his explanation of the inn's barn to the silent Christy. Once she returned with several bags of goodies, she said, "Let's go."

"Come on, Christy." Bradley confidently walked over and took her hand. The little girl let go of Stephanie's hand and followed him to the kitchen.

Stephanie's mouth gaped. "That's amazing." Her eyes moistened as she faced Mary. "Christy's had a difficult time. She doesn't trust very many people. She must feel comfortable with your son."

Mary smiled widely. "He has a gift for that. Sometimes I think he's a better innkeeper than I am." Remembering the overzealous new dog in the barn, she said, "Let's catch up with them."

Bradley had already instructed Christy in barn behavior, which had made Mary giggle since she continually had to remind Bradley. They entered the barn quietly, Christy hanging on to Bradley's hand.

The new dog barked and, tail wagging, trotted over to Bradley for a rubdown. "This is the new dog. We're calling her Frederica on account of she's a girl and not a boy."

Christy's eyes lit up as she ran her hands on the dog's back.

The sheep decided to join the party at the point, bleating their way over to the children. Bradley showed her how to pet them and she giggled as they nudged her. The chickens cackled from their coop, as if admonishing them for disturbing their domicile. The cow, horse, and duck just ignored them.

"You've got a regular zoo in here," Stephanie said chuckling.

"Yes, I know. The occupants come and go but we've always got an interesting mix." Mary gave Bradley one bag and Christy the other. He helped her to distribute the snacks, the children enjoying the sights and sounds of the animals." Mary's eyes kept going to the new dog, studying it. There was something different about her.

When she finally figured it out, she shook her head. *Just great.*

"They like you, Christy. See, even ole Bessie the cow's smiling at you." The girl's face beamed at the compliment. "Hey, after this you want to play a game? I've got 'Chutes and Ladders' and 'Connect Four.'"

Back in the house, the two set up at a table in the parlor with a pile of games to play while Mary offered Stephanie coffee. When the two walked through the dining room, Mary stopped at the sight of Natasha sitting at the table, perfectly groomed, her fingers rubbing her eyes.

"Miss Safina? We missed you at breakfast. Can I get you something?"

The woman let out a deep breath. "Yes. I would very much like to have cup of coffee. I may need gallon."

"You didn't sleep well, I'm sorry. Was something wrong with your room?"

"No. The tiny green creatures did not keep me up."

To the Stephanie's puzzled look, Mary whispered, "She's in 'The Grinch Who Stole

Christmas' Room." Stephanie nodded her understanding.

"It is work related."

"I see. Well, Stephanie and I were just going to have coffee in the kitchen. Would you like to join us for conversation?"

"Thank you, Mrs. Puletti, but the quietness of this room is what I need. And the coffee, much, much, coffee."

"I'll be right back with that."

Mary served Natasha and then sat at the kitchen table with Stephanie. "It must be interesting being in social services."

"If by interesting you mean sad, you're right. At least some of the time. If I didn't think I was making a difference, helping children get into safe, loving homes, I think I would have gone crazy by now. But it's my life. My calling."

They both sipped their coffee. Looking down at hers, Mary said, "I don't suppose you can tell me about Christy."

"Not much, no. Unfortunately, it's a common story. Neither parent is a fit human being, much less a parent." She shook her head in disgust. "That poor little one has scars it will take her years to get over, if ever."

"The eye?"

Her eyes met Mary's and she nodded. "It's severely damaged. She can't open it fully but we're hopeful it can heal." Mary guessed it was probably a result of abuse. She squeezed her eyes shut, her heart aching for the little girl.

"The poor thing hardly speaks. She has a stutter when she does." Stephanie sighed wearily. "She's only four but still has a lot of work to do just to catch up to others her age."

"Why is she going to the orphanage? No one has come forward to adopt?"

"That's right. We could go the foster home route but in her condition, I think it would be detrimental. She doesn't need any moving around. She needs a stable place to grow to begin to heal."

"So Tyler is the orphanage liaison?"

Stephanie smiled. "Yes. Anytime we need help with a child, we call the orphanage in Newport. They are wonderful about helping us out." She took a sip and said, "Tyler felt so bad about his SUV conking out on us, but he's pretty handy. I'm sure we'll be out of your hair soon."

"Nonsense, you're welcome for as long as you need to be here. We love having guests. Obviously," she said with a smile. "And with Christy here, Bradley is occupied. And I get to have coffee with a new friend." She lifted her cup in salute.

Stephanie chuckled and clinked her cup to Mary's. "I agree.

Outside, Tyler was about to pull his hair out by the roots. Muttering a few words under his breath, he threw his rag down and peered under the hood.

"You better not let Santa hear you talking like that. He might not bring you anything for

Christmas." Joe grinned as he walked to Tyler's side.

"I'd just be happy with getting to Newport safely." He blew out a breath, the cold air causing smoke to fill the air. "Can't understand it. I've checked the battery, the transmission, plugs, belts. I can't see what's keeping the darn thing from running."

Joe leaned over to take a look. He prodded, twisted, pulled, and felt. His only response was "hmm."

"Yeah. That's what I said." Joe raised his eyebrows. "Well, maybe I said it a little more colorfully."

"Why don't I call a mechanic? We've got a real good one about five miles from here. He can come take a look and give an opinion. Then we'll go from there."

"I don't want to put you out more than I have."

"You're not putting us out. Glad to have you." Joe pulled out his phone and made the call. Once he was done, he said, "Harv will be out in a couple of hours. He's bringing his tow truck just in case he needs to take it back to his station."

"Oh, man." Tyler leaned back under the hood.

"So what's the verdict?"

The feminine voice caused Tyler to jerk up, banging his head on the inside of the hood. "Ouch."

"Tyler? Are you all right?" Stephanie advanced placing her hand on his arm.

Like being burned, he jerked his arm away, dropping his pliers into the engine. "Yeah, I'm . . . okay." He reached down into the car trying to locate the missing pliers. His fingers finally found the tool but bringing it up, his arm was wedged in, trapping him there. He tried to produce a casual pose, crossing his legs, letting his other hand lean on the engine. "I'm fine."

Joe shook his head and bit his lip to keep from laughing. "Here, why don't I help you with those pliers." He reached in and helped ease his arm out of the engine, taking the pliers from the man.

Brushing his hands together, Tyler said, "We're going to have to have a mechanic take a look."

"It's that bad?"

"I'm afraid so." He looked for the latch to close the hood. Just in time, Joe saw that the man's flannel shirt was reaching inside the engine and before he could slam it on his shirt, he took hold of the hood. Tyler glanced at him. Joe's eyes went to the long shirt tale that was dangling in the engine. Tyler swallowed hard and pulled it out, letting Joe handle the hood.

"So, what does that mean?"

Joe slammed the hood and turned to see Tyler's eyes big and dreamy on Stephanie, just staring. He was afraid the young man would start drooling. Wanting to help, he said, "Tyler, tell her what's going to happen now."

"Huh? Oh, the mechanic will come in a few hours. He might have to take the car in."

"We don't know how long we're staying here?"

Tyler was back to the staring. Joe elbowed him so maybe he'd focus on the conversation. "Ah, I guess that's right. I'm really sorry."

She gave him a warm smile and said, "It's not your fault. And if we had to be stranded anywhere I can't think of a better place." She chuckled. "Christy's having a ball." She turned to leave and Tyler let out a small sigh.

Once she'd left, Joe looked at the lovesick man and muttered, "Buddy."

Tyler moaned. "I know, I know. It's pretty bad. I thought I'd been doing a good job keeping my feelings hidden. But now? Having to be in her company for longer than a few hours? What if I blow it by doing something stupid?" Joe decided not to comment. "She's . . . she's beautiful, so beautiful inside and out. She could probably have any man she wants. Why in the world would she want to spend time with me?"

Joe had a warm spot for this young man. "I understand your pain." He put his arm around Tyler's shoulders and said, "Come on, let's take a walk and I'll tell you my story of how I caught the prettiest brunette with the softest heart I'd ever known."

"Well, what do you think?"

Angela watched Joe walk off with Tyler, her thoughts whirling. "I think it's a very good thing that Joe can befriend Tyler. It will be good for him."

She sat down at a small table by the window in the lounge. Sam joined her. "What do you think of our three couples?"

Sam reached up to stroke his white beard. "To be honest, I think the group of twenty preschoolers that Eldon and I entertained this morning were easier." Angela laughed. "The Matthews make me blush, you should have seen them in the van going to the ski resort, she couldn't keep her hands off him. Poor Tyler has a bad case of the 'clumseys.' I'm afraid he's going to seriously hurt himself. And those two musicians? Hate is a kind word to describe how they act toward each other."

"Yes, but things are not always as they seem."

"Hmm. Have you got plans?"

The edges of her lips lifted. "I always have plans. You didn't mention the new dog. She's a handful."

"Yeah, I heard. It's a lot. But Angela, this time is different." He paused and she cocked her head, waiting for him. "The little girl. I'm worried about her."

She gave a nod and teared up. "So am I. She deserves a wonderful Christmas, the start of a better life."

Sam sighed heavily. "Three couples, pregnant dog, a little girl. It's a lot. Is it all possible?"

"Sam. Haven't I taught you that all things are possible? Especially this time of year."

"We may need more help this time."

Angela motioned towards the window. “We have it. You saw Joe take that boy under his wing. I imagine Mary will do the same with Stephanie.”

Sam’s brows narrowed in thought. “You’re training them, aren’t you? Gonna teach them in our ways?

“Of course.” Angela smiled warmly, lifting a brow. “But they aren’t the only ones.”

Chapter Five

Franklin slammed his fingers on the baby grand in the music room. "You are impossible. Why won't you listen to a single idea I have?"

"Because your ideas are wrong."

"At least I didn't hit the wrong notes several times last night."

Natasha's eyes flared. "How dare you suggest I play wrong notes. I am professional. I know how to play Christmas music. Unlike others."

She was infuriating. There she stood, dressed in a pale blue pantsuit, makeup perfect, her shiny black hair in an elegant bun on top of her head. Her shoulders back, spine straight, did the woman ever relax?

Not wanting to argue, Franklin decided to switch gears. "Speaking of Christmas music, I thought we might try something else tonight." Her perfectly groomed eyebrows rose. "The little boy was completely bored with our performance. Let's play something for him and the little girl. Angela suggested 'Jingle Bells.' I'm sure they would both enjoy that, as would the adults."

Natasha frowned. "What is this . . . 'Jiggly Bells'? Never have I heard of such."

Franklin stared at her. "You've never heard of 'Jingle Bells'? You've got to be kidding." He proceeded to play a bouncing, fast-paced version of the song, watching Natasha. Amused that she had no recollection, he played it through again, slowing it down thinking surely she'd remember the familiar tune. Finishing with a flourish, he glanced up at Natasha and waited.

Her expression was bland, as if clearly unimpressed with his talent laid out in front of her. "That is 'Jiggly Bells'? I will not play silly song."

"Fine. You can listen while I play it tonight." Irritated, Franklin stood and crossed his arms.

"No. You will not take time away from my performance!"

"No problem, I'll play it during our break. That okay with you?"

They were standing toe to toe, glaring at each other. Natasha's eyes narrowed as she said, "Do you know you lose accent when angry?"

Franklin's gut clenched. Had he really forgotten? How could he let her get to him? His mind again focused as he remembered that his profession, his success was everything. Nothing or no one else mattered.

He took a calming breath, straightened his sweater, and sat back at the piano. Clearing his throat, he said, "How about we take it from page five, second movement, bar two. You missed the change in tempo there."

"I—" She worked hard to keep her composure and said, "It is allegretto, I see."

He counted off and they drifted back into playing, the notes melding together into a harmonious declaration of joy. A dissonant tone sounded, causing each to immediately stop playing. The sound, a ringing cell phone, came again and Natasha's face instantly paled.

"I must take this," she said quietly and pulling her phone from her bag, hurried out of the music room. He watched her go, wondering what could have put that look into her golden eyes.

Wondering why he cared.

Everyone was ready for dinner that evening. Mary served a wonderful meal of baked chicken with roasted vegetables, homemade biscuits, and sweet potato soufflé. The Matthews were glowing from their successful day on the slopes. Sam shared stories of his morning spent with the children at the day care center, while Eldon shoveled in the food, not paying attention to the conversation around him. Christy's eyes were bright, her smile wide as she sat next to Sam. Stephanie told Angela how Bradley had introduced her to all the animals.

Chuckling, Angela said, "Yes, the owner has an affinity for animals. He insists that we be a sort of refuge for those hurting or needing a place to . . . regroup." She and Sam shared a knowing smile.

"I don't see Tyler, Stephanie. He isn't joining us for dinner?"

"I think he's still speaking with the mechanic about the car."

"Hmm." Angela took a bite of chicken and turned to Natasha. "I couldn't help listening in to your practice today, Miss Safina. Beautiful. You and Mr. Murray are extremely talented and play so well together. The evening performance should be amazing. I do hope everyone will attend."

"I promise, Angela, that it will be extraordinary," Franklin said. "We've added a few more holiday tunes in keeping with the season."

"Hmmph. Tunes. I do not play tunes," Natasha said under her breath.

"Whatever you play, dear, I'm sure it will be exceptional." Angela smiled, then glanced at the door. "Tyler, we were beginning to wonder if you'd be joining us."

She watched the young man enter and swallow hard when he saw the only chair left was next to Stephanie. "Do you have any news on your car?"

"Ah seems it's got your mechanic stumped. He towed it in and will let us know." Tyler reached for the chair and the loud scratching sound of chair legs on floor as he pulled it back so stunned him, the chair flew out of his grasp and crashed into the floor, in a thunderous boom. "Sorry," he said, blushing.

"Harv is the best around. I'm sure if anyone can fix it, he can."

Tyler looked around and Angela felt bad to have to inform him that the food along with the plates was placed on the buffet for self-serving.

"Please, help yourself." Angela motioned with her hand and tried to get everyone's attention away from the young man by saying, "Tell us what we can look forward to in tonight's performance, Mr. Murray."

Franklin sat straight and said, "We'll be playing a version of 'The Christmas Song' as well as other favorites from The Nutcracker Suite." He glanced at Christy. "For the young ones, I'll be performing a solo of 'Jingle Bells.'"

Sam clapped his hands. "Oh, boy. Nothing I like better than a rousing performance of 'Jingle Bells.'"

"Hmmph. Jiggly Bells," Natasha murmured.

Tyler set his full plate on the table and, his ears pink, gently pulled his chair out to sit down, which probably caused more amusement than the previous crash.

"To end the parlor performance, we'll do an excerpt from 'The Messiah.'"

Angela put a hand to her heart and sighed. "My absolute favorite. Oh, Mr. Murray, I cannot wait to hear it."

"Tyler, would you like a biscuit? They're wonderful." Stephanie passed the breadbasket and he reached for it. His fingers grazed hers and as if burned by a flame, he jerked back, causing the basket to tumble on the table. The biscuits fell out, rolling across the surface like billiard balls searching for their pockets, all eyes following them. Except for Eldon, who continued eating. Nothing disturbed him when he was eating.

Swallowing hard, Tyler said, "Sorry."

"That's quite all right," Angela said into the hushed room. "It . . . happens all the time." She plucked the biscuit from her lap and set it on her plate. "If you wouldn't mind, Mr. Matthews, would you pass the butter?"

"How's everyone doing?" Mary asked as she entered from the kitchen.

"Excellent dinner, as usual. And tell Bradley that Mr. Murray will be playing 'Jingle Bells' tonight. I'm sure he'll be thrilled."

"How's the new dog doing, Angela?" Darren asked as he sipped his coffee.

"Fine, fine. We've put out the word in case her owner is looking for her. In the meantime she's getting used to the barn." Angela's eyes went to Christy. "And enjoying all the attention." The little girl grinned.

"I'm sure. She looked a little . . . heavy." Darren's eyes sparkled with mischief.

"That she is. Normal, seeing as how she's going to have puppies." Darren laughed, Christy gasped, and the others expressed their own amusement. Except Natasha who was uninterested and Eldon who was hungry.

And Mary who sighed. "I suppose I'll have to tell Bradley now. I was hoping the owner of the dog would show up first."

"Now Mary. We'd never turn away a homeless creature, especially one expecting. Especially at Christmas. Seems the thing to do, to make a home for her . . . in our stable."

"Yeah, I get the metaphor. No problem." But she sighed again. "Can I get anyone anything before serving dessert?"

"What are we having?" Eldon asked, wiping his mouth with his napkin.

"Hot apple crisp with vanilla ice cream. I'll bring it out."

The conversations were muted as Mary set deep bowls of hot apples with pastry, Joe following, adding a scoop of ice cream. Apparently Stephanie asked Tyler a question and he turned to her. Angela sucked in a breath as just at that moment, Joe had stepped between them, his scoop filled with cold ice cream. Tyler's elbow bumped into him, jerking the ice cream loose falling smack on Tyler's nose. For a second, no one spoke. Tyler froze, literally, his face turning red, threatening to melt the ice cream faster.

Then little Christy let out a giggle. First softly, and then louder, growing with her mirth. Stephanie stared at her and turned to Tyler, her eyes warming as they found his. His lopsided grin and chuckle made Angela's own heart soften for the man. Stephanie joined in the laughter, as did the others, while she used her own napkin to clean off Tyler's face.

For such an unpredictable start, dinner at the inn had ended on a high note, one she hoped would continue through the evening.

Everyone drifted into the parlor for a peaceful evening of music and quiet games. Even Bradley, who'd been informed "Jingle Bells" would be played, was happy, sitting at a table with

Christy, working on a Christmas puzzle. Angela settled back for a relaxing evening.

Tricia sighed with contentment, leaning against a couch cushion, ready to listen to the music of Ms. Safina and Mr. Murray. It had been a wonderful day. Darren had been so patient and loving as he taught her how to ski. They worked on the beginner slope and then had a quiet, lovely picnic lunch in the woods away from the crowds. Her lips still tingled remembering the touch of Darren's against hers. It had been so romantic. She pulled his arm to her and wrapped hers around it.

Laughter caught her attention and she turned to see Bradley and Christy. And her heart yearned. What would it be like to visit a place like this with their own child's laughter in the background? She could see it as she'd imagined it time and again.

Trisha studied Christy. She was a sweet, quiet little thing. She'd probably had a hard life. Such a shame. No child should have to endure a hard childhood. It just wasn't right. If she understood correctly, the little girl was going to an orphanage. To be grouped with others in her situation. Her heart went out to her.

The music started and she tried to concentrate on the beautiful melodies but her mind kept returning to the children. Franklin began to play "The Christmas Song" and the lyrics that described an idyllic family Christmas engulfed her. It was her dream, what she wanted more than anything.

In her heart she felt this trip was their last hope. What if she couldn't get pregnant? How could she deal with the death of her dream?

And what about Darren? He deserved to be a father. She wanted to give him a child so badly.

As the duo began performing songs from "The Nutcracker Suite," Tricia's mind wandered. She saw the ballet unfolding—a young girl, celebrating Christmas with her parents, her family. They were happy as they enjoyed the season.

Slowly, a new hope began to blossom in Tricia. Similar to a connect-the-dots game, she began to see another picture forming and an idea formed. Maybe they wouldn't be able to have a baby but that didn't mean they couldn't be parents.

Christy walked up to the social worker and whispered in her ear. The woman smiled and nodded. As she turned, a puzzle piece fell from her hands. Darren quickly reached down and picked it up. Smiling, he offered it to her, to which she shyly took it and skipped away. The small interaction caused a breathlessness to come over Tricia.

She listened to the music, her brain on full speed. Turning, she smiled at the little girl, Christy, and her heart began to pound. Was this the answer she'd been looking for all along?

To the applause of the room, Franklin stood and bowed. As Natasha watched, he said, "Thank you, ladies and gentlemen. Ms. Safina has consented to allow me to indulge in one of my favorite holiday traditions—playing 'Jingle Bells.'"

Bradley cheered and Christy copied him. "To the children inside all of us."

She edged over into the doorway as Franklin sat and with a slow arpeggio, launched into a bouncing, joyful rendition of the song. She glanced into the room, watching the happy faces. She didn't feel happy, or joyful, or full of the Christmas cheer that everyone was expected to have this time of the year. How could she when all she'd built, all she'd worked for her entire life was quite possibly collapsing, ending for good with her having to accept a life she'd despise with all her being? Probably, she was not meant to live the life of freedom that she so desperately desired.

She took a deep breath and leaned back in the darkened hallway, letting herself relax for just a moment from the heavy burden she carried. How nice it would be to be like the other people in the inn, enjoying a Christmas vacation, laughing, eating, and playing. But her life was never meant to be that. Her uncle had made certain of that.

She'd ignored a phone call from him earlier. There'd be hell to pay for that but she hadn't wanted to be late for dinner, to just be with normal people, hearing the conversations of normal life.

Even Franklin. With his pompous British accent, his very different views on music, he was his own man, not controlled and maneuvered by others. She could admire that.

Hot tears formed in her eyes and she immediately blinked hard to push them back. Mustn't spoil her makeup. She'd be needed for the final number. Sighing, she knew she'd perform it perfectly, with all the emotion that clogged her soul. It was her outlet, the only thing that kept her from going crazy.

The thunderous applause meant Franklin was finished. Time to go on. She stood tall, straightened her shoulders, and adopted the expression she always wore when performing—the ice queen, secure in her talent, untouchable. Unflappable.

Stephanie was having a good time. But more than that, Christy was. It filled her heart with joy to see the little girl that had been battered, beaten, haunted with no doubt unspeakable things, now laughing, interacting, and basically being a kid. When it happened, it was the best part of her job. If only she could find a loving home to adopt the girl. Stephanie's fear was that with Christy's past and personal challenges she'd get lost in the shuffle at the orphanage. She sighed.

Not finding a child a home—the worst part of her job.

After again checking on Christy, she saw Tyler leaning against a bookcase, next to the large parlor Christmas tree, listening to the music. She could have kissed him hard on the mouth when his mishap with the ice cream had caused Christy to giggle.

As if he knew she was thinking of him, his eyes met hers and there was a sudden . . . zing.

Wow. What was that?

She smiled at him and he grinned slightly. Her face started to heat for some unknown reason and she glanced down to compose herself. But strangely she found herself looking back up, his creamy brown eyes pulling her in. His grin was gone, replaced by a serious, intent expression that immediately stole her breath. Her pulse quickened, she swallowed hard. This wasn't happening. Her future was set, her career always came first. Men were just a distraction, an unwanted distraction. Certainly not a distraction to be trusted.

The edges of his lips curved just enough for a dimple to form in his right cheek. Her eyes were drawn to it and to the small dent in his chin, giving his young face a masculine sense. She was entranced.

Hands in pockets, Tyler pushed away from the bookshelves. Stephanie's heart raced. But as he took a step, a stray branch from the Christmas tree next to him snagged his sweater, refusing to let go. He turned and in the process of trying to detangle, accidentally knocked a few ornaments off. Strands of tinsel fluttered off, falling in his eyes, which meant he couldn't see when he stepped forward, right into the tree. Stephanie gasped.

The music had stopped at the sound of crashing ornaments and the men rushed over just in time to save the tree, and Tyler, from falling to the ground.

The room was silent, as no one knew exactly what to say.

Stephanie took only a second to decide what to do. She jumped up, picking up ornaments and tinsel and replacing them on the tree. No way was she going to look at him. She wasn't going to get lost in his eyes again. Knowing his propensity for accidents, the household might not be able to take it.

"Sorry," Tyler murmured, helping to set the tree to rights.

Angela joined Stephanie. "No problem, Tyler. These things happen. Please, go on, Ms. Safina. Mr. Murray. Nothing like Christmas music playing when trimming the tree."

The tension broken, the music continued. No one spoke as they worked on the tree, the strains of the piano and violin softly filling the room. It was a peaceful existence until a noise was heard outside in the distance.

Angela stopped and cocked her head, listening. The low, agitated cry became louder and louder. Turning, her eyes met Sam's. His were just as concerned.

The music grew to a crescendo and ended but no one applauded. The room was silent and all anyone could hear was the sound of a wolf moaning, the sound getting closer.

"What is it, Mama?" Bradley asked, going to stand next to Mary.

Angela continued to stare out the window. "Joe?"

"I'll go check on the animals in the barn. Make sure it's locked up."

"We'll go with you," Sam said and Eldon nodded.

"Me, too," added Darren.

"Be careful, honey," Mary said, her face etched with worry.

Angela's spirit echoed that worry.

Chapter Six

Bradley bounced into the dining room the next morning just as Sam, Eldon, and Angela were finishing breakfast. "You ready to go tubing, Sam? I'm ready. I've had my breakfast and all my chores are done. Mama says we can go anytime."

With a chuckle, Sam said, "Very soon. Let me help with the animals this morning. And I, ah, thought we'd ask the others if they'd like to come. They seem to be sleeping in this morning."

After the disturbing cries of the wolf the night before, no one had been eager to retire for the evening, as nerves were on edge. Later, business in the bar had been exceptional.

"Hey, here comes Christy." Bradley ran to the little girl who held Stephanie's hand tightly. "You want to go tubing with us this morning? It's going to be lots of fun."

She looked at Bradley, her good eye huge. "What about the w-w-wolf? Will h-he eat us?"

"Of course not. He's probably sleeping during the day so he won't bother us, will he?" Bradley asked Sam.

"No. He won't." Sam and Joe, along with Angela, had discussed the situation the previous night and come up with a tentative plan but Bradley didn't need to know the details. "Ah, Mr. and Mrs. Matthews. We're going tubing down the hill behind the inn this morning. Would you like to join us?"

"Well, we thought about heading to the slopes again today."

"Trails are closed this morning. Weather too rough on the mountain," Eldon said not looking up from his food.

"They hope to reopen this afternoon. Please join us."

Tricia glanced at Christy's happy face and smiled. "We'd love to join you and the children for tubing. Sounds like fun, doesn't it, honey?"

When Mary brought out more toast, Stephanie said, "I don't seem to be able to get cell phone reception this morning. Could I possibly use your phone to make a few calls, update everyone on our situation?"

Mary wiped her hands on her apron. "I apologize for that. A storm came over the mountain last night and decided to stay for a while. When that happens our phone reception goes out. Including the landline."

"I'm sure you'll be able to get a bar or two of reception while outside," Angela said. "In the meantime you and Christy can have fun with us." Stephanie glanced at Christy with concern. "Now don't you worry about her. We'll all be there to help watch. She'll have a wonderful time, I guarantee it."

Later, too much later according to Bradley, the children ran out of the inn giggling and squealing. Especially when dropping into the new fallen snow. The sounds of their laughter filled the quiet countryside that had seemed determined to sleep in.

"Wait until you slide down the hill, Christy. It's lots of fun!"

"It's s-s-so pretty."

"Haven't you ever seen snow before?" Bradley asked, frowning.

Stephanie put her arm around the girl and said, "Christy lived in the city. I'm sure the snow-covered Vermont countryside is a new experience for her."

"Oh. Well, you're gonna love this!" He bounded into the storage shed and helped Sam hand out the inner tubes. Grabbing several, he walked back to Christy. "I've got a small one for you. Come on!" With a small inner tube on each shoulder, he grabbed her hand and headed toward the small hill beside the inn.

The group trudged to what Bradley deemed the perfect spot. A second later, he ran and plopped down on his tube, hollering as he skidded down the hill. The others laughed while Christy watched the scene, her expression full of amazement.

From below them came the sound, "Come on down, you guys! It's great!"

Darren shrugged and said, "He doesn't have to tell me twice. Come on, honey." He sat on his tube at the hill's edge, holding out his hand for his wife, who sat next to him in her own tube. Pushing off, the two followed Bradley down the hill, their laughter filling the air.

Stephanie leaned down to Christy. "Doesn't that look like fun?" She didn't say anything but nodded just the same, her eyes on the hill. "Are you ready to try?" She shook her head. "Okay. We'll just watch for a little while." Stephanie wrapped her arms around the young girl as they viewed the others.

"What do you think?" Darren asked, his eyes bright, his smile wide, as he and Tricia walked back up the hill.

"Wonderful." She linked her arm with his, returning the smile. "Almost as much fun as skiing," she said, clearly tongue in cheek.

"Do I detect a note of sarcasm in that tone, young lady?"

"Maybe just a bit. It is fun though." Tricia's eyes went to Christy who was watching the tubers. "Darren. How about taking Christy down the hill with you. She looks like she wants to but isn't quite sure. She probably needs someone to go with her."

Darren glimpsed Christy and furrowed his brows. "You're probably right. Okay. How about she and I race you?"

Laughing, Tricia said, "You're on." She hurried over to Christy and leaned down. "Would you like to go down with someone, Christy?

Darren will let you ride with him. He'll make sure you're safe, okay?"

Christy had her finger in her mouth. She looked up at Darren, as if gauging whether he was trustworthy or not.

"Come on, princess. What do you have to lose?" He kneeled and whispered, "And I bet with your help we can beat Tricia. How about it?"

Tricia's heart melted at her husband's tenderness with the girl. When she took her finger out of her mouth and nodded, Tricia wanted to cheer. This was working out. It could be the beginning of her answer, her wish come true. She tried to hold her excitement in.

After a word of encouragement from Stephanie, Tricia took the little girl's hand. "It will be so much fun, Christy. Darren is always so much fun."

Darren set his large tube down on the edge of the hill, sat, and stretched out his arms for Christy. Tricia's heart lightened as she led the girl over and got her situated in Darren's lap.

"All right, Mrs. Matthews," he joked. "You need to get in your tube so we can beat you."

"Hey, Bradley. How about we give them a little help?" Sam asked going to stand behind Darren's tube. "You give Mrs. Matthew's tube a push, and I'll give Christy's a push."

Eager to help, Bradley situated himself behind Tricia. "On three. Ready? One . . . two . . . three!" Sam and Bradley pushed and the two tubes went flying down the hill. Tricia enjoyed the frosty wind in her face but even more than that, she enjoyed the laughter of her husband and the squeals of joy from the little girl riding with him.

They were all laughing at the bottom of the hill but stopped when they heard barking. "Now, what's she doing out here?" Darren stood, hands on his hips as the dog, Frederica, bounded as best she could toward the couple.

Tricia and Darren immediately gathered her to them, stroking, speaking gently. Turning, Tricia saw Christy watching and said, "Come on, sweetie. Frederica loves to be petted." She took the girl's hand and guided it to the dog's back. The dog gave her a doggie grin, which made the girl smile.

In Tricia's mind, the interaction was a piece of heaven.

Stephanie was having a ball. Not in tubing, which was a great deal of fun, but in watching Christy. She'd ridden several times with Darren and once with Tricia. She'd gone by herself, with Bradley riding his own tube next to her. The giggles and smiles from the little girl brought tears to Stephanie's eyes. This was what Christmas holidays should be like for every child—carefree, fun, enjoying the season with friends and . . .

If only Christy had a family to share this with. Again she felt a sense of failure that she hadn't been able to find a family to love the girl. If she hadn't been a single, career driven individual she wouldn't have hesitated to take Christy in but she knew in her heart it couldn't be her.

The ping of an incoming text brought her thoughts back to the moment and she pulled out her phone to see that she had two glorious bars of reception.

"Would you like to go try your calls?" Angela asked walking up to her.

"Yes, I . . ." She glanced at Christy, having so much fun carrying her tube back up the hill.

Angela patted Stephanie's arm. "Why don't you take a walk and see if the reception gets even better. We'll watch Christy."

"I don't know . . ."

"Now don't you worry, dear." Angela gently nudged her away. "The girl will be fine here. You'll be able to see her and get your work down and she'll get to continue to play."

Stephanie gave her a small smile and walked away, punching in numbers. Everyone involved needed to know what was going on, although she didn't quite know what to tell them.

"Tyler, what have you been doing this morning?"

The man ran his fingers through his mussed hair and looked around at the vast white countryside. "I guess I overslept this morning. Can't seem to get any reception on my phone."

Angela grinned. "It's a bit unreliable when we have a storm. I hear it's really coming down up on the mountain this morning but I believe if you walk down the driveway, you be able to get make a call."

"Great. I need to check with the garage and see what they say."

The news was not good. The problem had been narrowed to the carburetor, the starter, or the battery. Tyler wasn't hopeful. He swore soundly as he shoved his phone back in his pocket.

"Bad news?"

The sound of Stephanie's voice hit him like a gust of arctic air, sending him falling back in a deep drift of snow.

"Oh! I'm so sorry. I didn't mean to startle you." She moved to him and reached out a gloved hand to help him up.

His mouth was dry and his heart was racing. How did she always do that to him? And he always responded by appearing as a fool. Great. "Thanks," he muttered when he finally stood with her help.

"Were you talking to the mechanic?"

"Ah, yeah. He's not sure yet what the trouble is." He shoved his hands in his pockets. As always, he was nervous around this woman.

She was everything he'd always dreamed about in a woman. She was perfect—the right height, the right age, the right . . . everything. Her blonde hair cut short above her shoulders, her bright blue eyes that told every emotion she seemed to have. Her delicate heart-shaped face with porcelain skin, as beautiful as a priceless doll.

And that was nothing compared to the kind and gentle heart she had. As long as he'd known her, which was a few years, she'd always been selfless, extremely protective of the children in her care, loving and caring to the max. She was . . . just everything. Even now, with her brows lifted, her eyes wide she was mesmerizing. Wait, had she said something? Was she waiting for an answer?

"Tyler?"

"Ah . . . what did you say?"

She cocked her head. "You look a little flushed. Are you feeling okay?" She moved closer to him, placing her hand on his forehead. "Are you coming down with something?"

Her nearness had his heart leaping and he jumped back at her touch. Right into the trunk of a large maple tree, briefly knocking the breath out of him. The impact caused the snow on the branches to flutter down, covering his hatless head.

A moment passed as he absorbed the embarrassment. He was getting quite used to it. But then the lilt of her laughter had his spirit soaring. "Oh, Tyler. I'm so glad if Christy and I had to be stranded, we're stranded with you."

She ran her hand over the top of his head to scatter the snow and their eyes met and held for a second. A long second in which nothing existed in the world other than the two of them. He couldn't breathe, couldn't move. He wanted to go on looking at her forever.

"Hey, Tyler," Darren called out. "Got a tube over here with your name on it."

The intimate moment gone, he stepped away. And started breathing again. Had he imagined the interest in her eyes that surely echoed his? Probably just his vivid imagination.

But in the deepest part of his heart he couldn't help the glimmer of hope that maybe, just maybe she saw him as more than the bumbling orphanage helper.

It was Christmas, after all. A times for wishes.

From the window of the music room Franklin watched the group riding down the hill on tubes. It wasn't something he'd ever done as a child and probably would never do as an adult. It did look fun, though.

He glanced at his watch wondering where Natasha was. She was never late and in fact usually prided herself on being punctual. Of course, it would give him something to hold over her head. That was always fun. It was fast becoming his greatest source of entertainment—to irritate and get the best of Natasha Safina. At least it kept him from noticing how beautiful she was.

He watched the "tubers" for another few minutes until she came fluttering into the room, holding sheet music. As always, she was groomed to perfection. Today she wore a silk shirt in the color of emeralds and a black pencil skirt with black heels.

"I do not understand the 'Jiggly Bells.' The words, they confuse me." She read the words aloud to demonstrate her point. "Is no fun to ride through snow. Is cold, very cold. Uncomfortable." She shivered at the thought. "No one sings. No one opens mouth because is cold, very cold."

He couldn't contain his amusement. "I suppose that where you come from that's true. But in most countries a ride on a sleigh is a pleasurable experience. It's fun, romantic even."

"Romantic? When eyes water and nose is red? And body shakes from coldness?"

Franklin grinned. "Ah, but warming up someone you care about is very romantic."

"Why not go inside and sit by fire? That is not more romantic?"

Perplexed, Franklin said, "Well, yes. Of course sitting by the fire is romantic but a sleigh ride is . . . well, it's just fun. People love it."

"Then people are fools." The noise outside the window seized her attention and she walked to stand next to him, looking out. "What is going on?"

"The others are tubing. They're sitting on inner tubes and riding them down the hill. Again, it's about having fun." He was about to add "something you know nothing about" but stopped when he caught a look at her eyes. The gold flecks seemed to sparkle as she watched the group. Behind the usual hardness, he glimpsed longing. And hurt. For a moment he wanted to comfort her, wanted to pull her outside and push her down the hill, wanted to hear her just once cut loose with a squeal of joy, demolishing that perfect, polished image.

In a flash, her eyes hardened to their normal temperature—frigid. "Shall we get to work?" She didn't wait for an answer but moved to her violin and began tuning the instrument.

Her ringing phone seized her attention and Franklin saw her body tense, her jaw clench. "I must take this call. Please excuse me."

He nodded and sat at the piano doing a few exercises to warm up the fingers. Just to get a rile out of her he started playing "tunes"—"Frosty the Snowman" and "Santa Claus is Coming to Town." He anticipated with delight the fire that would glow in her pretty eyes.

Finishing with a flourish and an arpeggio he waited. What he heard in the silence stunned him.

A quiet sob, like that of a wounded animal came from the hall. He jumped off the piano bench and found her in the hall, crumbled in a sitting position on the floor. The shock turned to concern immediately.

"Natasha? What's wrong?" He knelt beside her, ready to carry her to her room if she was sick or hurting.

She said nothing for a long time. Franklin felt completely helpless. He gently rubbed her arm, hoping the gesture would somehow convey support.

Finally, she lifted her head and sniffed delicately. However, her eyes stayed down, not looking at him. When she sniffed a second time, he reached into his pocket and pulled out a handkerchief for her. She quietly thanked him and wiped her eyes and nose.

"Did you get bad news?"

Her eyes met his and he watched with fascination her struggle to compose herself. "What?"

"The phone call. Was it bad news?"

She cleared her throat and stood, refusing his help. Yes, the strong façade was returning. Clearly.

"Nothing I was not expecting. Come. We have rehearsal. Tonight's performances must be perfect, I will accept nothing less."

He took a quick minute in the hall by himself. She may have recovered but he hadn't. Whoever called had devastated her and as much as they argued and disagreed, he hated to see anyone in that much pain.

Especially beautiful violin players.

Angela and Sam watched the others race down the hill as Joe walked to them. "Did you see anything?" Sam watched, keeping his voice down.

"I saw some tracks at the end of the cross country trail, coming down from the mountain. Could have been a wolf."

"We've never had a wolf this close before. What could have drawn it here?" Angela asked.

"Haven't a clue. Sam?"

He sighed. "Could be several things. Wolves are usually fearful of people and try to avoid them, but there are several reasons for a wolf coming near humans and I'm afraid none are good."

"Go ahead," Angela said when Sam hesitated.

"One, the wolf could be rabid. Two, it could have been provoked in some way by a human. Three, it could be hungry and looking for food." Sam sighed and said, "Finally, it could just be predatory, aggressive, ready to fight off whatever it feels is threatening its existence." He stopped and lowering his voice added, "Like I said. None of the reasons are good."

"What should we do?" Angela asked.

"I'll make sure the barn is locked tight before the sun goes down."

"Do you think it might come during the daylight?" Angela glanced around her in concern.

"I doubt it. But we should all be alert," Sam said. "And the children shouldn't go out alone." His eyes went to Joe.

"I've got it covered." Joe reached his hand to pat the inside of his coat. "I'm carrying a gun just in case."

Angela blanched at the news.

Chapter Seven

After playing in the snow and eating lunch, Christy was more than ready to take a nap. Stephanie decided to take a break in the parlor, maybe work on a puzzle. Mary had lent her a baby monitor so she would know as soon as the girl awoke.

Holding the monitor she walked into the room and was surprised to see Tyler sitting on a sofa reading. She took a minute to watch him, remembering the morning. They'd talked about the next few days and getting Christy to the orphanage as they'd walked back to the tubers. All morning she couldn't help watching him, whether it was racing the others down the hill, throwing snowballs with Bradley, or building a snowman with Christy. He really was a special man.

Now he was clearly immersed in the book he was reading. Who would have thought that the quiet, hardworking man from the orphanage would be a reader?

She walked quietly closer to get a peek at what he was reading. *War and Peace*. "Wow." At her comment he dropped his book on the floor and when they both bent to retrieve it, knocking their heads together. "Ouch."

"Sorry," he murmured, picking up the book and finding his place again. "Christy okay?"

"Yes. Angela suggested I take a break in here. Mary loaned me the baby monitor," she said showing him the device.

She sat next to him, pulling one leg underneath her. "You're reading *War and Peace.* I'm very impressed."

He shrugged. "I guess I was just in the mood for a story about Russian aristocracy during the Napoleonic wars. Just a little light reading." He gave her a lopsided grin.

Returning the grin, she was enchanted. "I've never read it. Is it good?"

"If you can get past the language to the plot, it's not bad."

"I suppose next you'll tell me you've read Homer's *Iliad*." When he looked down and grinned she playfully punched his arm. "You did, you really did! I'm jealous. I tried to get through it in college but ended up reading the *Cliff Notes*."

"You probably got as much out of it as I did."

"Do you normally read heavy literature during your free time?"

He thought about it for a moment. "I've enjoyed reading ever since I learned how to read. The workers in the orphanage showed me how I could travel to different places, have a ton of adventure, be anything I want by reading good books."

She smiled. "They were wise."

"And right. Books . . . got me through a lot of tough times."

As she frowned she wondered about that. "You grew up in the orphanage, right?" He nodded. "Did you ever know your mom or dad?" He shook his head.

Seeing his forehead crinkle as if trying not to think of the past, she tried for a lighter tone. "And look how well you turned out. It gives me hope for Christy."

He hesitated. "She'll be fine, Stephanie. I'll make sure of that."

"Thank you for that. I hope you're right." Stephanie sighed. "I just wish I could have found her a home, a family. I . . . somehow feel like I've failed."

"No you haven't. I know you and I know you've done your very best to find the best situation for her. If that's the orphanage, I'm sure she'll do fine there. We've got special teachers who'll help her speak and grow and learn. She'll catch up to the others in no time."

With a heavy sigh she said, "I'm sure you're right. It's just that . . . it's not right. Every child should have a loving home to grow and prosper in and I won't stop until every child in my care has just that." She swallowed hard and forced herself to take a deep breath.

His eyes seemed to study her and then he surprised her by taking her hand and holding it between his. "Why is a home for each child so important to you?"

She wanted to reply that of course it was important, it was her job but she saw in the depths of his eyes that the question went a whole lot deeper than that. A warm sensation filled her body, making her want to curl up next to him and confide in him her awful past. She wanted to let someone else be strong for a while, to carry the burdens for these children with her, to release her from the feelings of inadequacy from her past.

No, she wouldn't burden anyone with her own problems. Hadn't she learned to cope and fight her own battles? She'd been given a job to do, a mission to help each child brought to her and to her dying day that's what she'd do. And not even a caring man with delicious chocolate eyes was going to distract her from that calling.

Once again, she swallowed hard. "It's my job, of course."

To her chagrin his eyes continued to probe hers but now they seemed to sharpen with an appreciation and . . . was that affection?

"The children are very lucky to have you," he said softly.

Okay, so she'd indulge in looking into those wonderful eyes. For just a second. Maybe a minute. Or two.

Of its own accord, her body started to move toward his, seeking to be close. She glanced at his lips, straight and serious and enticing.

A phone shrilled causing her to jump back, her face heating at what had almost happened. "It's the mechanic." Tyler's gravelly voice indicated that he was as affected by the near kiss as she was.

What had she been thinking? The answer was evident, she hadn't been. The mental scolding started just as she heard Christy stirring on the baby monitor. "Christy's up. I'd better go to her." Stephanie hurried from the room, glad to be away from the situation. Glad to focus on her job.

Glad to put some distance between Tyler and herself. At least that's what she told herself.

"What do you think, honey? Want to try out the slopes this afternoon?"

Darren looked out the window from their suite, trying to check the weather on the mountaintops. "I think the storm has moved on. Could be good powder up there. I'll take you up to a beginner trail, you're ready."

"Hmm." Tricia sat at the foot of the bed brushing her hair, a habit that relaxed her. He teased her about loving to brush hair so much that their cats were the best groomed animals in all of Atlanta.

"I don't know, sweetie. By the time we get all the way over there, we won't have much time before they close for the day. Besides." She put her brush down and said, "I'd like to talk to you about something."

He mentally sighed. Not again with the talk about babies. Couldn't they go for one day without bringing the subject up?

Her bright eyes, which always captivated him, had him sitting in an armchair, ready to listen. "All right. What's up?"

She set her hands on her lap and took a breath. When she still hesitated he tried not to get nervous.

"I've been thinking." Another long pause. He was starting to sweat now. "It may be a long time before we have a baby. I mean, the doctor said . . . well, you know. It could happen this month or not for ten years. Or ever." She took a deeper breath. "So, I was thinking maybe we should stop thinking so much about having a baby."

Euphoria invaded his system like floodwaters over a low valley. His system embraced it and his throat clogged with gratitude so that he was barely able to speak. "You mean it? You're easing up on the idea?"

She gave him a tentative smile. "Yes. I think it's the best thing."

Darren leapt from his chair and wrapped his arms around her, kissing her hard as they fell back onto the bed. "I know this hasn't been easy but I'm so proud of you." He proceeded to kiss her cheek, her neck, her ear.

When she giggled, he smiled, nibbling on her earlobe, which he knew she enjoyed. Until she spoke again.

"But that doesn't mean we have to let go of our dreams of parenthood. In fact, I think I may have come up with a different solution."

He sat up, confused, getting a bad feeling about where this was going. "What do you mean?"

With a smile, she also sat up and took his face in her hands. "There's no reason we can't be parents now. Especially when a sweet little girl needs us."

More confusion. "Huh?"

"Christy. She needs a home, not an orphanage. If we can provide one for her, why not do so? Darren, we could adopt her, we could have our own little girl. Isn't that exciting?"

He stood and hands in his pockets walked to the fireplace and back again, letting the idea sink in. "You're saying we should adopt the little girl? The one we only met a couple of days ago? The one we know nothing about?"

"I'm sure that Miss Singer could tell us all we need to know. Darren, it's the perfect solution. She needs a home, we need her."

Darren frowned, rubbing the back of his neck. "I wouldn't exactly say that we need her."

"Well, of course we do. This is the answer to all our problems. Adoption."

His gut tensed. "I wasn't aware that we had a lot of problems."

Tricia shook her head. "Maybe I'm not explaining this right, I'm sorry. It's just that I think . . . well, it's an alternative. An option. Please don't say no without giving it some thought."

He paced the room again, taking deep breaths. He could tell by Tricia's eager tone, her bright expression that she already had her hopes on this . . . solution. But this was too serious to jump into. He sat on the edge of the bed and reached over to take her hands. "Sweetheart, I know you're excited about this but there's something you haven't considered."

"What's that?"

"Christy." She shook her head in puzzlement. "This little girl has obviously been through a great deal. Things we haven't a clue about. She's going to need a lot of help."

"And I'll be glad to get that help for her."

"I know you will. But I'm concerned that this will only hold your interest until and if you get pregnant. Does that mean if we do have a baby that we'll send her back? That she's simply a stopgap until we get what we really want? If that's so, it's not fair to her. In fact, it's downright cruel."

Tricia bolted to her feet, clearly offended. "Do you think that I'd be so insensitive to a child? What kind of mother do you think I'd make?" Now Tricia was the one pacing.

"I didn't mean to hurt your feelings, honey, I just want you to think this all the way through. If we were to adopt Christy, it would mean that we'd give her our all. She'd be our daughter forever and whether we had other children or not, we'd be responsible to care and love her just as much as the others. That's all I'm saying."

Her arms around herself, Tricia stopped pacing and thought. "You don't think I'd love her like I would our other children?"

He walked to her and wrapped her in his arms, smiling. "I think you have an abundance of love to give. It's one of the things I adore about you." He tenderly kissed her cheek.

With a sigh, she laid her head against his chest. They were silent for a few moments, enjoying the embrace. Finally, she said, "Will you at least think it over?"

"I'll think it over." He kissed her head.

"Thank you," she whispered. Lifting her head, she kissed him. "Now, why don't you head over to the ski slopes and see if you can get a few runs in today."

"You're not coming?"

"No. I think I'll just relax here until dinner."

After another kiss, Darren contacted Joe for a ride to the ski resort and donned his ski gear. On the ride over, he replayed their conversation. He said he'd think it over and he would. However, he was concerned that Tricia was only replacing one obsession with another and where did that put him? Or their marriage?

Then again the little girl did need a good home. They were more than equipped to give her that. Maybe it was the right thing for them.

But as he pondered the idea he'd continue to shower his wife with love and attention. He'd continue to invest in their marriage because it meant more to him than anything.

Her head was pounding. If only she could get a decent night's sleep she could logically think through everything and come up with a viable plan.

Natasha peeked through the rooms looking for someone. Feeling a little embarrassed, she eased the kitchen door open and saw the innkeeper mixing a salad. The homey scents and colors of the room drew her in.

"Excuse me."

Setting down her work and wiping her hands on her apron, the woman smiled. "Miss Safina. What can I do for you?"

"I am sorry to trouble you but do you have . . . ah . . ." She pointed to her forehead. "For hurting . . ."

"Oh, you need pain reliever for a headache?" Natasha let out a breath and nodded. "Of course. I've got some right here." She went to a cupboard and pulled out a bottle, then a glass and filled it with water. "Here you go."

"Thank you. I will pay you, of course."

"Not at all. No charge."

Natasha downed the pills and water just as Angela came into the room. "Mary I think we should—oh, Miss Safina. Everything all right?"

"Yes. Ms. . . ."

"Mary." The woman smiled.

"Uh, Mary was just giving me . . ." She held up the bottle.

"You have a headache, I am so sorry. If we can help in any other way, please let us know."

"Actually, I heard there is a spa in town. Would it be possible to get a message?"

Angela crinkled her brow. "A . . . message?"

"Yes. I believe my body could use good . . . rubdown."

"Oh, you mean a massage. Well, of course, we have a wonderful spa at a nearby hotel. However, appointments must be made a day in advance but they will come here to the inn."

"Very well. If you could get me an appointment I would be grateful."

"Certainly." Angela paused. "In fact, I just had a wonderful idea." She chuckled. "Mary, how about we talk to the other women. See if we can order the 'Girls' Day' package. Have them come out for massages, facials, manicures, pedicures, and the whole deal. What do you think?"

"I think that's a wonderful idea. Sign me up for a couple of hours."

Angela turned to Natasha. "What about you, Miss Safina? Are you interested in having the complete package?"

She rubbed her forehead. "Is fine." She turned to leave and then said, "Oh, Mr. Murray and I will not be joining you for dinner. We are behind in rehearsal."

"You've got to eat, dear."

"We must be at our best for the performance tonight." She lifted her chin, an effort, as the pain reliever hadn't kicked in yet. She vaguely heard Angela say, "Perhaps we can make up a couple of trays and bring them into the music room."

She nodded and left.

After rousing a napping Franklin and bullying him to the music room, she set up her music and started her warm-up.

"You still have not given me a satisfactory answer to why we need this extra practice."

"Because practice this morning was short. And weak."

"Weak? I thought we sounded wonderful."

"Because you have no ear." She turned the strings on her instrument to tune them.

"I beg your pardon, but my ear is fine. As is my appetite. Dinner is soon and I'm famished."

"Fine if you want to give adequate instead of great performance tonight. For me, I will practice until I am worth money paid to me."

He blew out a frustrated breath and sat at the piano. "Fine. Let me warm up."

They went through the first piece to be performed that evening—a medley of famous Christmas works. She could feel his eyes on her and stopped in the middle of the second page. "Is there problem?"

"Your playing seems tense. Are you still upset from the phone call earlier?"

She clenched her jaw. "I am not upset. I am not tense. Please try to keep up." Pointing to a spot of his sheet music with her bow, she said, "We begin here. One, two, three, four."

The music continued but this time on the next page Natasha missed a note and trying to catch up pulled them both off beat. Franklin stopped. She stopped and cursed in Russian. "I think we should slow the tempo there."

"No, the music calls for allegro. Would you like to practice the bar a few times to get the feel of it?"

"No, I do not want to 'get the feel of it.' My 'feel' is fine. Again as before." They played and got past the troublesome part on into another page. But here Natasha felt her timing off a bit and frustrated she furiously drew her bow back and forth. "Argh! Is not right. Is not perfect."

His voice calm, Franklin said, "Perhaps if you took something for that headache you could concentrate better."

"I did." She narrowed her eyes at him. "How did you know I had head pain?"

"You get a couple of lines on your forehead between your eyes." His fingers went to his head to the spot.

For a moment she contemplated the fact that he seemed to know that fact about her. It seemed a little . . . too cozy. Of course she had slobbered all over him after her phone call that morning and how embarrassing was that.

"My head is fine. Let's continue," she said wanting to get back to work.

They played on, working their way to the finale. The grand sweep of the music took over and she could feel herself getting lost in the sounds when thoughts of the future snuck in and she found herself playing harder to keep them at bay. The piano accompaniment slowed as she got faster. They were soon playing at different spots, creating a cacophony of discord.

"No, no. Stop! What is matter with you? End must be grand, moving, exciting. But you play like for church or wedding."

"Excuse me, but you were playing as if the hounds of hell were chasing you."

"I do not know hounds of hell but they would like better than your slow dirge."

"Slow dirge?" Franklin stood and ran a hand through his hair. "These songs are meant for the audience to have the time to appreciate, to reflect. You were running so fast through them no one would be able to even guess the titles, let alone be moved by the music."

"Not true. Must be played with a tempo that is alive. The problem is you have no bravery. You are afraid to take chance." They were standing toe-to-toe now.

"Afraid? Afraid to take a chance? Listen, honey, we're both professionals here and your interpretation is flawed, it doesn't mean I'm afraid."

"You are coward. Your playing lacks passion, it lacks fire. Is better for elevator play!"

She could tell from his gasp and the flaring of his eyes that she'd said the wrong thing. But the tension in her head, the frustration in her heart dulled her understanding and instead spurred her on.

Her hands fisted at her sides and her eyebrow rose. "Also, your accent has disappeared. I wonder where it goes. Maybe explains much. I never did want to work with you. Is like torture to spend time with you. Why would I want to be with boring and arrogant man?"

Recovering his voice, Franklin said, "Arrogant? Really? Sure you want to go there, sweetheart?" His eyes were now flames of fire and if she wasn't hurting so much she would have been fascinated.

Instead, she pointed at him. "Aha. There it is. No British accent. Clearly American. So who are you, Franklin Murray? Wait, maybe Franklin Murray is not real name!"

He fell back, his eyes dulled and his complexion paled. He looked down at the piano keys in contemplation, leaving her feeling a mixture of confusion, regret, and pain.

She was breathing hard after her rant and wanted to desperately retreat to her room to let the medicine take away the last vestiges of pain and to keep from saying anything more hurtful. Instead, she stood her ground, ready to do battle once again if needed. To fight against this man, since the one she really wanted to fight wasn't available.

Or maybe she couldn't bring herself to fight him. In truth, she was the real coward.

Franklin straightened and turned to her, taking a few steps until they were too close in her opinion. His voice was low and sent a chill down her spine.

"I'm not sure why you feel the need to be such a witch. Probably because of that call this morning that had you sobbing like a hurt animal but I'm not going to pry. You can have all the privacy you want, precious. And I hope you're happy with the isolation you bring on yourself. It's well deserved."

He took a breath but wasn't finished. His eyes searched hers. "I happen to think you're miserable being an ice princess, by not letting anyone near you but again, none of my business. It boggles my mind, though, that a woman could be so beautiful and talented and yet close herself off, like she was an exhibit in a museum behind glass. Well, baby, some of us don't like to work with pieces of art. We prefer the flesh and blood type of woman. No matter how gorgeous they are."

After one last glare, he stalked to the door. "We've practiced enough. I'm going to dinner. See you at the performance." He closed the door with enough force to cause her heart to jump.

She stood frozen, his words echoing in her mind. As hard as she tried, she couldn't break free from two little words he'd attributed to her—beautiful and gorgeous. Of course she'd heard herself described that way numerous times but always with a speaker's hidden (or not so hidden) agenda.

But not Franklin. He'd stated the words with passion and conviction.

And for the first time in months, she smiled.

Chapter Eight

It was a beautiful evening in Vermont. The temperature was a “mild” 30 degrees. There was little wind, making the stillness of the night wrap around Tyler like a warm blanket.

He walked across the front porch and leaned against the railing, looking over the countryside, illuminated by the moon overhead. As a grin crept on his face he relived that afternoon in the parlor when he and Stephanie had almost kissed. A chuckle escaped his lips at the wonder that she had actually seemed eager to kiss him. Almost as eager as he’d been to kiss her. His heart swelled with happiness. To have even just that small moment of joy, that the woman of his dreams would be attracted to him . . . well, it was almost too much to handle.

Leaning his elbows on the rail, his eyes on the snow, he wondered what would have happened if they hadn’t been interrupted. Would they have kissed? Would it have been as wonderful as he imagined? Tyler shook his head. Not possible.

Maybe if he could get her alone again they could . . . continue. He sighed heavily thinking the odds were against him. She had little Christy to care for. It wouldn't be easy to be alone. But maybe once they were at the orphanage and Christy was settled. Perhaps he could ask her to coffee. Or dinner, if time allowed.

He was so busy planning a strategy to be alone with Stephanie that he didn't hear the quiet click of the front door or the soft footsteps nearing him.

"It's a nice night, isn't it?"

Tyler turned suddenly, losing his footing and stumbling, catching his balance just in time to prevent his falling on his bottom. His face heated as he avoided looking into the blue eyes of the object of his thoughts. "Ah, yeah," his voice cracked. "Real nice out tonight."

She walked to stand next to him at the rail, apparently ignoring his clumsiness. She was probably getting used to his accidents. Sometimes he wondered if she'd be safer just to avoid him. Still, he couldn't help being glad she was next to him. Alone. In the night. His mind started buzzing with what to say, what to do. He felt like a teenager trying to string two words together so he wouldn't appear as dorky as he felt.

"What's Christy up to this evening?" That was good, right? Talk about the little girl.

Stephanie smiled. "Having the time of her life. She's in the parlor playing games with Bradley, Angela, and Sam, who she insists is Santa Claus." With a laugh she added, "I try to tell her that Sam is Santa's helper but she doesn't believe me. Anyway, she's happy as a clam."

After an uncomfortable pause, at least uncomfortable for Tyler, he said, "I've always wondered why a clam is so happy. I guess maybe they don't have much to worry about since they spend their day chilling in the ocean. That is unless someone catches them and they get eaten or something." Did he really just say that?

He pressed his lips together to end his brilliant observations when she giggled. Actually giggled. He felt ten feet tall.

"Oh, Tyler. You're so funny. I'm really glad we've been stranded here so I could get to know you better."

He swallowed hard, his spirit light. "Me, too."

She leaned back against the rail and breathed deeply. "This is such a nice place."

"It is. It's so peaceful out tonight. Not like the other night when we heard that wolf." When her face tensed, he congratulated himself on being a mood wrecker. "But surely it's long gone by now."

Stephanie glanced at the vast landscape, visible only in shadows. "I hope so. Angela said to stay on the porch anyway."

"Good advice." His eyes studied the dark blue of hers. Did she know her emotions showed through them, the light to her soul? He could gaze at them all night long.

"Tyler?"

"Huh?" Had she been speaking? Great, she'd caught him staring at her. "I'm sorry, what was that?"

Her bemused grin eased his embarrassment. "You never told me what the mechanic said about the van."

"Oh. We need a new part for the carburetor. They don't carry any here, no surprise as the van's about fifteen years old. It's going to take a while to get it in."

"How long?"

He shrugged. "Probably a week. With the holiday season and the weather everything's slow."

With a frown, she shook her head. "How are we going to pay for staying here that long? There isn't any money budgeted from my office. And I'm sure the orphanage can't spare any extra. Especially at this time of year."

Her concern touched that protective instinct in him. Very carefully he touched her arm, a friendly gesture, to relay his solidarity with her. "I'll think of something. Maybe Joe could use some help with the animals in the barn or the inn. I'm pretty good with animals and I'm the fix-it guy at the orphanage."

"Maybe Christy and I could help also. We could do chores in the kitchen and such."

His hand lightly rubbed her arm. "Sounds like a plan." Her gleaming eyes met his and smiled and again he was captured, not wanting to look away but unsure of doing anything else that would scare her off.

A burst of wind came out of nowhere and whipped her coat around, pushing her into Tyler. "Oh! I'm sorry."

He wasn't. His hands were on her shoulders allowing her to get her balance as his heart pounded at her nearness. "That's all right," he said softly. "But you've got to button up in this weather." He reached for her coat and buttoned the few buttons at the neck, loving being this close.

Until his watch got caught in a few errant strands of hair, seeming to attach him to her person. He tugged which got an "ouch" from her. "Sorry," he muttered trying with his other hand to release the hair.

The light sound of her giggles had him looking up. Her face was alive with humor?

"Let me help." She reached for the trapped hair, freeing it, as their hands seemed to meld together, the touch turning soft and caressing. When their eyes now met, the humor was gone, replaced with a simmering warmth that was quickly heating. He swallowed hard. The time was now. The setting couldn't get any more perfect. He wasn't going to wait any longer.

His eyes still on her, he slowly lowered his head, giving her enough time to refuse him if she wanted. He really hoped she wouldn't. Her eyes darkened and he continued, watching so that he didn't do anything stupid like miss her lips.

The first touch had fireworks shooting in his brain. He pressed a little harder, loving how her lips seemed to soften. Heat shot through him and the porch didn't seem so cold anymore.

In order to breathe, and how embarrassing would it be if he keeled over about now, he leaned back slightly. Her words took him by surprise. "I'm really glad you did that."

Clearing his throat, he said, "I've wanted to."

"You can do it again."

He grinned and proceeded to do just that, his last thought being that he had been wrong.

Kissing Stephanie was more wonderful than anything he could have imagined.

Natasha wasn't so sure about a girls' spa day. Not having any close girlfriends, she didn't know how she would handle a day having to make polite conversation. She'd never been close to any woman after her mother had died, her uncle had seen to that. There had been no slumber parties, no long telephone talks, no conversing about hair or fashion or boys. Only music. Always and only, music.

A spa day with other women was so out of her realm of experience. Maybe she could sneak away to practice for a couple of hours. She wondered where Franklin would be. They really needed to practice that medley of Christmas hymns set for tonight. Angela had said she was especially looking forward to them. Nothing like a little pressure from the one paying your salary.

She wandered through the inn looking for Franklin. Since their blow-up yesterday, their interactions had seemed to mellow. She was glad that the energy of bickering with him had somehow been replaced with a genuine desire to work with him. The thought might have disturbed her but she wasn't going to waste time analyzing. If it resulted in a better performance, well, that was the important thing.

As she neared the parlor, she recognized the voices of Angela and Franklin and hesitated. She didn't want to barge in. What could they be doing? She peeked in and watched in amazement. Angela was sitting on the couch, chatting easily while wrapping yarn into a ball. Franklin sat next to her holding the yarn around his hands, smiling at Angela. A cheery fire warmed the room and it looked like they each had a cup of coffee or tea on a dainty tray in front of them.

Franklin's face was relaxed as he listened to Angela. It was unlike any expression she'd seen on him. Usually his eyes were intense, his brow furrowed slightly as he concentrated on his music. Or battled with her.

There had been times when she'd chanced a glance of him while he played something he apparently enjoyed, like the "Jiggly Bells" song. The happiness that poured from him would slam into her like a brick wall. As much as she loved to play the violin, she couldn't remember ever feeling that happy. Maybe if she thought very hard she could remember a time with her parents, but those thoughts were few and far between and as the years passed were even harder to remember.

"Tell me, Franklin, where did you get your love for music?"

This question from Angela had Natasha craning her head to hear the answer, ignoring the idea that she was interested in Franklin's past.

"From my mother. She had music playing in our house all the time as I grew up."

"That's so nice. Music is so important."

"Yes. In fact, I sat with her many times just like this, holding yarn for her, while we listened to Chopin or Bach."

"I thought you'd done this before. Did your mother knit?"

"All the time. She made sweaters, caps, mittens, and scarves for my siblings and me."

"That's so nice."

"Yes. In fact, the brown scarf that I have today was a Christmas gift from her years ago."

"How special. Do you get to see your family much?"

Natasha leaned in a little. A quick flicker of his eyes told her he was about to tell a lie. "Not that much since they live so very far away from me."

"Where in England did you say they lived?"

Another flicker. "I didn't. It's a small . . . village. I'm sure you've never heard of it."

"You are lying, Mr. Franklin Murray," Natasha whispered. "I wonder why."

"And you met Miss Safina at the symphony in New York?"

This time his eyes didn't flicker but changed somehow. Natasha frowned, straining to hear more.

"Yes. We also have the same American management team. I suppose that's how we ended up here at your charming inn."

Angela smiled. "Yes. That's how."

"I can't tell you how wonderful it's been to be here. The inn is enchanting and the countryside is breathtaking. I think this engagement is doing me a world of good."

"I'm sure it is." Angela watched her ball of yarn grow as her head cocked. "I'm not sure that Miss Safina agrees with you. She doesn't seem to be enjoying herself."

Natasha's ears perked, watching, waiting as Franklin formed his answer.

"Natasha is . . ." *Yes, yes, what will you say about me, Franklin Murray?* "She's a brilliant musician. Not only does she have a natural talent that others can only dream about but she has a work ethic that I've never come across in my life." Natasha's heart warmed at the praise.

"Hmm. I agree with you. However, she doesn't seem . . . very happy in her work."

Her warmed heart felt a jab of pain, as if pierced by an arrow. "I think she has things going on in her life that are hard. Not that I really know as she is a very private person."

"Yes."

"I can tell you that behind the façade I believe there is a kind and generous person. I know that she routinely plays in the free performances we give to inner city schools. And any time a group is being put together for a trip to a senior citizen home or children's hospital, she's always first to volunteer. Everyone connected with the symphony respects her and in the competitive world we live in, that is saying a great deal."

"Yes," Angela agreed. "It certainly does."

Natasha stood still, unable to move. She didn't realize tears were streaming down her cheek until a few dropped to her hands clenched in front of her. Was that what people really thought of her? It couldn't be, Franklin was just making that up. But why? Why would he lie? There had been no flicker in his eyes so could he be telling the truth?

And to hear it from this man. She'd given him such grief since they'd arrived and here he was defending her. A lump formed in her throat that made it hard to swallow.

"Miss Safina?" She jumped at Joe's voice. "Is there something I can help you with?"

She tried to inconspicuously sniff. "No. I wanted to speak with Mr. Murray but didn't want to intrude."

"I'm sure they wouldn't mind." Joe started to lead her into the room but she stopped him.

"That is fine. I will speak with him later."

"He's going to the mountain to ski while you women have your spa day. Is it anything that can't wait?"

She gave one last glance back at the parlor, sighing, as her spirit seemed to settle for the first time in a long time. "No. It can wait."

As she hurried back to her room, she thought about Franklin's words and felt the warm sensation of them surround her like a hug—

something she could remember about her parents. They gave incredible hugs.

In her room she sat in the large armchair and wrapped her arms around herself, replaying the conversation between Angela and Franklin. A smile curved her lips as she thought of that new image of herself and the man who had spoken it.

Maybe her image of him was changing as well.

Chapter Nine

Women's laughter filled the solarium along with scents of lavender and jasmine. Angela sat with a mudpack on her face, cucumber slices on her eyes, her feet in a footbath, enjoying the sounds. She knew this had been a wonderful idea.

The three women from the Mountain Serenity Day Spa were miracle workers. The owner Jessica worked out of a resort hotel near the ski slopes and always catered to the needs of the Sleep In Heavenly Peace Inn. She was currently giving Stephanie a pedicure and regaling the women with humorous stories about her business.

Millie, her assistant was working on Tricia, while Katrina, another employee, was giving Mary a massage in the music room that they'd converted for the day. Angela smiled thinking that Natasha wouldn't be able to sneak away to that room to practice.

Natasha was sitting next to Angela, her face also covered with mud, waiting for her manicure. Christy, her little face covered with mud, her hair wrapped in a large towel after being conditioned, sat at a nearby table coloring, content to be in the presence of these women—a big step for the abused little girl.

Everything was going swimmingly, in Angela's opinion.

Jessica, with her thick New England accent, finished with her story and Millie, a champion talker, took over.

" . . . Then this huge linebacker of a man asks me if I can go a little deeper on the massage. I'm telling you, he had muscles piled on top of muscles and I'm on the small side but since Katrina was working on someone else and I am certified in massage therapy, I thought I could handle it. I had to climb on top of the table and lean my whole weight into the man. When that didn't go deep enough, I crawled on top of him and positively bounced." The other women all giggled.

"As I was bouncing, here comes Jessica." Millie was laughing so hard she could barely talk. "I was pushing with all my might, totally into it, and the linebacker was whimpering. Jessica calls out, 'Millie!' I stopped and looked over and saw her giving me the eye like 'what the heck are you doing.' The linebacker looks up and says, 'Don't stop now. I was just starting to feel it.'" Everyone laughed out loud. "I had to bite my tongue from laughing in his face."

"I'm not sure if I should be laughing." Angela felt the heavy mud caked on her face. "I can feel my face cracking."

Jessica chuckled. "I always think that laughter of any kind is the best medicine for the complexion. Even better than mud facials."

"You know Jessica is thinking of adding a real mud bath to the spa. Not only would you have the mud mask but you'd be completely submerged in mud." Millie sighed. "I want to be the first to try it since I've heard about them in the European spas."

Angela removed the cucumbers on her eyes and turned to Natasha. "You've traveled quite a bit, Miss Safina. Did you ever see a mud bath?"

"What?" She seemed surprised that someone was speaking to her. "Yes, I have. Near Basel, Switzerland is superb spa that specializes in mud baths."

The woman all "oohed."

"Did you try it, Miss Safina?" Millie asked. "What was it like?"

Natasha considered her answer as if it was of world importance. "It was relaxing. My skin felt soft afterward and I was . . . how do you say . . . the stress was gone." Everyone sighed.

"What did the mud feel like?" Millie voice revealed her excitement.

"When I gave the helper my robe and stepped into the bath, it was thick."

"You were naked? In the mud?" Stephanie asked.

"Yes, that is how it was. Then I lie flat on my back. The helper put more mud on my top until I am covered to my chin. I lie there for one hour, not moving. It was wonderful."

"Hmm." Millie thought it over. "Could you move your hands?"

"No. The mud is very heavy."

"Well, what do you do if your nose itches?"

Several snickered but Natasha didn't notice as she thought hard. "I do not know what you do if you must itch. Perhaps you turn your mind to thoughts other than itching."

Everyone giggled and Angela was gratified to see Natasha joining in."

Millie sighed. "Ah, I envy you, Miss Safina. Working with that hunk. Mom and I came over a couple of nights ago for a performance and I couldn't stop watching him." Her eyebrows wiggled. "I'd love to make some music with him." More giggling. "He is dreamy."

Angela watched Natasha's reaction. "Yes, he is very talented," she said with no emotion.

"Is he seeing anyone?"

"Seeing anyone?"

"Yeah. Does he have a girlfriend?

Natasha's mind was humming. After a moment she said, "I do not know the answer but . . ." She gave the young woman a survey. "He may."

Millie's face fell. "Oh, blast. It seems the best men are taken."

Angela watched Natasha's confused expression. Thinking to change subjects, she said, "Stephanie. What's the latest on the van?"

"It seems we're here for a while until some part comes in." She quickly added, "Tyler and I've spoken to Mary and Joe about doing some work to pay for our rooms."

"Don't you worry about it, honey. It'll all work out."

"Speaking of good looking men, that Tyler is a real cutie. He helped us bring in all our supplies this morning." Everyone stared at Jessica. "Relax, not for me. I've got a niece that would be perfect for him. She's the right age, teaches Sunday school to first graders. A real sweet girl."

"He'll be going back to Newport as soon as our van is repaired," Stephanie replied a little too quickly. Seeming to catch herself she added, "Because, you know, that's where he lives."

"Well, just the same, maybe I'll bring her over soon. Introduce the two of them." Angela watched Stephanie frown and her breathing grow shallow.

Apparently Jessica noticed also. "You okay, honey? You seem tense. Let me get you a glass of ice water."

"All done, Tricia." Millie stood and wiped her hands on a towel, admiring Tricia's bright red toes. "Who's next?"

"Why don't we let Christy go next?" Tricia walked over to the little girl. "Are you ready to have your toenails painted, sweetie?" The little girl looked up at her, her face devoid of emotion. Tricia crouched down beside her, smiling. "It's fun. It even tickles and when Millie's done, you'll have beautiful feet." She stuck one foot out and pointed. "See?"

Christy glanced at her foot and then stared at her. "Want me to take you over?" Tricia held out her hand. The little girl looked at it, hesitated, and finally took it. Tricia's smile beamed as she walked her over and lifted her gently into the chair that Millie had added a bolster seat to. "There you are. Now you're going to have beautiful feet and hands just like all of us."

To that comment, Christy gave Tricia a small smile.

"Well, now I know how one of my noodles feels." Mary hobbled into the room, followed by Katrina.

"How was it?"

"Oh, Angela. I can't remember the last time I felt so relaxed. Katrina, you're marvelous."

"We aim to please. Be sure to keep drinking water. You want to get rid of toxins in your system." She glanced around. "Who's next?"

"I guess I am," Tricia said. She rubbed her hands together. "Let's get rid of those toxins."

Millie set Christy's feet in a footbath and began working on her nails. "So, little princess, what do you want for Christmas?"

Christy just looked at her with no emotion, her one good eye blinking underneath the mud mask. Sitting in a chair next to her, Stephanie leaned over, her hand patting the little girl's arm. "It's all right, honey. Millie is a friend."

"Of Santa's?" she whispered.

Stephanie paused. "Um, yeah, I'm sure Millie is a friend of Santa's."

With a deep sigh as she sipped iced water with lemon slices, Mary said, "I can vouch for that. This whole spa day is an early Christmas present." She winked her thanks to Angela.

The spa day continued until everyone had been massaged, exfoliated, buffed, and polished. Afterwards, Angela led the women to the hot tub in the back of the property, with Jessica, Millie, and Katrina joining them since they were officially off the clock.

"Where's Stephanie and Christy?" Tricia asked looking around.

"I told Stephanie it might be a little too hot for children so she took Christy inside to get her dressed."

The bubbles worked their magic as the women all leaned back, eyes closed and enjoyed the churning sensation of the water. Steam filled the cold air creating a cozy cloud.

"I think I could stay here for hours," Millie murmured. It was the quietest she'd been all day.

"Yeah. Anytime you want to book us, Angela, just say the word. We love coming to your place."

"I've got to tell Darren we need one of these. Can't think of anything as relaxing as coming home after a hard day at work and stepping into a hot tub." Tricia opened an eye and looked around. "Although I'm not looking forward to getting out into the cold with just a swimsuit on."

Angela and Mary glanced at each other and burst out in giggles. "It can be a problem. Especially if the water is lukewarm," Angela said. The others groaned in agony.

"Yes, it happened a couple of years ago. It seems the temperature gauge was, ahem, acting up." Mary looked sideways at Angela, who gave her most innocent expression. "Seems to me it was especially cold that year." Mary and Angela giggled.

"Funniest thing I ever saw was the two of them trying to put their clothes and shoes over wet bathing suits and run back to the house before they got frostbite."

Millie sat up straight. "That's not—"

"No worries. This tub is staying hot." Angela leaned back and sighed.

There was a crash from the barn and before anyone could say anything, the door pushed open. The new dog flew out, a little clumsy with her extra weight, and excitedly ran circles around the yard while barking.

"What do you suppose is wrong with that precious dog?" Tricia asked.

Mary scowled. "Joe put her in the barn while he was gone so she wouldn't be out causing trouble." Another crash behind the shed had her wincing. "I'm afraid she's found trouble." She stood, reached for a towel, and carefully stepped out.

"The poor dear probably needed some exercise." Mary smirked at Angela.

The dog flew past the hot tub and headed for the back door. "Hey, hey, hey. You are not going to track up my clean floor anymore!" Mary wrapped the towel around her middle, quickly pulled on her Ugg boots and ran to choral the animal.

Thinking it was a game, the dog took off and, if Angela wasn't mistaken, she was smiling widely. The chase was on as the dog zigzagged across the yard, behind the barn, around the shed, and past the hot tub. The women watched from the safe distance of the steaming water.

"Do you suppose we should get out and help?" Millie asked.

"Probably." Jessica said and leaned back in the hot water.

The chase continued for a few more minutes and just as Mary seemed to be gaining, the dog made a last burst near the hot tub. Mary lunged trying to grab her but tripped in a patch of . . . mud. Splat!

She landed face down, stretched out in the mud. Everyone looked over the side of the hot tub, no one speaking.

Finally, Millie said, "Well, Mary. Guess you got that mud bath after all."

A beat past and everyone burst into peals of laughter, including Mary.

Just before dinner, Joe, Darren, Bradley, and Christy walked to the barn to check on the animals. It was the second time Darren had made it to the barn and it was quickly becoming a highlight of his vacation.

They laid out the food, taking time to check on each animal. Frederica was tuckered out after her exercise with Mary so she lay down, happy to be petted and groomed.

Darren ran a brush through her thick hair as Christy sat next to him, gently running her hands over his side. He smiled and said, “Christy, would you like to brush the dog?”

She turned to him and stared. Slowly, she nodded and Darren gave her the brush, thrilled that she’d interacted with him, even if in a small way. He gently instructed her, even guiding her hands over the dog’s body.

“That’s a good job, Christy. Ole Frederica likes it.” The girl smiled tentatively at Bradley.

“Heard you had a big day with the ladies, honey. Did you have fun?” Joe asked. She kept her head down but nodded.

“I know Tricia really enjoyed it. What is it with women and spas? I’d much rather be out on the slopes any day.”

“I hear you.” Joe shrugged. “Still, if it makes them happy.”

Darren shook his head. “I can’t think of enough to keep me occupied for all afternoon in a spa. What did they do?”

Joe’s eyebrows furrowed in concentration. “I’m not sure. I think I heard something about a mud bath.” He shrugged. “But it was worth it. Mary was happy and relaxed when I got back today. And you know, happy wife—"

"Yeah. Happy life." Darren stood back and watched the two children rubbing on the dog then turned to see Joe smiling. "You've only been married a couple of years, right?"

His smile brightened. "That's right. Best decision I ever made."

He glanced at Bradley. "It wasn't hard, suddenly becoming a father?"

"Huh? No. Well, I'd known Mary and Bradley for a while so it wasn't a shock." Joe's eyes took on a warm glow as he watched Bradley. Quietly, he said, "Bradley needed a father. I was crazy in love with Mary. It was just the right decision."

"He accepted you, no problem?"

Joe frowned. "I guess our situation is a little different from others. You see, Bradley's father was a friend of mine. We were in the military together." His tone became somber. "He didn't come home from the Middle East."

"I'm sorry."

"Yeah." He paused to remember. "But really I think even if I hadn't known him, me and Bradley would still have hit it off."

"Why is that?"

Joe leaned back against a stall railing. "Because we like each other. We spend time together. I guess that grew into love." He cocked his head and said, "Why do you ask?"

"Just curious." Darren studied Christy. Could he have that kind of relationship with this precious little girl? It was what she deserved, what she needed. Maybe Tricia was right and this was the answer to their becoming parents. Still, he wasn't ready to make any decisions.

"Let's get the hay out for the horse."

Darren followed Joe to the back of the barn as the children continued to pet and groom Frederica.

"You should have been with us today, Christy. Mr. Tom at the hardware store showed us about a zillion different screws. He even gave me a grape lollipop. It made my tongue all purple. See?"

Christy studied Bradley's colored tongue and smiled. "I h-had fun too. They put m-m-mud on my face."

Bradley's eyes got huge. "You got to play with mud? I didn't know you did cool things like that!" Christy gave him a satisfied grin.

The dog sighed and lay her head down, eyes closing. Bradley put a finger over his lips. "Shh. Let's let her sleep. You know she's tired a lot on account of she's going to have puppies."

"Really?"

"Uh huh. Papa says it's going to happen soon so we've got to take good care of her." He took her hand and stood. "Come on. Let's visit Pokey the horse."

They stood on the railing and the horse instantly came over to greet them. "Hey Pokey. How's it going?" The horse gave a soft neigh and the kids giggled. Bradley touched the horse's nose, patting him gently. "You remember Christy? She's a friend that's staying at the house."

Christy started to reach out. "Christy!" She pulled her hand back and turned to see the men bringing over a bale of hay.

Joe dropped his side and went to her, putting his hands on her shoulders. "You've got to be very careful when approaching a horse, honey. Sometimes they'll nip at you." He took her hand and opened it. Inside of his strong one, they reached out and gently touched the horse's head. "That's right. Ole Pokey here likes a soft touch. See how his head leans towards you? That means he likes it." Christy's face brightened. When the horse nuzzled his head with hers, she giggled. "Well, look at that. I think this horse is falling in love with you, sweetheart. What do you think of that?"

Her smile big, she looked at the horse and then Joe. "I-I-I like him."

Joe chuckled and gave her a little hug.

While the men gave Pokey his dinner, Bradley and Christy said goodnight to the other animals. The horse neighed, the cow mooed, the chickens cackled, and the duck quacked. Christy ran her hand over the soft wool of the sheep as they "baaaed" their approval.

They peeked in on Frederica, watching her snore in her little stall. Bradley sighed and said, "I want a dog for Christmas. I asked Santa and everything. Sure hope he gets my letter in time."

"Can't you t-tell him at d-dinner?"

Bradley sighed in frustration. "I'm telling you, Sam's not Santa. Mom explained it to me. He's only Santa's helper. But you're right, it couldn't hurt to tell him too. Hey, what do you want for Christmas?"

She watched Bradley, her expression thoughtful. She glanced around and turned back. With a sigh, she leaned in and whispered in Bradley's ear her deepest Christmas wish.

His eyes got big. "Really? That's what you want?" She nodded. He petted the lambs, thinking. "Mmm. Well, Santa's had harder things before, I'm sure he can handle this. Are you sure it's what you want?" She nodded. "Okay. But you gotta believe. Sam taught that to me. If you don't believe in a miracle, a miracle can't happen."

"W-what's a m-miracle?"

"It's when something really good happens, something that you wanted really bad."

"Oh."

"Just the same, I think we should tell Sam about it. He might have some ideas."

"What about A-Angela? She looks like a angel to me."

Bradley thought about this. "Really? I always thought she was just a nice lady."

Chapter Ten

"She was so cute with her little face all covered in the mud mask. And she picked the same color for her nails as I did, the red. Isn't that cute?"

Tricia had not stopped talking about Christy from the moment Darren had returned to their room to shower before dinner. Her excitement filled him with joy since she'd struggled for so long with her emotions.

"She couldn't go to the hot tub since young children shouldn't be in them for long and the rest of us had a nice long soak. Which reminds me." Eyebrows lifted in her best hopeful expression, she said, "How about we get one for our backyard?"

"A hot tub?"

"Yes. They're very therapeutic and you've said how your back is sometimes sore after a day at work." She stepped to him, running a finger down the front of his shirt. "Can't you just see it? You and me, relaxing in our very own hot tub."

He took her in his arms and kissed her neck. "Sounds very . . . relaxing." He kissed her again. And again. "I'm thinking the idea may be inspired." He took her face in his hands and gently kissed her lips.

She smiled at him. "Of course, we'd have to make sure that Christy was in bed while we were in but we can buy one of those baby monitors to hear her."

Darren stepped back and grabbed a comb to run through his hair. "We're still thinking that through, aren't we?"

Her expression through the mirror was one of confusion. "I thought you agreed it was a good idea, the best idea."

"I said we needed to think about it. I'm not ready to make any decisions yet."

"Well, for goodness sakes, what do you need to decide? She's a sweet little girl who needs a home. We're good people who want to be parents. What more do you need to know?"

"Lots." He set down the comb. "Look, I'm not saying it isn't a good idea, but it's too important to rush into." Before Tricia could speak, he took her shoulders and sat with her on the side of the bed. "We need to spend more time with her, talk with Miss Singer about her needs, we need to . . . seriously think how this will impact our lives."

"It will make them better. Don't you think?"

"Maybe." He narrowed his eyes. "What are we going to do during the day? Are you going to give up managing my office to stay home with her? If not, you want to put her in childcare all day? That might not be the best idea with all her problems."

"But she's going to an orphanage if we don't help."

"And the orphanage probably has access to all the professionals that will be needed to help her get over her past."

Tricia's tone softened. "Darren. We can help her get over her past."

He rubbed his wife's arm. "I believe you. But again, I want to make sure before we commit our lives to her." He stood and finished buttoning his shirt. "Lord knows she's been through enough changes in her life. That little girl needs stability. And love."

Tricia came up from behind and wrapped her arms around his middle. "And we're just the mother and father that can give it to her."

He smiled at her in the mirror.

But a side of him couldn't help thinking that they needed more time. He'd give it a few more days. Tyler had said they were there for another week, maybe two. They'd have plenty of time getting to know the little girl.

The inn was finally quiet after a busy day. Lights in the halls and parlor were left on low as guests settled down in their rooms for the night.

Franklin sat in his "White Christmas" room and studied the music before him. His attention, however, kept slipping to the past day. When had he experienced a day so full, so happy? He'd gone to the ski slopes with Darren. While the man had gone to the long trails, he had taken a beginner's class. Even after a few falls, he'd fallen in love with the sport and after a couple of hour's time had met up with Darren and even attempted a few intermediate trails. His family would be so amazed—him at a fancy ski resort, snow skiing. He had to remember to get a postcard and send to his parents.

After his time on the slopes, Mary's meal of chicken and dumplings had seemed like a banquet. He'd been ravenous. Dinner with the other guests had been totally enjoyable.

He thought of the real pleasure of the day. Natasha. Something was different about her. She hadn't balked about him going skiing while she had a girls' spa day. She hadn't argued when they'd had a short, late afternoon rehearsal. And she'd been cordial all during their evening performances. She even interacted with several of the women.

What had gone on during the spa day?

Yes, she was still Natasha, with her hair and makeup perfect, her clothes tailored, her performance flawless. But there was a quietness about her today, almost as if she was deep in thought. It was a different side to her that interested him. But if he were honest, every side of Natasha was fascinating to him, something he definitely wasn't going to admit.

Shaking his head, he got back to work, looking over the copy of "Christmastime is Here." It could be a piano solo, but the strains of a violin in the background would add such a deep layer to the piece, he had to talk Natasha into playing it with him. In his mind he could see her nimble fingers expertly manipulating her instrument into music that would charm the devil himself. Her talent was unlike any other he'd ever encountered. He looked out the window into the dark night. The moon was behind a cloud, plunging everything outside into darkness. It reminded him of Natasha's hair.

Enough with thinking about the woman! As if he didn't have plenty to keep himself busy, now he was fantasizing about Natasha Safina?

He turned back to the music, imagining the performance. When his eyes again saw Natasha next to him, playing the violin, he decided maybe if he just asked her now about accompanying him with the piece, he could stop fantasizing about the woman.

Grabbing the music, he left his room and walked down the hall to hers. Hopefully she wasn't in bed yet. He'd knock quietly a couple of times and if she didn't answer, he'd go back to his room and force himself to get some sleep.

He was surprised when his first tap against the door had it creaking open. Why had she left her door open? Even though they weren't in a big city, it still wasn't safe to sleep in an unlocked room. Didn't she know that anyone could happen by? Grateful for the anger that now surged in his blood, a more comfortable way to deal with Natasha, he walked into the room.

Suddenly a chill skidded down his spine. Had something happened to her? Was she all right? His stomach plummeted with the possibility that she wasn't well.

All the lights were on but there was no Natasha. When he heard her in the bathroom, his body heaved with relief. "Natasha, it's Franklin. What do you mean by leaving your door open? You live in New York City, don't you know you always, always lock your door? You never know when—"

The words stopped in his throat when the door opened and she walked out. "What is it? Has something happened?"

He didn't hear her. His body was too busy absorbing her presence. She wore a short red silk robe that stopped high on her thighs revealing her lovely, long toned legs. The robe, obviously hastily put on, was slipping off one creamy, white shoulder. Her hair—he'd never seen it down, never knew it was so long. Obviously still damp from a shower, it flowed around her face, and down to the middle of her back, in shiny riotous waves that made him think of the churning ocean in the dead of night.

But her face. Her golden eyes were wide and innocent. There wasn't a smidge of makeup on that exquisite face, showing high cheekbones, dewy skin, rose red lips. He was completely mesmerized.

Perhaps if he swallowed, he'd regain the use of his tongue but he highly doubted it. Nor did he want to stop the spell. He just wanted to stay where he was and savor her beauty.

She pulled her robe tighter. "Did you need something?"

His mind was working overtime at the answer to that question.

"Uh . . . uh."

Her eyes seemed to soften, just for a moment, causing his pulse to accelerate. His hands itched to reach out and touch her. To pull her into his arms and hold her close.

Until she blinked twice and cleared her throat. "There must be a reason for this . . . bust into my room. Why are you here?"

"Here we are. Your key, just like—oh, Mr. Murray. I didn't know you were here." Angela stopped, turning back and forth between Franklin and Natasha.

His voice returning, he said, "I, ah, had to give something to Ms. Safina." He waved the sheet music as if to verify his presence.

"Thank you, Angela for the key."

"No problem, dear. You must have left it on the table after dinner. Well, I'll say goodnight. See you in the morning."

Once she'd left, Natasha turned on Franklin, her hands fisted on her hips. "What is this about sheet music? You could not wait until morning?" Her eyes narrowed. "Why do you look at me like this?"

He hesitated and said, "I was worried."

This seemed to puzzle her. "What?"

He shook his head to clear it. "I came to have you take a look at this, maybe something we could do together. When I knocked, the door opened and I was worried when you hadn't locked it."

Her expression eased and her body relaxed. She took a step closer to him, letting out a breath. "Oh. I . . . well, that is . . . nice."

When their eyes met, a tension filled the room, thicker than the clouds on the mountain. Neither seemed to be able to look away but neither seemed inclined to move closer.

"I'll just . . . leave this music here. When you get a chance, look over it. I think you could probably play an echo during the second verse." She nodded, not speaking.

He placed the music on the dresser, next to a plush Grinch that went with the room's theme. In the mirror he saw the Dr. Seuss classic Christmas story open on her nightstand. So, she was reading it. He smiled and turned, surprised that his movement had moved him closer to her. She smelled of apples and peaches, probably a shampoo or body wash, but either way, it attracted him like a bee to honey. Her wide-eyed expression made him think of the wonder of first love. He wanted desperately to move closer, to—

Outside, a wolf cried out. Not a sad cry, not a lonely cry, but one of anger, of aggression.

Natasha moved instantly to him, her hands coming to his chest. "It is back."

His hands were around her, holding her firmly. "It appears." His heart thudded at her nearness, at her softness. He would have liked to go on holding her just this way but a commotion sounded in the hall. They hurried outside the room to find Tricia holding tightly to Darren, his arms around her, a crying Christy in Stephanie's arms, who was trying to console her. From below, Tyler bounded up the stairs, running to put his arms around the two girls. "You all right?" he asked Stephanie, who nodded.

Joe came from the attic apartment buttoning his shirt, followed by Mary and Bradley. "Everyone here? No one's outside?" After getting confirmation, he hurried downstairs. Angela, who lived in the other apartment on the third level also came down. Seeing the worried looks, she said, "I'm sure everything will be fine. The wolf probably won't even come near here."

No one looked convinced.

"How about we go downstairs and I'll make a pot of tea. Stephanie, would Christy like a glass of milk?"

"That'd be nice."

Bradley walked to Stephanie and patted Christy's arm. "It's okay, Christy. My papa will make sure that bad ole wolf doesn't come here. Let's get some milk." He turned to his mother. "And Christy could probably go for a Christmas cookie. Don't you think, Mom?" He gave her his sweetest smile.

Mary grinned. "I see what you did there. Okay. We'll break out the Christmas cookies. But you can choose only one."

Bradley didn't argue.

Morning was a miserable affair. Everyone was grumpy from lack of sleep along with worry over the wolf. Angela watched the guests try to eat their breakfast of pancakes and bacon. And plenty of coffee. Lots and lots of coffee.

She lifted the coffee pot and noticing it was nearly empty said, "I guess I'll go to the kitchen and refill the pot. That is, if anyone wants more coffee. All the adults immediately chimed in their urgent need of the caffeinated liquid.

In the kitchen, Mary was asleep standing, her head leaning against an upper cabinet. Angela gently touched her arm. "Mary?"

She startled awake. "What? Oh, I'm sorry." She yawned. "I didn't get much sleep last night."

Angela looked towards the dining room. "That seems to be the theme of the morning. Bradley have trouble?"

"Some. He insisted on sleeping with me until Joe got back. To protect me. He was wrapped around me and I didn't have the heart to take him back to bed once Joe came. Even still, he slept in fits." She yawned again.

"The poor dear."

Mary glanced at the door to the dining room. "How's Christy this morning?"

"I do believe she may be the only well rested one of the bunch. She was very excited for the apple pancakes this morning. Seems to be very hungry. Stephanie is keeping her close to her side."

"Of course."

The back door opened and Joe walked into the mudroom, stomping snow off his boots. His expression was somber. He nodded at the women.

"Joe, tell me what you saw last night."

He headed straight for the coffee pot and poured a cup, taking a sip of the strong black brew, sitting at the little kitchen table. “I turned on all the outdoor lights. We should think of getting motion detectors.”

“Absolutely. I’ll get you the money.”

“I didn’t see it, but I heard it. Right in the woods behind the inn. I went into the barn to check on the animals. They were pretty shaken, so I gave rubdowns and such. Made sure they had fresh water. Tried to settle them down. Then locked the barn back and came inside.”

“And watched outside for the next three hours,” Mary added.

He gave a tired grin. “Maybe two.”

Angela sat next to him and patted his arm. “I’m grateful. What about this morning?”

Joe leaned back in his chair and rubbed his eyes. “I’ve called animal control and alerted them. I called all the authorities I could think of. Hasn’t been any trouble at the ski resort or downtown Stowe.”

“That’s good.”

“Yeah. I called the Lesters,” he said mentioning their nearest neighbors. “They heard it but said only off in the distance. Thought it might be some stupid kids playing a prank or something.”

“Is that possible?” Mary stood next to her husband, her hand on his shoulder.

Joe shook his head and took her hand in his. “I’m afraid not.” He glanced to Angela. “I saw its trail.”

The air seemed to be sucked out of the room at the news.

"How close?"

"At the edge of the woods." He took a deep breath. "On our property."

Both women gasped. "Our property! He was coming here?"

Frustration was evident in Joe's voice. "Looks like it. We need to do something, Angela, and barring sitting on the back stoop with my gun and having target practice when it gets close, I don't know what to do."

Mary's other hand gently massaged his shoulder. "Joe," she said to calm him.

He sighed loud and long. "Sorry. I'm worried. About my family. Our guests, the animals."

"Of course." Angela was baffled and she hated to be baffled. This certainly wasn't the plan for the holiday season, to be concerned about a crazy wolf creating havoc.

"Why don't you go get some sleep? The both of you. I'll clean up breakfast and see about Bradley." Angela looked around. "Where is he?"

"Sleeping in his own bed. Probably not for long."

"Well, send him down when he wakes. I'll think of something fun to do today to get our minds cleared."

"Good luck." Joe yawned. "I think I could drink a gallon of coffee."

"Coffee! Oh my, I forgot. I'm supposed to be getting coffee." Angela jumped up and grabbing the pot hurried back to the dining room. You'd have thought she was the rescue squad come to save those trapped inside by a blizzard by the welcome she received. She poured cups, glad to see that the java seemed to be slowly helping everyone perk up.

As they drank coffee and nibbled at breakfast, Angela wracked her brain with cheerful news for the folks. "Mary's got a nice coffee cake this morning." She went to the buffet and brought the cake back to the table. "It should go very well with the, ah, coffee."

Everyone looked at the cake with not much interest. Except Christy. She brightened and Angela couldn't help chuckling as she cut a piece for the girl.

Once she sat again, she took a breath. "Franklin, we're going to have a full house tonight for your performance in the parlor." His eyes went to Angela. "Our friends at the spa have told everyone they know and are bringing over a group tonight."

"It will be our pleasure to perform for them," Franklin said in his dignified British accent.

"I suppose I'd better warn you. Millie, from the spa, seems to have her eye on you. Thinks you are quite a catch."

Natasha's head popped up. "Catch? What is catch?"

"It means she thinks Franklin is attractive, a nice man that she'd like to get to know."

"He lives in New York City. Is woman going to move to be near him? Or follow him around when he tours? How does she know he is catch if she does not know him?"

Everyone stared at Natasha. Especially Franklin. As always, her makeup was impeccable, showcasing a flawless face, except for the slight black circles under her eyes that even makeup couldn't hide.

Angela, with a sweet smile, said, "I think that is the object—to get to know him."

"He is busy performing." Natasha realized that everyone was watching her. Especially Franklin. Her eyes flickered briefly before she said, "I will not have my performance gone wrong because woman is . . . bothering you. Will not happen. Is clear?"

Franklin's eyes warmed slightly. The edges of his lips lifted. "Clear."

"I'm sure she doesn't mean to bother anyone. She was just telling me that she and Jessica's niece were very excited about coming—"

"Jessica's niece?" Stephanie asked, suddenly interested.

"Yes. Seems she'd like an introduction to Tyler." The man in question dropped his fork, making it clang against the china plate. He looked around, obviously hating to be the center of attention.

"Jessica was so impressed by you the other day when you helped bring in her supplies. She wants you to meet Cammie. I've met her, she's a very nice young lady."

"Oh. Well." Starting with the tips of his ears, his face turned bright red. "That's . . . ah, something." He turned to Stephanie and took her hand, causing her to gaze at him. "Stephanie and I'd be glad to meet Jessica's niece."

So, he was stating his position, Angela thought. Good boy.

Her eyes roamed the table and landed on Tricia who was smiling at her. The woman gave her a wink clearly understanding Angela's intent in bringing up the two women coming that evening. Angela tried to give her best "I don't know a thing" look but just couldn't resist returning the smile.

Conversation died out. The Matthews didn't want to go skiing, as Tricia was concerned they'd meet up with the wolf on one of the trails. The others didn't seem eager for any activities either. Stephanie and Tyler were waiting for assignments from Mary and Joe but Angela explained about their sleepless night and that they were napping.

Just as Angela was running out of ideas, Sam and Eldon, who'd eaten earlier, came into the dining room.

"Morning, folks. We had a couple of inches of fresh power overnight. It's a great morning to take a walk. Who's up for snowshoeing?"

Chapter Eleven

It was the perfect idea, Angela thought as they stomped through the field next to the inn, a bright white wonderland waiting to be explored. The air was sharp and invigorating, just what everyone needed. Thoughts of the wolf had evaporated just like the wisps of smoke from their breath. She heard pleasant voices and chuckles as they trudged on. It was good.

Sam led the way and Eldon brought up the rear, adding a feeling of safety for their little group. Behind Sam was Bradley who held Christy's hand. The boy was talking a mile a minute pointing things out and giving a running commentary on the countryside. Angela smiled, happy that little Bradley was taking his job as host seriously, helping a damaged little girl to heal. Her heart puffed with happiness.

Christy was fast becoming a different child from the one that had appeared one snowy evening last week. Her cheeks were rosy, as a child's should be, and she smiled more easily. She was trusting with Bradley and was getting more comfortable with the adults around her. The bad eye was healing and was slightly open now. Her words were still few and not very clear, but she was trying. Angela was very proud of her.

As for the others, well . . . she was cautiously optimistic. So far, each couple seemed to be closer and that was good. But with all relationships, they would be tested and her loving heart hoped they had the strength to make it through those tests. Time would tell.

Stephanie walked beside Tyler, enjoying his nearness. They hadn't had much opportunity to be together since their kiss, which had been the most phenomenal kiss of her life. Who would have guessed that quiet, sweet Tyler was so romantic? There was certainly something electric between them and she was eager to find out what it was.

He walked closer, brushing up against her and she was pleased to see him grinning at her. She took his arm and held his hand, loving the strength she felt from him.

They walked along in silence for a while when he said, "I'd like to see you."

She giggled and replied, "You're seeing me right now."

Shaking his head and frowning, he said, "No. I mean I'd like to . . . you know, see you. As in date."

The nerve endings in her body seemed to come alive with excitement at his words. Despite the cold temperature, she could feel her hands getting sweaty. She felt the glow of her cheeks and realized she was giddy with expectation. "I . . . I'd like that too."

"You would?" He seemed surprised.

"Of course. I'd like to explore what's between us." Her thoughts veered towards their situation and sighed as she said, "But I'm not sure it's going to be easy."

"Why not?"

"Well, for starters, you live in Newport and I live in Burlington. That's not next door."

"I know." They trudged on. "But we've both got phones. We can take weekends to see each other. I've seen people make long distance relationships work. They can work."

"Maybe. But Tyler, my job is very demanding. I put in a lot of hours working for these kids. It's my passion, my reason for living. I'm not sure about being . . . distracted."

He squeezed her hand. "I know. That's one reason you're so special." He hesitated. "I would have loved to have had you on my side when I was a baby." Frowning, he said, "I mean, not really because then you'd be a couple of decades older than me." She laughed. "But you know what I mean. I admire how hard you work for these kids. It's beautiful. It makes you beautiful."

No one had ever spoken those words to her or understood her purpose in life. No one until Tyler. At the moment she wanted so badly to grab him and kiss his breath away. Her throat heavy, she said, "Thank you."

"I wouldn't in any way interfere with what you do. If anything, I'd like to help. That's what I try to do at the orphanage, try to work for our kids, like you do at social services."

She stared at this man that was beginning to mean so much to her. "You are very special, you know that, Tyler?"

He shrugged the comment off. "Not really."

"Oh, you are. Those kids are mighty lucky to have you." He grinned. She lowered her voice and said, "And if we weren't with a group of people right now, I'd kiss you silly."

His adorable blush started and she laughed. "Okay. We'll try the long distance relationship. See where it goes."

To her surprise, he leaned over and gave her a quick kiss on the lips. His voice was low, filling her insides with warmth when he said, "Good decision."

He wrapped his arm around her, pulling her to his side as they walked on. Stephanie giggled and said, "Do you realize that you haven't had any . . . accidents since you first kissed me?"

"Hmm. There must be a lesson in there somewhere." His eyes brightened. "Maybe as long as I'm kissing you, I'm not a walking disaster. You could save humankind a great deal of trouble by continuing to kiss me."

She laughed out loud. "Well, if I must, I must."

They were still gazing at each other when Tricia walked up. "Hey, you two. I can see this walk was a good idea, especially for you guys." She waggled her brows up and down.

Tyler cleared his throat and looked away, Stephanie giggled and said, “I think we all needed some fresh air.”

“Indeed.” Tricia’s eyes went to her husband who had lifted a chuckling Christy off her feet and set her on his shoulders. “I think there must be healing powers in the air up here. Or maybe it’s in the inn. It’s a special place.” Both Stephanie and Tyler agreed with her.

“Listen, I wanted to talk to you about something, and . . .” Tricia took a deep breath. “I figured this was as good a place as any to do it.”

“Okay.”

“You want privacy?” Tyler motioned that he could walk with the others.

“No. You’re also responsible for Christy’s future so you should stay and hear what I have to say.”

Stephanie was getting uncomfortable. Had Christy done something? What could this woman possibly say about Christy? Clearly she was nervous, her hands jittery, her breaths uneven, her eyes unsure.

“Darren and I . . . well, we’d like to start the process to adopt Christy.”

Stunned was a mild word for the way Stephanie felt. Maybe numb. She’d never seen this coming. But how could she, they hadn’t been at the inn for a week and Tricia was ready to take Christy home to raise?

She’d dealt with all kinds of women before—abusive mothers, struggling mothers, women who were becoming mothers both naturally and through adoption. It was a very sensitive subject so she knew she had to tread carefully.

"I see." She glanced at Tyler and saw him quietly watching her, deferring to her, although he did squeeze her hand in support. She was thankful for him at the moment.

"Tell me what you're thinking."

"Oh, Stephanie, I've been so excited, I don't think I've slept for the past two nights. You see, Darren and I have been trying to have a baby for several years and . . . well, nothing has happened. We came to Vermont for Christmas thinking if we just got away and concentrated on each other . . . But when we saw Christy . . . She needs a home and, no offense," she said to Tyler, "but it would be much better for her to have a loving, two parent home than be one of many in an orphanage. Right?"

"Well, yes."

"We can give her that home. We can be her parents. We're established, upper middle class. She'll never want for anything. I just know we can be a family together." She blew out a breath. "What do you think?"

Stephanie looked ahead to see Christy giggling as Darren bounced over the snow. She smiled at the little girl's delight. Was it possible? Was this the answer for Christy? A few thoughts bothered her mind.

"It seems rather sudden. Have you pursued adoption before?"

"No, that's just the thing," she said, as if it explained everything. "We'd never thought of it until Christy. Maybe that proves we were just waiting to meet her. That it was meant to be."

"What does your husband think about the idea?"

"He's excited, like me." She sighed, her eyes going to Darren and Christy. "Just look at the two of them. Don't they look perfect together?"

Her mind wavered back and forth between good idea and horrible idea, the answer to placing Christy and a terrible mistake for the girl. It absolutely would be ideal for her to have a home. But why hadn't both Tricia and Darren approached her? Christy needed love and she'd definitely seen that between Tricia and Darren but did they realize all that would be involved with her healing?

There was a lot to discuss.

"Christy has been through a great deal. There's scar tissue, both physical and emotional. It's going to take time, patience, and professionals to help her heal."

Tricia's voice softened. "And love. You forgot that, which I think is the most important thing. We're ready to give her everything she needs. Will you help us?"

Stephanie eyed Tyler, who watched her, encouraging her. The woman seemed sincere. Everything she had seen in the Matthews did point to the idea that they would be good parents.

Still she was hesitant.

"The adoption process is a long one. There are forms to complete. There will be visits to your home to evaluate you and Darren, interviews to do. Plus the fact that you live in a different state adds more paperwork and I'm afraid time."

"You mean we can't just take her home with us?"

Tyler's brows furrowed. She understood. She wanted to tell Tricia that Christy wasn't a dog that they could just pay for shots and a collar and carry off but she held her tongue.

"No. Like I said, it's a long process. Are you willing to go through that?"

Tricia looked over the horizon and back at her husband and Christy. A warm, authentic smile appeared, instantly softening Stephanie. "Yes. We're willing."

"Well then, I guess I can print out the initial request at the inn. You can start on that mountain of paperwork."

With tears in her eyes, Tricia said, "Thank you. So much."

Franklin walked beside Natasha. They hadn't spoken much since they'd been out, a few words of idle chatter. He wondered what was going through that captivating brain of hers.

"It's a lovely day out."

"Yes," she replied, her eyes scanning the countryside.

"Is Russia as beautiful?"

"Yes. There are spots where beauty makes you cry. It stretches out and welcomes. And sky is so blue it hurts eyes."

"Do you miss it?"

She considered the question. "I think I miss country. At times. Is beautiful."

"Do you miss the 'jiggly bells'?" He grinned at her and was pleased that she smiled back.

"Is cold in Russia. You Americans know nothing of cold weather with playing in snow and snowmen and 'Who people.'"

"Ah. Have you finished *The Grinch Who Stole Christmas*?"

"Yes. Is interesting book. I like ending when heart grew. It made me like funny green character. It all right he is all over my room."

Franklin laughed. Then frowned. "Why do you say that I'm an American?" he uttered in his most precise British accent.

Natasha grinned at him, her eyes sparkling. "Is none of my business why you pretend. If you want to be British, be British. I prefer Americans."

"Really?" Realizing he'd slipped again, said, "I don't know what your speaking of," crisp and regally. "But for argument's sake, why do you prefer Americans?"

Her eyes glowed with hope. "Because Americans love freedom. For me, is most wonderful word of all."

"Why is that?"

"Because . . . very hard for me to have." She glanced at him as if trying to gauge how much, if any she should share with him.

"You're not free?"

Her eyes misted over and he almost hated asking the question and making her sad.

"I am not free. Not really." His arm went around her, to comfort and encourage. "My parents died when I was young child. My uncle took me and continued musical education. He recognized my desire and my teachers told him I had special talent. He made fortune with it."

Anger quickly formed in Franklin's chest. "He made a fortune with it? How so?"

"He is manager. He controls money. He controls everything—my passport, my green card, my career. He did not want me to come to America but to stay in Russia but money here was good."

She sighed, having no idea the fury Franklin was trying to contain. "My uncle is not good. He has friends who watch me in New York. They will not be happy when I return."

"You ditched them?" he said, snickering. She frowned and he clarified. "You left without letting them know?"

"Yes. My uncle was not happy. I tried to tell him that my American agent was responsible, even though I was happy to get away. He is threatening to bring me back to Russia." She shook her head. "I do not want to go."

Franklin's hand on her shoulder tightened. "Of course not. You shouldn't go anywhere you don't want to go."

Her big golden eyes searched his. "Really? You do not think I am ungrateful for wanting more?"

He wanted to pull her into his arms and hold her, whispering kind, sweet words to her. The idea that anyone had so controlled this woman and destroyed her self-worth made him furious.

But it made sense. No wonder she was always striving for perfection. An attitude that was, no doubt, a gift from the uncle. No wonder his calls upset her so much. No wonder she was so closed off from everyone else. She was constantly being watched and judged. How could anyone deal with that every day and not crumble?

He wasn't sure what to say, what to do. Going with instinct, he pulled her a little closer to his side. "You're not ungrateful. You are a strong, brilliant musician. And, I think, a sweet woman. With a growing heart."

Wondering if she'd get the Grinch reference, he watched her from the corner of his eyes. She slowly turned and blandly said, "Are you comparing me to green book character?" The sparkle in her eyes told him she wasn't offended.

"Ah, also a very intelligent woman. The way I see it, you're only missing one thing."

"Which is?"

"You need to learn how to have fun. Think I'll give you a lesson." Franklin stopped and reached down for a handful of snow. He balled it up, watching her confusion.

"This is a ball of snow," he explained. "Most people, American and British, occasionally enjoy using it to play with others."

He watched her back up, probably uncomfortable with the gleam he was sure was in his eyes. When he started after her, she shrieked and hurried away, hampered by the large snowshoes on her feet. He easily caught up to her and pushed the ball of snow on her neck, letting pieces drift down her back. More shrieks. Franklin laughed so hard, he was bending over.

He didn't notice her forming her own ball. When he looked up, his face met an icy snowball. He would have been impressed with her aim if he wasn't so adamant about making another snowball to form.

Before he could throw it, she let go of another snowball. He had just enough time to duck, meaning the snowball meant for him, piled into the back of Darren. Still holding Christy, he turned around to see what was going on. Franklin laughed and turning, saw Natasha, her eyes wide, her hands covering her mouth in shock.

Recognition shone on Darren's face and he lowered the little girl. He bent to the snow and said, "Oh, it is so on."

And that began the epic snowball fight of the season.

Bradley hooped and hollered as he threw snowball after snowball. Tricia took Christy's hand and helped her form her own balls to throw. Stephanie and Tyler got into the thick of it, throwing snowballs and taking the time to cover each other in snow. Sam and Angela laughed loud and long. Eldon just shook his head, until Bradley landed a perfect shot to his chest. Then he was in the middle, hurling snowballs as fast as he could make them.

In the midst of the battle a happy bark was heard across the field. Bradley turned and yelled, “Hey, look! It’s Frederica. Here, girl.” He gave a barely audible whistle. The dog bounded toward the Matthews, barking and jumping at flying snowballs.

Laughing, Darren gave the dog a rubdown. “What are you doing out here? I thought you were nice and warm in your stall in the barn. Why do you want to come out here in the cold in your condition?”

“She just wanted to get the jitters out.” Bradley joined him in petting the animal. “Least that’s what Mom says to me all the time. Come on, Christy. She likes it when you pet her.” The girl walked over and with a small smile began running her hand over the back of the dog.

The walk and snowball fight turned out to be a wonderful way to break tension, Angela thought, happy that everyone was having a good time.

Then in the near distance she saw buzzards flying.

Chapter Twelve

Sam seemed to see it at the same time as she did. He and Angela exchanged glances as the snowball fight fizzled on account of exhaustion from the participants.

She walked to Sam and said, "What do you think the buzzards are doing here?"

"I'm afraid it's exactly what we think." He turned to see the little group laughing, talking with each other. "I'd hate to spoil this pleasant moment for everyone. How about you and the others head back to the inn? Eldon and I will check out what's got the buzzards so excited."

She nodded and paused to put on her best smile. "Well, how about we head back to the inn? We can warm up with coffee or cocoa and make sure our escaped little mama has a fresh bowl of water."

The others agreed and started the trek back to the inn. Sam and Eldon lingered behind and, when everyone was out of sight, set out for the woods, uneasy about what they'd find. The snow was deeper as they got closer, their steps getting slower. Even with the trees missing their leaves, the forest loomed ahead, a foreboding that Sam felt in his soul.

A large group of birds seemed to be making a meal of something lying on the ground. "Turkey vultures," Sam said. Eldon nodded.

They inched closer and saw that the birds, hissing and grunting, were feasting on a deceased deer. Sam looked closely, his feet crunching in the snow and scaring the birds, most of them taking flight or scattering. He and Eldon got closer and saw deep teeth marks over the lifeless body of the deer. Sam cringed. "Something got a hold of this deer and it wasn't these vultures."

"Nope." Eldon's eyes went to Sam's. "You know as well as I what it looks like."

"Yeah." In the back of his mind Sam had been hoping that perhaps the calls they had heard in the night had been from a misplaced wolf and not an angry, aggressive one. He was afraid he was wrong.

Sighing, he backed away. "We'd better get back to the inn, give Angela and Joe an update."

"This isn't good, Sam. That wolf is getting too close." With his eyes sharp, Eldon looked around. "If it's violent, it's not thinking too clearly. What's to say it won't come closer to the inn. And in daylight?"

"I know, I know. We've got to formulate a plan, keep everyone safe." Being extremely careful, they made their way out of the forest and into the open field, keeping alert to their surroundings.

Angela was eager to hear the news when Sam and Eldon walked in the back door. She noticed the smile Sam put on his face when he saw the children.

"Well, what do we have here?"

At the table Bradley and Christy sat forming small pieces of dough into balls and setting them on cookie sheets. Bradley grinned up and said, "We're making chocolate chip cookies."

With a smidge of dough on her cheek, Christy smiled and raised her tiny ball of dough. "Cookies."

Sam chuckled. "Wonderful. You can never have too many chocolate chip cookies in the house."

Angela saw the nervous look he gave her and Mary, who stood by the children, rubbing their backs and encouraging them. "Yes. We're about to put the first batch in the oven. The others are having coffee and cake in the dining room. Would you like to join them?"

"Sounds good." Sam gave Angela a barely perceived nod and she followed them out of the kitchen.

At the table sat Darren and Tricia, Stephanie and Tyler, and a bleary-eyed Joe. He was chuckling as the others told him about the snowball fight.

"Wish I had been there." He took a sip of coffee and shook his head. "Can't figure out how that dog is getting out? She should have been secured in the barn."

"She just wanted to play," Tricia said, her head resting against her husband.

All eyes went to Sam as he, Eldon, and Angela sat down. "Sorry you missed it, Joe. Did you get any sleep?"

"I did, thanks." His eyes flared slightly, as if feeling the tension they brought with them.

Turning to Stephanie, Angela said, "You should see the cookie baking that's going on in the kitchen. Christy is so proud."

"Really? I've got to see this." She hurried out of the room.

Tricia covered a yawn. "If you'll excuse me, I think I'm going to take a nap. I'm exhausted."

After she left the room, Darren's expression grew somber. "You want to tell us what you found out there?" When the others looked surprised, he said, "Tyler and I saw the buzzards too. What did they get?"

Sam folded his hands on the table and lowered his voice, in case little ears were listening. "A deer. From the looks of it, it'd been attacked."

It was silent for a moment. Tyler voiced what they were all thinking. "By the wolf."

Following a beat of quiet, Joe said, "You guys are guests of the inn. Don't worry about this. We'll take care of it."

Darren ignored him. "There must be a reason for that wolf. This isn't usual behavior."

"No," Sam said. "It's not."

"What can we do to help?" Tyler chimed in.

"We've mentioned motion detectors." Angela addressed Joe. "I think you should go to the hardware store and get them today."

"Check. I'll also look into traps while I'm there."

"Traps? Couldn't that hurt the other animals around here?" Darren asked.

"I'm keeping our animals close by for the time being but I think a few traps just inside the woods might be helpful." Joe added, "I'll go by animal control. They've got traps that don't maim animals."

"Speaking of the animals, that dog seems to be able to get out of the barn. Any way to secure it better?"

Angela studied Darren. "I'm amazed at your concern. I've always thought it took a special heart to care for the animals of our world."

Darren shrugged. "I've always loved them. At one time I thought I'd become a vet, like my older brother."

"Why didn't you?"

Angela thought she saw a hint of depression in Darren's eyes. "My dad needed help in his dental business. I enjoy it, I make a good living." It almost sounded like he was trying to convince himself of those facts.

"I'll get better locks for the barn. Come to think of it, I'm getting better locks for the inn as well. How does that sound, Angela?"

"Good. Sam, any other ideas?"

"No. Eldon and I'll keep our eyes and ears open outside."

"I'll check on the animals in the barn," Darren said.

"I'll go with you to the hardware store," Tyler added.

"Sounds like a plan." Everyone stood to get started and Angela went to Darren. "I'd like to thank you for your help. I know this wasn't probably what you'd planned to do while you were staying at the inn."

Darren gently touched Angela's arm. "Glad to help. Actually, I've had a ball with your animals. Makes me wish I could have my own barn in Atlanta." He chuckled as he left.

Angela couldn't help a twinge of pity for the man who so clearly was not fulfilling his destiny in life.

In the music room, Franklin was oblivious to the threat of the wolf. As he and Natasha played, he smiled. Their practice session was going well, the music flowing through their fingers with a lightness, just what the song "Let it Snow" needed.

When they finished, he glanced up to see that same lightness on her shining face. "That was wonderful. I think we should go for a walk every morning before rehearsals. It seems to help our practices."

He grinned at her. "See? Having fun can actually improve performance. I think I'll write an article on it."

She chuckled, still a new sight and a welcome one. "It took three cups of coffee to warm. And one hot shower and dry clothes. I am still cold."

"But it was worth it, wasn't it?"

She seemed to think it over. "I will tell you when toes are unfrozen."

"I don't understand it. You're from Russia, you should be used to the cold weather, not abhor it so. How did you ever live and function there?"

As if the answer was essential, she thought. "Is not easy. I stayed cold." She sighed. "I dreamed of beaches, hot, sunny beaches where I could wear bikini and lay in sun."

Franklin could see it. He could see it all too well. "I should take you." Her eyes flew to his. "I mean, after this engagement we should take a few days off. The beaches of the Florida Keys or the Bahamas are beautiful."

For a second her eyes appeared hopeful then all too quickly they shaded. "Is not possible. I . . . have another performance."

"Where?"

"In Russia."

"Where in Russia?"

"Ah, in Moscow. A benefit." She was flustered and began working with her strings, as if they needed tightening. He knew she was the one too tight. Probably because she was lying. But he'd leave it alone.

"Oh. All right." He began playing quietly as she continued working on her instrument, trying to hold his tongue and not ask her any more questions about herself. It was difficult not to want to know more. Not want to spend more time with her. Her giggles from the snowball fight still rung in his ears, the sound as delicate as an angel's song.

Then she would get that lost look back in her eyes. He wanted so much to take it away and let her know she was safe with him.

And that frightened him as much as whatever she was dealing with. He had no business having feelings for this woman especially since nothing could ever come of them. She was indebted to the miserable man she called uncle, bound to a country that offered her nothing. In his way, he was indebted also, bound in a way that made the idea of a relationship with any woman laughable. Especially one so exquisite as Natasha.

Thinking to lighten the mood, he said, "You haven't made fun of my accent lately. Ready to just enjoy the deep, melodious timbre of my voice? I have been known to make a few women swoon, you know. But I won't brag."

She chuckled, as he'd meant for her to do. "Few women? Were they old and deaf?"

"Very funny. Most women like a man with a dignified speaking voice." He toyed with a few piano keys. "Don't you?"

She gave a small shrug. "Actions are louder than words. Is not saying?"

"Yes, very good. I suppose you're right." He fingered through his sheet music and pulled out several pages. "How about we work on Bach's Christmas Oratorio? I think the tempo is good but let's raise the volume here at the—"

"Franklin."

His name on her lips stopped him. It was so seldom that she used it, it sounded odd. He looked up at her and waited.

"I was thinking." She was clearly nervous, a first, so he waited patiently for her to finish her thought. The edges of her lips lifted slightly, something he probably had no business looking at. "I would like to try the 'jiggly bells' song. Please."

"You . . . what?" Franklin put a finger in his ear, thinking he'd surely heard wrong. "You want to play 'Jingle Bells'?"

"Little boy and girl, they like. Maybe others like. May I try?"

Like warm honey on a hot biscuit, his insides felt . . . cozy, that was the word. He could feel a smile bursting so wide it threatened to break his face.

Without thinking, he rose and walked to her. He took her shoulders in both his hands and pulled her forward, giving her a quick kiss on the lips. "Natasha, my dear, you are coming around, aren't you. Before long, we'll even have you 'dashing through the snow.'

He froze. What had he done? He'd kissed her. He was touching her, holding her. He was in trouble.

Her eyes were wide and glassy, and as he watched, they slowly darkened into something he could only hope was interest. She was too close. Her enticing, exotic scent wrapped around him, pulling him like a magnet, closer. The taste of her lips lingered on his and he wanted more.

Warning bells sounded in the far side of his working brain. As if awakening from a deep sleep, his mind slowly pulled him back to reality. This could not happen. He cared about her, he'd admit that, he wouldn't use her to satisfy any carnal desires.

He eased back and tried to give her a smile, patting her shoulders before his body took over and he pulled her into his embrace. As if walking through molasses, he shuffled his heavy legs back to the piano bench and lowered himself.

Looking at the keys, he said, "Bradley and Christy will like it very much. Shall we try it in the key of G?"

And before he could say anything stupid, before he could do anything stupid, he launched into a peppy, upbeat version of the song, letting her pick up the rhythm and tune. He settled his racing heart and concentrated on what he was best at—performing.

Anything but being who he really was.

Chapter Thirteen

The parlor was crowded for tonight's performance. Guests and neighbors from Stowe had packed the inn to hear Natasha and Franklin.

Stephanie was serving cider and cookies as fast as Tyler was bringing them out. She glanced around the room and saw Christy sitting on Angela's lap. The child was content, looking through a large Christmas picture book with the woman. Tricia and Darren sat on the couch next to them with Tricia occasionally speaking to Christy, pointing out things in the book. Stephanie cocked her head. Could she see Christy with the Matthews? Could it work? When Christy grinned at something Tricia said, it calmed her spirit. Christy was slowly becoming more comfortable with the Matthews. That was good. She'd have to remember to give them the preliminary request to adopt papers for them to fill out.

As Natasha and Franklin played to the quiet room, she leaned back against the large stone fireplace. The beauty of the music filled her, reminding her of the joy of the season. Sometimes she was working so hard she forgot.

Tyler slipped into the room and set another plate of cookies on the table before her, giving her a warm smile. Her insides wanted to just melt to the floor. Who would have thought that she'd find romance during a business trip across Vermont? And with Tyler Buchanan. She'd always thought him very nice, very respectful and helpful but she'd never taken the time to look at the person behind the friendly face. What she saw was very appealing.

Her abusive background made it hard to spend any amount of time with the opposite sex but Tyler had always been gentle, kind, easy to be around. He made her feel safe. It was a different feeling and one that she was coming to enjoy.

Maybe they could make a long distance relationship work. Then, maybe he could find a job in Burlington and they could deepen their relationship. Of course he'd have to understand the long hours that she put in the job. That was paramount. Her job was how she dealt with her past, how she made everything right. She couldn't ever think of leaving it.

The twosome finished their last number, "Jingle Bells," for their performance in the parlor and the crowd applauded loudly. "Thank you, thank you ladies and gentlemen. Miss Safina and I greatly appreciate your kindness. For those who would like more, we'll be performing in the lounge in one hour. Again, thank you."

The assembly grew loud, talking among themselves and congratulating the performers. The refreshment table was swamped and

Stephanie found herself busy, passing out goodies with a smile.

As the crowd lingered or made its way to the hall or to the lounge, she searched for Christy. Angela was gone but Christy was sitting next to Tricia, who had her arm around her, and Darren. Both were talking to others.

Something in Christy's good eye made Stephanie stop. The little girl was staring at a couple standing nearby. The woman stood, arms crossed, brows and lips in a hard line. The man's eyes were narrowed, pining her with a stare. They were discussing something and obviously neither one was happy.

Stephanie's eyes went back to Christy, who was watching the couple. She could tell the girl's little body was tensing, as if waiting for a blow.

The couple continued to converse, their voices getting louder. She was now able to make out something about the woman's habit of spending too much money and his habit of spending too much time at his club.

The little girl slid off the couch, out from Tricia's arm and inched away while Tricia and Darren continued talking to others. Stephanie felt her stomach tighten. She knew exactly what Christy was feeling, waiting for the first blow to be delivered. Her throat became heavy and dry. Before she could go to Christy, dizziness started to cloud her vision with her own memories.

"How's everything going out here?" Mary asked, touching her arm. "Honey, are you okay? You look a little pale."

Stephanie heard a few whimpers. At first she thought they'd come from her but then she saw it was Christy hiding behind a table.

"Christy needs help. I need to go," she mumbled, rushing from the refreshment table.

Before her eyes could fill, she scooped up the sobbing child in her arms and fled, not stopping until they were safe in their room. Stephanie sat in the big armchair, cuddling Christy closely.

"It's all right, sweetie." She wondered if she wasn't also comforting herself as she rocked back and forth while Christy whimpered and clung to her. She wouldn't let her mind go back to that dark place where she was simply a pawn in her parents' life, juggled back and forth, used as a piece of property between two unhappy "adults." Concentrating on Christy, she tenderly kissed her head, brushing her hair out of her eyes.

They sat like that for minutes, or hours, she didn't know, when a soft knock sounded. "Stephanie?" Mary poked her head in. "Is everything all right?"

"We'll be fine." Her voice croaked out the response.

Mary came in and knelt by their chair, her hand covering one of Stephanie's. "You're crying." She hadn't realized that tears had streamed down her cheeks. Now she was embarrassed.

After sniffing, she said, "Really, I'm okay. Christy had a scare, that's all."

Mary gently stroked the little girl's hair. "I saw. And heard. That couple arguing really upset her, didn't it?"

She was glad for Mary's simple understanding. Not able to answer, she just nodded.

"The poor baby." Mary continued stroking Christy. Then looked to Stephanie. "What can I do?"

She sniffed again. "Nothing, thank you. I just need to settle her down and let her sleep."

After one last stroke, Mary said, "Okay." Her voice was soft, gentle, and compassionate. "I'll be in the kitchen or the lounge. If she . . . or you need me, please don't hesitate to find me. Promise?"

Mary saw too much. Still, she was grateful. She gave a half smile and nodded.

A few hours later, Stephanie jerked awake. She'd finally gotten Christy asleep and had stretched out next to her with a book and fallen asleep herself. Nothing could have prepared her for Christy's scream.

The little girl thrashed back and forth, first fighting and then cowering, completely immersed in a nightmare. Stephanie used all her training to subdue the child, all the time calmly telling her to wake up.

"Christy, it's Stephanie. You're safe. No one is hurting you, sweetheart. Wake up."

The screaming continued until Christy was exhausted. Then the crying began—deep, primal sobbing that ripped the last bit of control from Stephanie. She took the girl's face in hers. "Christy.

It's me. Are you awake now?" The little girl nodded.

Stephanie pulled her into her arms and held tightly, the both of them crying their hearts out. All the pain of her own childhood came flooding back as she tried to comfort the little girl. All the questions, the fears, the inadequacies rocked her and deluged her until she felt she could hardly breathe.

Unexpectedly, two arms wrap around her along with the voice of an angel saying, "You're not alone, Stephanie. Never alone. You are loved."

She turned her head slightly to see that it was Angela, her face so filled with love and compassion it tore at her soul. Causing her to cry harder.

They stayed like that until Christy finally quieted down and settled back into sleep.

And then the anger came. It so filled Stephanie's soul that a child would be subjected to such injustice and grief she wanted to cause pain to every mortal that uttered an unkind word to a precious child. She wanted to find every boy or girl that had to endure the brutality of adults and cocoon them in her arms until they knew every thing was all right.

It made her want to work harder at her job, spend more hours, whatever it took to protect the children of Vermont, America. It was her mission, her passion, the reason she'd made it through the horrible cycle of abuse—to be the rescue for the children, the ones that had no voice.

Which meant she had no time for anything else. Including a relationship with Tyler. She squeezed her eyes together. The truth was how could she trust anyone in a relationship after what she'd seen and experienced?

The initial awareness hurt but solidified in her mind. It wasn't that she believed Tyler was an abusive adult or would ever damage her or a child, far from it. During their acquaintance he had proven how dedicated he was to the children of the orphanage. But no matter how good a guy he was, she couldn't trust that he wouldn't change, that he would be there to protect and love her when she needed him. She couldn't trust.

She wiped her eyes, the pain like a sharp knife in her heart. "Could you stay with Christy for a few minutes? There's something I have to do. Immediately." Before she lost her righteous indignation and let her attraction to him take over.

"Wouldn't you like to get some sleep? Whatever it is you need to do will still be there in the morning and you can look at it with a rested perspective."

"No. Now." As gently as she could, considering her own emotional upheaval, she lay Christy down on the bed and turned to leave. "This shouldn't take long."

"Watch your words, honey." Stephanie turned to face Angela. She couldn't possibly know what she was going to do, although the way the woman was peering at her she couldn't be sure. "Words can damage the soul."

Something she knew only too well.

The huge crowd that had enjoyed the music in the parlor now crowded the lounge. Darren had been lucky to snag two stools at the bar and as Natasha and Franklin played a mellow version of "Have Yourself a Merry Little Christmas" he was glad he had.

Tricia hadn't mention babies or adoption all afternoon. He felt he'd finally had an opportunity to breathe, to relax. It was like he'd gotten his happy, interesting, charming wife back. The morning snowball fight had brought back good memories of their early trips to the Smoky Mountains to see snow. Her laughter from the morning still made him smile.

She'd gone with him to care for the animals in the barn, laughing and talking the entire time. The sheep had been fascinated with her, or in her cashmere sweater. As they fed the chickens, she'd clucked along with them. The dogs adored her, especially when she scratched behind their ears. Frederica seemed to be drawn to her, the dog's eyes following her wherever she went, with an expression of admiration. Maybe it was her gentle voice as she comforted or her soft hands as they rubbed, but all the animals seemed to think Tricia was a gift sent from heaven.

He agreed with them.

This vacation had been the best thing for their marriage. Not that they'd been having serious trouble, it was just that Tricia had been so singularly focused on the baby issue that it was all that mattered. But just now, looking at the way the light shone on her silky hair, the way her eyes sparkled while she listened to the music, the contented smile on her face, he was one happy man.

And he couldn't wait to be alone with his wife.

The song finished and the crowd applauded for the duo. But Darren's interest was fixed on the woman in front of him.

"Would you like another drink?"

Her bright eyes found his. "No, I'm good." She sighed, leaning back against the bar. "I'm having such a good time. You?"

"How could I not? I'm here with the most beautiful woman in the place. And I even get to take her home with me."

Tricia giggled. "How many drinks have you had?"

"Just the one." He held up his glass. "But I'm drunk on your beauty, under the influence of your potent charm, intoxicated by the power of your smile."

She laughed and he joined in. "I can tell you're flirting skill needs a lot of work. You're so out of practice."

Taking her hand in his, he said, "You're right and it's a shame." He kissed the hand he held, lingering an extra second. "A man should flirt with his wife. I'll make a point of doing more of it, get better at it. Like when we met and started dating." His eyebrows lifted, a grin appeared on his face.

Tricia leaned in and kissed him softly. "I'm so lucky."

They kissed again as the music started up. Neither noticed at first when Stephanie entered but soon saw the wide-eyed woman standing in the doorway, searching the room.

"What do you suppose is wrong with Stephanie? She seems upset."

Darren shook his head. "I don't know."

Stephanie spotted them and made her way through the crowd to get to them. Breathless, she said, "Have you seen Tyler?"

"Not lately. Is something wrong?"

"It's not Christy, she's okay, isn't she? I saw you take her earlier in the parlor. Was it her bedtime?"

She paused as if not sure what to say. "Yes. I . . . I just need to talk with Tyler."

Darren glanced around. "He was in here a minute ago. The place is so packed he was helping Joe out. If not here he's probably helping Mary in the kitchen."

"Okay, I'll check there." She turned to leave, then stopped. "Oh, Tricia. I printed out those preliminary adoption papers you asked me about. I can give them to you in the morning."

Darren's mind stopped working at the words. *What did she say?*

"And I think we should talk about what happened with Christy tonight, she had a setback."

Tricia's face fell. "A setback? What do you mean?"

"It's something you and Darren will have to work through when you adopt her. She was scarred pretty badly and things like this are bound to happen but I can't go into it right now. I'll explain everything in the morning. Right now I have to find Tyler."

Darren barely heard the words as blood was pounding through his veins and his heart was banging against his ribs. Had Tricia really started the adoption process without his consent?

When Stephanie hurried away, Tricia frowned. "The poor little thing. I wish I'd been there to help. What do you suppose—"

Darren saw her expression change from concern to surprise. And back to concern as she gazed into his eyes.

Chapter Fourteen

"Honey, why are you looking at me like that? Is something wrong?"

He took a fortifying sip of his drink and set it down, proud of himself that he didn't slam it. "Why is Stephanie giving you adoption papers?"

"Because that's the first step in the process."

He nodded his understanding. "And when was it that you talked to her?"

"This morning on our walk. It seemed like the perfect time, you were playing with Christy. I didn't want to wait any longer so Stephanie and I talked." Her frown deepened. "Is something wrong?"

Was this what they'd become? So singularly focused on being parents that their own communication was nonexistent? What had happened to his perfect world of a few minutes ago? Had it just been an illusion, something he'd desperately wanted to see instead of what was? The resentment, the disappointment, the sheer frustration washed over him like a winter flood and he had to take a minute to compose himself before he did or said something he'd probably feel sorry for.

"And when were you going to inform me that we were adopting?" He was amazed his voice could sound so unaffected.

"Inform you? Honey, we've talked about this. It's no coincidence that we're here and Christy showed up needing a home. It's a good thing, we agreed. Why are you so upset?"

Maybe he wasn't hiding his feelings as well as he thought. He swallowed hard but knew his voice was still low and menacing. "We were still at the thinking stage. *I* was at the thinking stage and I seem to recall that you were going to wait to talk to Stephanie until I was finished thinking it over. *If* I agreed to it."

"Was I?" A flash of realization came in her eyes, as well as concern. "Oh, honey, you're right. I guess I was just so excited, especially during the walk and you were getting along so well with Christy that I didn't want to wait."

"You didn't want to wait to see if it was something that I wanted?"

"What? Of course it's what you want, it's what we both want. It's just—"

More applause sounded as Natasha and Franklin finished their last set for the evening. The crowd chatter grew and many headed towards the bar for another drink, causing the room to be extremely noisy.

Just as well, Darren thought. He needed to cool off. Maybe he should take a walk, jump in the snow.

Tyler came into the room carrying a bin and dishtowel, obviously trying to keep ahead of the cleaning.

Tricia called out to him. "Tyler. Stephanie was looking for you. We sent her to the kitchen, did you see her?"

"No. I was in the parlor." He cleaned a table, putting the dirty glasses in his bin. "I'll head back to the kitchen."

Darren wanted to get back to their "discussion" but people had crowded around them waiting for Joe to fill their orders and conversation was almost impossible.

From the other corner of the lounge, loud voices could be heard over the fray. Angry voices. "And I said to get her hands off her."

"Now don't be ruffling up you feathers, James Bond, I just want to talk to the lady."

Franklin's eyes narrowed, his nostrils flared. He had to remember not to show his ugly past as he dealt with this loser. But the brute had a hand on Natasha's arm. Her troubled eyes clearly told him she wasn't the least bit interested in the idiot. "And I will repeat one more time. Mate. Take your bloody hands off Miss Safina."

"Franklin," Natasha said quietly. He wasn't sure if she was placating him or giving a plea for help. He decided it was the latter.

"Now don't go on so, Shakespeare, the lady doesn't have a ring on her finger. She can choose a real man if she wants."

He saw red, his mind whirled. It was the very last thing the man should have said to him.

Stephanie walked back into the lounge and scanned the room for Tyler. Mary said he was in the parlor but she'd checked and hadn't seen him. Where could he be? She didn't want another moment to go by until she'd settled this. She'd never be able to get to sleep with it hanging over her head.

Things had changed in the few minutes she was away from the lounge. Franklin seemed to be in hostile discussion with someone, Natasha not looking too pleased about it. Darren and Tricia were in their own intense conversation, neither very happy. And the room was loud and boisterous with people milling around.

Tricia saw her and called out, "He was here. He went to the kitchen to look for you." Her shoulders stooped and she turned to return to the kitchen, desperate to find him.

Tricia went back to attempting to calm her unreasonable irate husband. "We both agreed it was a good idea."

"In theory, yes. The little girl needs a home and we want a child. But there's more to it than that."

"We'll love her. What's more important?"

Darren huffed out a breath. "Tons more. The little girl has been through hell. What do we know about it? What do we know about helping her to heal? I'll tell you, we know nothing."

"But we could learn, work on it as we go."

"While Christy suffers?" Silence hung between them.

"Tonight, when we were in the parlor she slipped away from us when we were talking. *We* let her slip away. Not a good habit for parents."

"I saw Stephanie go to her. It must have been her bedtime, no big deal."

"And what was Stephanie talking about tonight, Christy had a setback? What does that mean? Are we going to be able to cope with her problems?"

"Of course we are. We're both intelligent, loving people—"

"Patricia, you're not listening to me!" His harsh tone shocked them both. "You're so locked in on becoming a parent that you don't think about anything else." *Or anyone else*. "You've become obsessed, it's all you ever talk or think about."

Tears formed in her eyes at the accusations. She didn't like the picture he was painting of her, nor of his assessment of the situation.

Someone bumped into him hard and he pushed him away. "You want to watch it, buddy?"

"Sure. If you're done, maybe you could give your seats to someone else. How about it?"

"Well, we're not done so just shove off."

Tricia was shocked. Darren was never like this. He was usually the most patient man in the room. It was so unlike him to pick an argument with a stranger.

"You don't own this place, fella. I got just as much right to be here as anyone."

The temperature of the room was rising quickly and Tricia didn't like it. She jumped from her stool and said, "Here, take mine." To Darren she added, "We can share. It's no problem."

Before he could respond to her, Tyler entered the room, confusion covering his face at the unease in the room.

"She went back to the kitchen looking for you," Darren yelled.

Tyler nodded and hurried out, surely glad to have a reason to escape the tension of the room.

"A real man, is it? What would you know about a real man? In my opinion, a real man is someone who doesn't force a lady to do anything she doesn't want!"

"Franklin."

If he'd been looking, Franklin would have seen Natasha's eyes water, he would have heard the soft appreciation in her tone. But his body was too busy keeping himself from pummeling this guy into the ground.

"Just want to let the lady know her options."

"She knows her options and she'll let you know if she's interested in a loser like you." Probably not the right thing to say.

The man's face reddened and as he stepped forward, his fist rising, another voice joined the fray. "Excuse me but I just had to meet you."

Franklin turned to see an attractive redhead staring at him. "Um, yes?"

"I'm Millie. Hi, Miss Safina."

"Hello." Franklin noted a chill in Natasha's voice.

"I just wanted to say how much I enjoyed your playing." Her hand went to her heart. "It made me so happy. It must be wonderful to bring such joy to people."

Franklin glanced around. Natasha seemed to be scowling at the woman. The man hanging around seemed interested in the conversation and joined in. "What I was just thinking. Hey, how about the four of us double date?" The man took Natasha's elbow. "I know a really nice bar that stays open until two. We could have a few drinks, a few laughs." His eyes went to Natasha. "What do you say, honey?"

Natasha's eyes widened and Franklin shoved in front of her to come eye-to-eye with the man. "Natasha is not going with you, anywhere." Franklin looked at Natasha and quickly added, "That is unless she wants to." His intense eyes implored her to agree with him.

She smiled. "No. I do not want to go with him."

Satisfied, he turned back to the man. "I find myself repeating that you're bothering Miss Safina. Perhaps you'd like to ask someone else before I'm forced to make an example of you."

"You want to try, buddy?" The man stepped closer, his eyes gleaming from too much emotion along with too much alcohol.

"Uh, why don't we all settle down?" Millie said. "There's no reason for tempers to fly."

"I agree. If this idiot would just step back and leave Miss Safina alone I'd even be glad to buy him a drink."

"I don't take orders—hey, did you say a drink?"

Stephanie walked back into the loud, heated room, frustrated. Seeing the Matthews still at the bar, she walked to them, shaking her head.

"Maybe you should stay put until he makes the loop back in here," Tricia said, causing a small grin from Stephanie.

"Yeah, and since you're here, you'd better hold on to those adoption papers for a while. We're not ready to commit to anything yet."

Tricia's eyes flew to her husband's. The general tension of the room was tripled between the couple. Stephanie had the feeling she was in the middle of a major disagreement. Trying to diffuse the energy, she said, "Well, we don't have to do anything tonight. In fact, it's late. I think we all should probably get to bed, get some sleep."

Tricia turned to Stephanie, her eyes still spitting anger. "I thought you had to see Tyler."

"I'm sure it can wait until tomorrow." It couldn't but at the moment she wanted to get this couple calmed down. Then she could search out Tyler. "Tyler's not going far. We can just as easily—"

"Stephanie?"

The familiar voice had her spinning around. "Tyler! Where have you been? I've been looking all over for you."

The smile on his face had her stomach dropping to her feet. This wasn't going to be easy or enjoyable but still had to be done.

"Thank God. I was getting dizzy watching you two going back and forth through the house chasing each other." Darren finished his drink and motioned to Joe for another.

"Let me finish cleaning up, Stephanie, and we can go talk on the porch."

"No." Not the dark, romantic porch. It would be so hard to explain things with his chocolaty eyes staring at her in the moonlight. She stopped him with a hand to his arm. His strong arm. "This won't take long." Taking a deep breath she said, "Tyler . . ." Her eyes went over his shoulder to see Tricia and Darren watching them, hanging on their words. "I, ah, think maybe the parlor would be better."

"Uh oh, sounds like bad news." Clearly Darren had one too many drinks and wasn't choosing his words carefully at the moment. "Take it from me, kid. When a woman gets that tone, they've already made a decision about your future, one that you had no part in. Women are good at that, deciding things for you."

Tyler frowned as Tricia scowled.

"Stephanie? What is it? Just tell me."

To get at least a little privacy, she turned slightly, taking him with her. "Tyler. You are a wonderful man and I like you very much. However—"

"There's a 'however'?"

"I'm afraid so. I . . . can't see you, socially."

"Sure you can. We talked about it, we can call each other, I can drive over on weekends or maybe we can meet halfway. We can make it work."

"No, you don't understand. I . . . can't." The spoken words made her feel weak, it transported her back to when she was a child, cowering away from the ones who were suppose to protect and love her. The ones who were suppose to demonstrate what a real relationship was like.

They'd given her a demonstration, all right. And ruined her for any kind of a happily ever after. She knew they didn't exist.

The realization gave her back her strength. "I'm not going to have a relationship with you, Tyler." Her back was straight, her voice strong, and her resolve firm. "We are only work associates. And that's all we'll ever be."

Chapter Fifteen

"Joe, would you be good enough to pour this man a beverage of his choice?"

"I'll have a beer. You're not so bad, Winston Churchill." The man turned to Natasha. "What do you say, honey. After this drink I know a great spot opened late for dancing. With your great stems I'll bet you can dance for hours."

"I do not understand." The whole evening was confusing to Natasha—the boisterous crowd, the man that wouldn't go away. Was she always to be dominated by men?

Then there was that woman flirting with Franklin. And Franklin. He seemed furious with the man who was currently guzzling his beer. Franklin acted as if he objected to the man and wanted her to have a say in where she went and with whom. It was . . . sweet.

Maybe that emotion surprised her the most. Franklin Murray kept surprising her and she found she was enjoying it.

His hand went gently to her arm. "Nothing to worry about, it's all settled. This . . . gentleman will finish his drink and leave." His eyes glared at the man. "I would advise you not to return as long as Miss Safina and I are in residence."

The man wiped his mouth with his arm, his eyes sharpening. "No one tells me where I can or can't go. Especially not you, Sherlock Holmes."

"Sherlock Holmes?"

Franklin shook his head, a warning for Natasha to stay out of it. His hand gently but firmly held her back, his eyes stayed on the man. "I find myself growing tired of dealing with you. Perhaps you'd like to go outside and finish this off."

A shock of terror jolted her body. "Franklin, no!"

"That would suit me just fine." To Natasha's horror, the two men stepped away from the bar, toward the door.

"Franklin!" She was desperate to stop him. "Your hand, you must not hurt your hand!"

He turned to grin at her and at that moment, the other man brought his fist up hard into Franklin's chin, knocking him back. The sound of the contact added to the heightened tension of the room. Murmurs grew, drinks spilled, people shoved to get a ringside seat.

Franklin shook his head and before Natasha could ask him if he was okay, he threw his own punch, landing squarely on the surprised man's nose, knocking him onto the floor.

Only stirring up the unruly crowd.

The commotion at the other side of the bar had Darren, Tricia, and Stephanie turning. Tyler's eyes were still locked on her.

They were ending before they had even begun? What had happened? He wanted to shout, vent, tell her she was wrong, they weren't only work associates. What was between them was right and good and had potential to be something special. How could she just throw that away?

It was all so predictable. He'd never had anyone love him before, why would he expect anyone to start now. Oh, he knew he was respected at the orphanage, but in the deep recess of his heart he yearned for someone to love him, to want to build a life with him. But his parents hadn't. It appeared neither would the girl of his dreams.

The crowd continued to press making it impossible to try to reason with Stephanie. Amidst voices, the sound of a bark rang through the room. Tyler watched as both Darren and Tricia heard it too, their eyes searching the room.

Frederica pushed her way through and went to the couple; both immediately knelt, enclosing it from the shrill crowd.

"What are you doing here, you sweet thing," Tricia said, her arms holding the dog closely.

"I can't figure out how she got out again." Darren ran his hands over the animal, making sure the dog wasn't hurt in any way. The dog kept licking both their faces as they spoke gently to the animal. Tyler's hurt was momentarily lessened at the picture.

Until he saw a large man pushing his way through the crowd, stumbling toward Stephanie.

Mary was concerned by all the noise coming from the lounge but nothing could have prepared her for the actual turmoil. People were yelling, laughing, pushing, shoving; clearly the crowd was out of control or nearly there.

She moved quickly behind the bar to Joe who was studying the crowd. "I don't like the looks of this. What should we do?"

They both watched a large man throw a wobbly punch toward Franklin, who easily dodged it. With a wry grin, Joe said, "Hide the cookies."

Thinking of a memorable lounge altercation a couple of years prior, Mary huffed out a laugh. "Agreed. Then what?"

They watched Tyler grab Stephanie and pull her out of the way of a towering man before he crashed to the floor, which seemed to stir those around him, adding more fists and bodies in the fray.

Across the room, Franklin and Natasha were making their way back to their instruments as fights were breaking out around them. Natasha made a leap for her violin and bow, holding them safely over her head as the swarm of people moved around them, Franklin trying to protect her with his arms around her.

"Look there." Joe pointed to a pair on the other side of the bar, near the floor. Tricia and Darren.

"Are they okay?" She asked and then saw the furry creature they were protecting. "Is that Frederica?"

Joe sighed. "Seems to be."

"What is she doing in here? We must be violating so many codes." His bland expression had her wincing. "I know, not the most important thing at the moment." Her face tightened. "What are we going to do?"

After a quick moment, Joe said, "I've got an idea." He cupped his hands around his mouth and hollered out, "Hey, the Village Saloon is giving free beer for the next hour. Free beer!"

It only took a few repeats of the announcement before the landscape of the room changed and the chaos of the fighting turned into a stampede for the door. Everyone rushed out, cheering and eager. Even from behind the safety of the bar, Mary reached for Joe, who pulled her protectively against him.

The mad dash lasted for a tense-filled few minutes until the lounge emptied out leaving an eerie, surreal quiet, like one would expect after the end of a fierce wartime battle.

And its only inhabitants being the resident guests and bewildered innkeepers.

Angela stood in the doorway holding Christy's hand. The little girl had awoken and wanted Stephanie so she'd brought her downstairs to find a mass exodus occurring from the lounge. Thankfully they were out of harm's way as everyone rushed out of the room, down the hall, and out the front door.

As confusing as that was, it was nothing to what she and Christy found in the lounge. It was a mess of overturned tables and chairs, broken glass, spills on the floors. Mary and Joe stood behind the bar, their arms around each other, relief in their eyes. Stephanie was against the wall and Tyler had his back against her, his arms back as if protecting her from a vicious charge of wildebeests in the savannah. Tricia and Darren were huddled on the floor their arms around . . . was that Frederica? What was she doing in there?

And at the piano, Franklin and Natasha stood on the bench, his arms around her, hers holding her violin and bow high, like protecting them from flood waters. And both involved in a sweet and lengthy kiss.

Angela shook her head.

Glancing down at Christy who was rubbing a sleepy eye, she wondered what it looked like from her viewpoint. Probably sensing her perusal, Christy looked up at her and cocked her head.

"I have no idea," Angela muttered. She let out a deep sigh. "But Sam's never going to believe this."

Chapter Sixteen

The sun was barely making its daily entrance and Mary was busy stirring oatmeal. Joe came down the back stairs and kissed her cheek. "I'm not sure why I'm cooking so much for breakfast. After the spectacle of last night, everyone probably wants to sleep in."

Joe chuckled. "Any noise from the guests this morning?"

She sighed. "Stephanie came down with Christy and jumped at the chance for Sam to take her to see the animals in the barn." Mary sighed. "Her eyes were red. I'm sure she's been crying."

Joe shook his head and poured himself a cup of coffee before he sat at the table. "Were we that miserable when we fell in love?"

With a chuckle, Mary said, "Yes, I believe we were. Amazing how hard some people fight against honest emotions." She set a bowl of oatmeal in front of Joe and put her hand on his shoulder. "How long did it take you to clean up the lounge last night?"

"Too long. I'm thinking we should stock paper cups and cover the floor in plastic, removable floor mats. Thought it'd take all night to get the lounge set up again."

"Same goes for the parlor," Mary said, returning to the stove. "I hope Angela thinks again before she allows the whole county to come for the evening. We're all out of cider and cookies. I'm going to be busy all day stocking up again."

"I'll be glad to make a run into town if you need supplies. Just make me a list."

"I will. Seeing the mess our guests were in last night, perhaps we should check on our supply of aspirin."

"True." He tried to hide a grin. "And while I'm out, I have a little Christmas shopping to finish."

Mary didn't even try to hide a smile. "Oh? For anyone I know."

"You might." He took a sip of coffee. "Any last minute suggestions you'd like to add?"

She thought about that. How could she want anything else? She had everything—a loving husband, precious son, a good job, good friends. However, deep in her heart she did have a desire, one she hadn't shared with even Joe. And wasn't going to share today. She'd be too busy making cookies!

"No. I'm good."

He put his mug down and went to her, pulling her in for a hug. "You sure Santa can't bring you something special? You've been a very good girl this year."

With a soft chuckle she said, "Thanks. But really, I have everything I could ever want." Her eyes met his and held. "I'm so thankful for you, Joe. Every day I thank God for the gift that you are to me. And Bradley."

He took her face in his big hands and kissed her tenderly. "I love you, Mary Puletti. You and Bradley are the best things that ever happened to me. I'm the one that's thankful." They kissed again.

A throat clearing had them quickly parting, seeing Darren standing in the kitchen doorway. "Excuse me. I don't mean to intrude. Just thought I'd go check on the animals this morning, if that's okay."

Mary felt a wave of compassion for the man and saw from Joe's expression, he did as well. It was evident from the bloodshot eyes, the slump in his shoulders, and the bruise on his cheek that he was another casualty of the night.

"Sure." Joe walked to him and put his arm around his shoulders. "Come on. I think Sam and the kids have beat us to it but there's always something to do."

Mary watched them and said another prayer of thanks for her thoughtful, kind husband as he led Darren through the mudroom and back door. Joe had filled her in on the troubling conversation the couple had before hell had broken loose in the lounge. It concerned her deeply.

So she said another prayer, this one imploring divine help for Darren and Tricia Matthews.

Sam watched with joy as Bradley and Christy scattered chicken feed for the clucking hens. Bradley was gentle as he instructed the little girl and the delight on her face was enough to thaw out the coldest of hearts. This was good.

He'd been surprised when the two had been adamant about him coming with them to the barn that morning. Until they'd told him the reason. Bradley had been excited and Christy had been . . . resolute, so unlike the quiet little thing she normally was.

She'd pulled up a folding chair and pointed, saying, "Sit." When Sam obeyed, she climbed up on his lap and recited her Christmas list again . . .

Adding something that made his head spin. When he glanced at Bradley, the boy was nodding his head, his face serious and earnest.

And Sam's heart melted for these little ones. How he wanted to make all their Christmas wishes come true. If he only had the power to do that.

When he gave the usual platitudes—"We'll have to wait and see" or "That's a little hard for Santa to put in his bag"—Bradley had brought his own words back to him.

"You said before that Christmas was a time for miracles."

"Yes. I did."

"And that to get a miracle, we had to believe in a miracle."

The back of his neck was starting to sweat. "Yes. I said that."

"Well?" Bradley lifted his arms and dropped them to his sides, as if to say, "Duh, this is one of those times."

Sam gathered both kids in his arms and carefully said, "This . . . wish isn't something like a new doll or game."

"Course not," Bradley agreed. "It's more important."

"Yes. Yes, it is. And others are involved. I'm not sure . . . It can be . . . We'll have to . . ." The words clogged his throat looking at their hopeful faces."

Christy's little hand went to his face and she gently patted his beard. Her damaged eye twitched and her good eye was wide, a deep, pleading blue. "P-please, Santa. I've been a g-good girl."

And Sam was completely undone. The arm around Christy pulled her tightly against him and he closed his eyes to keep from bawling like a baby. Christy patted his back and he swallowed a sob. He would have done anything in the world for this precious little girl, who'd had to endure such a hard, unfair life. She deserved to have a childhood with all the love and joy available in the world.

"So, Sam, what do you think?"

He cleared his throat and turned to Bradley. Although only seven, the boy had a certain maturity, a certain optimism that warmed his soul. Words Angela had spoken earlier about the inn's future resonated inside of him.

Suddenly hopeful, he glanced at both children. "You know what? It is Christmas, a miraculous time of year. I'll believe with you, okay?"

"Great, but we need a plan, too."

Sam chuckled at the boy's matter-of-fact tone. "I suppose we do. You two mind if I share this with Angela? She's much better at plans than I am."

"We were going to her next," Bradley said. He and Christy went to get the chicken feed, content that the problem was solved.

Sam sighed. What was Angela going to think? He should have the kids there with him when he spoke with her, even have Christy on her lap. How could she refuse to help that sweet little girl?

Of course, he knew when dealing with the wills of adults nothing was for sure. They'd have to tread very carefully with the children so as not to damage their faith. It would be a delicate balancing act.

The barn door opened and Joe and Darren walked in. "Morning." Sam's cheerful greeting went unreturned as the two men merely nodded and went towards the horse's pen.

Knowing Christy was in good hands with Bradley, he moved to get a bale of hay for the horse's morning meal.

Darren was rubbing the horse's head, checking his eyes and his teeth. The observation didn't go unnoticed by Sam. "You seem to know a lot about animals, Mr. Matthews."

"Please call me Darren."

"Of course." Sam smiled. "How did you come of your knowledge?"

Darren pulled out a sugar cube from his pocket and let the horse take it. "My brother's a vet. I go to his place now and again and help out. I guess you could say it restores my soul. Gets my perspective back. Sometimes it's so much easier to deal with animals than people."

Sam knew about the Matthews' argument in the lounge the night before and felt bad for the man. Maybe he could help smooth things out. "You ever take your wife with you?"

"Tricia? To the animal hospital?"

"Why not?"

Darren thought about it. "I guess I never thought to ask."

"She seems very gentle and caring. From the way she talked about your cats, the way Frederica seems to adore her, I know she's an animal lover. I bet she might enjoy going to the animal hospital with you."

"Hmm. Not sure Tricia has animals on her mind."

"Have you asked her? You might be surprised." Sam ran his hand along the back of the horse. After a beat of silence, Sam said, "Talk to her. Talk about what you both want and need. I know there's a compromise in there somewhere."

Darren's eyebrow rose. "Hard to see it."

Patting the horse, Sam said, "There's always compromise in marriage, give and take. No place for selfishness."

"No," Darren muttered.

Sam turned to see Joe watching the two children and when the sheep started to get loud, he laughed and said, "I think we have some hungry customers."

"Can I get the food, Papa?"

"Go for it." Joe held out his hand to Christy. "What do you say, Princess? Want to go calm those starving lambs?" With a smile, she nodded.

The door cracked open and Tyler came in, his eyes droopy, his hair unkempt. Sam's heart immediately went out to the lad.

"Oh. Didn't know anyone was out here yet. I'll just get going."

"No, come on it, son. Never too many people to care for the animals. Help me get the food for the dogs, will you?"

Tyler nodded and followed Sam, not saying anything.

"Heard you were busy last night. I know Joe and Mary appreciate all your help."

He shrugged off the praise. "It was nothing."

"Just the same, it's good of you to help out." They poured food into the dogs' bowls and Tyler got a bucket to fill with fresh cold water for their water bowls as Sam studied him. Something was definitely wrong.

"Is something troubling you, Tyler?"

His shoulder went up in another shrug and he couldn't seem to make eye contact. Instead of pressing, Sam walked to him and put his hand on his shoulder. "Have patience with her, son."

Tyler's eyes widened as he stared at Sam. "How do you . . ." He didn't finish his sentence. As if a weight was pushing him down, he lowered onto a nearby stool and sighed. "I thought . . . I thought we were . . . that we might . . ." His puppy-dog eyes pinned Sam's. "Could I have done something wrong? Was I too forward or too clumsy or . . . too . . . me?"

Sam pulled another stool over and sat, folding his hands in front of him. "You're a fine man, Tyler. I can't imagine that you could have done anything that would be wrong. Stephanie seems enamored with you."

"I thought maybe so. But now she doesn't want to have anything to do with me."

"What did she say?"

Tyler shook his head back and forth. "A lot of nothing. Nothing that made sense, anyway. I got the standard 'It's not you, it's me' but isn't that what people say whenever they want to spare your feelings?"

"Not necessarily. Tyler, do you know anything about Stephanie's life in Burlington? About her past?"

"Not a whole lot. I know she works really hard for children's services. She has a great reputation, everyone likes her. All of us at the orphanage admire her. She'd give her life for those children, no doubt about it."

"Have you ever wondered why she cares so much for the children?"

Tyler frowned in thought. "Other than she's a wonderful person I hadn't thought much about it."

"Sometimes, a lot of times, our choice of vocation stems from our childhood. Something that inspired us or deeply affected us will cause us to turn in a certain direction. So much of our reactions to . . . different circumstances are directly a result of our past. Maybe if you knew her past, it would explain the difficulty she's going through now."

"She says she doesn't want to get to know me, Sam, how much more explanation do I need? I've only got so much ego." Sam's heart warmed for this young man.

"I'm saying if what she needs right now is a friend only, be a friend." His tone became serious. "Don't throw away a friendship because she's hurting. Or you're hurting."

Tricia's head pounded. She needed aspirin.

The argument she and Darren had had the night before was worse than anything they'd ever been through. Had she really messed things up so badly? She'd thought they were on the same page, or at least getting there.

Still, she remembered the disappointed look on his face. She'd somehow let him down and she still wasn't sure how.

They hadn't spoken since leaving the lounge the night before. Hadn't spoken this morning. Darren had left early, not telling her where he was going. Her guess was the barn to care for the animals.

She glanced at herself in the mirror. Had she become all her husband suggested? Had she stopped listening to him in favor of her own agenda? She hoped he came back soon, they needed to talk.

Actually, she needed to apologize. Yes, she'd jumped the gun. He wasn't ready to commit to adoption, she realized that now. It was just that they had so little time with Christy before they returned to Atlanta and Christy went to the orphanage.

Her mind kept going back and forth, between Darren's anger and Christy's situation when the door opened. She sat up in bed and smoothed her hair back, ready to talk to her husband.

He looked so good, wearing jeans and a soft plaid shirt and she had to swallow in order not to drool. Even after ten years of marriage, the man could still make her melt into a gooey puddle.

She watched him pull off his watch, probably to take a quick shower after working with the animals. The room was eerily silent, tension filling every corner. She supposed it was left to her to start the conversation and even though she wasn't sure exactly what to say, she started with the basics.

"I'm sorry."

He stopped what he was doing, his body seeming to relax a bit. When he didn't reply, she crawled to sit on the edge of the bed. "I shouldn't have spoken to Stephanie. It was wrong of me and I apologize."

His dark, green eyes pinned her with an intensity that rocked her soul. "I love you, Tricia, you know that, don't you?"

Without warning, her eyes filled. She nodded, unable to speak.

"I love you so much that I'd sell my soul to give you anything that you wanted." A tear streamed down her cheek. She adored this man.

"I was just . . . hurt that you didn't . . . seem to love me enough to take into account what I felt."

"Oh, honey." She reached for him and he sat next to her. As she rubbed his arm, she felt the strength there, strength that had always been there to hold and comfort her. "You're wrong. I love you with all my heart. Ever since the night we met." She grinned and quickly sobered. "I was thinking only of myself. Can you forgive me?"

Those green eyes warmed as they studied her. He took her shoulders in his hands and kissed her, first softly and then with a passion that had her trembling.

He pulled back and took a deep breath. "I know this means a great deal to you, therefore it means a great deal to me. I will consent to starting the adoption process with one caveat."

Her heart stopped, as did her breathing. Did he just say he wanted to adopt Christy? Her mind quickly catching up, she said, "One caveat. What is that?"

"This little girl has been through too much already. She's having to deal with too many changes. I don't want her to know that we're seeking adoption until it's a done deal. No reason to add more stress and possible pain to her little life."

The tears fell from her eyes now. He was such a good man, so thoughtful and loving. He would make the best father ever. She nodded quickly and sniffed. "Absolutely. I promise that we won't tell Christy until it's certain. We'll just spend this time getting to know her. Letting her get comfortable with us."

Darren nodded once, obviously content with her response.

Excitement built in her at the prospect that her deepest wish could finally be fulfilled. Joy bloomed inside, traveling north and erupting into a giggle. She threw her arms around Darren and the two of them fell over against the mattress, both laughing like giddy teenagers.

Chapter Seventeen

Darren and Tricia wanted to play outdoors with Christy, so Stephanie went to supervise and observe as they made snow angels. The change in the couple, or specifically Darren, the eagerness to hand in the preliminary paperwork and spend time with Christy was causing her head to spin.

She needed more aspirin.

Last night had been one disaster after another, starting with Christy's meltdown, her meltdown, the confrontation with Tyler, and the absolute chaos in the lounge. Sheesh, if word ever got back to the office about her being in the middle of a bar brawl . . . What would everyone think?

The Matthews laughed as Christy drew a halo on her snow angel but Stephanie found it hard to concentrate on them. Her mind was filled with Tyler—his deflated, sad look, his puppy-dog eyes staring at her. She'd hated to hurt him.

How did she think she could ever have a healthy relationship with a nice guy? She had no background for it. In her job she saw the worst examples of relationships. She was simply not destined for the happiness that came with loving and being loved.

"Step-anie!"

Christy was calling out to her, the pronunciation of her name without the "f" sound was endearing. It was clearly progress that she was talking at all. Stephanie smiled and waved. "Your angel is beautiful, sweetheart. Good job."

A little smile brightened her tiny face, warming a part of Stephanie's cold heart. She again gave herself a pep talk, reminding herself of her mission. If it worked out with the Matthews, Christy would have a loving home to belong to and her job would be done. Then she'd move on to the next sad case.

A noise sounded from the side of the inn and she turned to see Tyler dumping a couple of trash bags in the garbage cans. His face was etched with misery. He appeared like a little lost boy. She was sorry for that, she really was, but what could she do?

As if he sensed her presence, he looked up. Their eyes held for the briefest of moments before he turned without a wave, a grin, any acknowledgement, and walked away.

Her stomach dropped. Seeing him was worse than she thought it would be and she indulged in a little self-hate thinking of how she'd hurt him.

She turned back to watching Christy playing happily with Darren and Tricia. That should lift her spirits. But it didn't. Her mind stayed on Tyler and when she heard him return with more trash bags, her eyes couldn't help but to watch him, missing being near him, talking with him, sharing, kissing.

"Come p-play!" Christy called out.

Stephanie pasted on a smile and started over, taking one last look at Tyler. But before she'd taken two steps, one of her boots got stuck deep in the snow causing her to stumble. She let out a yelp just before her bottom hit the cold ground. She saw Tyler start to run over but really didn't want his help so she quickly stood, brushed off the caked snow from her pants and jacket and with the little dignity she had remaining, turned and walked to Christy.

Knowing that her face was a flaming red.

"Anyone like a cup of hot chocolate?" Mary and Joe came out carrying trays of mugs steaming with the hot drink.

Her cheeks peek, a wide smile, Christy lifted her hand and said, "Me!"

Mary laughed and when they set the trays down, she lifted a mug. "All right, young lady, you get the first." She held it as Joe took a can of spray whipped cream. "And because such a special young lady should have a special cup of chocolate, Joe here is going to put the finishing touches on it."

He made a mock salute and shook the can. While Tricia's hand settled on Christy, the young girl watched as Joe sprayed the whipped cream into a swirling heap on top of the drink. "Oh, boy!"

Everyone laughed. Mary carefully held the cup out to Christy. "It's very hot, honey. Let me hold it for you while it cools a bit." She took her first sip and smacked her lips. "It's g-good!"

Her excited reaction eased the pain in Stephanie's heart. This was so good for Christy and as she watched Tricia and Darren speak gently to her, all smiles, she deemed it very good indeed.

Franklin had insisted they get some fresh air before practicing. At the moment Natasha would have agreed with anything he said.

Last night had been the first time any man had ever stood up for her and the idea was intoxicating. She was used to men using her—using her talent, her money, and her fame for their own benefit. Franklin wasn't like that at all; he had his own talent, money, and fame. She found herself, amazingly falling for him.

"Look over there." Franklin pointed to the Matthews, the little girl, and Stephanie. They seemed to be falling in the snow for some strange reason.

"What is going on?"

Franklin chuckled. "They're making snow angels. Here, let me show you." He dropped her arm that he'd had wrapped around his and she immediately missed the warmth. He found a patch of snow and dropped backwards, moving his arms and legs back and forth. Standing, he brushed off the snow. "See the angel?"

Natasha walked closer, gazing at the image stamped into the snow. The vague impression of a robed being with wings could be seen. She laughed out loud. "I see it. I see wings right there," she said, pointing. "Now I try."

He chuckled. "Okay. Now you try."

She stood next to his angel and then fell back, moving her arms and feet as he'd done.

"Perfect." Franklin smiled and reached down to help her up. This time he kept her arm in his. "See? It's great."

Natasha felt a warmth and peace that had eluded her for many years. Just to be in this beautiful place doing simple things with this man was almost more than her heart could take.

When Mary brought out the hot chocolate, she motioned to Natasha and Franklin to join them. They stood in the snowy yard, chatting, laughing and drinking the most delicious chocolate she'd ever had.

After a while, she saw that Franklin was staring at her. "What? Is cream on my face?"

He grinned and shook his head. "It's just nice to see you enjoying yourself."

She took another sip of the hot liquid. "Maybe is something good to playing in snow." And she grinned back.

Mary was in the kitchen cooking a creamy crab Newburg for dinner. Christy was "helping" her make biscuits, sitting at the table using a small jar lid to cut out the shapes from the rolled out dough. Stephanie grinned thinking of her enthusiasm as she headed to the parlor to set out clean cups for the hot apple cider to be served later.

She wasn't prepared to encounter Tyler.

But there he was, running the vacuum cleaner over the large braided rug. Well, apparently the talk she needed to have with him would come now instead of later. Just as well. She hated to be so distant from the man she admired so much. Besides, very soon they'd be driving to Newport and how awkward would that be sharing the ride and not speaking to each other. After setting down the cups, she gathered her courage and prepared to confront him.

Tyler turned off the cleaner and reached for a newspaper left on the floor. Now was her chance to get his attention. Quietly, she cleared her throat and opened her mouth to speak but before anything came out, the vacuum started again.

She walked into the room and waited but evidently he didn't know she was there. The machine stopped again and she said, "Tyler?" But that again got lost in the noise of the loud vacuum as he switched it back on. He was really going to town on the rug, running the vacuum over and over it again as if his life depended on its cleanliness. Was she the cause of that? Probably.

The guilt seemed to trickle through her body, remembering the lost expression on his face when she'd told him she didn't want to date him. He was such a great guy, she'd hated to do that. She wished things were different.

So much for waiting for him to stop the vacuuming. She cleared her throat again and said with a loud voice, "Tyler, I'd like to speak to you," just as the vacuum turned off, causing "speak to you" to be yelled loudly through the downstairs.

She could feel her face burn with embarrassment as he jumped at the noise. "Sorry," she said quietly. "Uh, Tyler. Could I speak with you for a moment?"

His eyes didn't meet hers as he bent to retrieve the machine cord and wrap it around the vacuum. "Seems you said everything last night. I've got to finish cleaning the floors."

Why did she feel like she'd kicked a puppy? Maybe it was his slumped shoulders or his hooded eyes. Whatever, she hated this feeling. "Surely you can spare five minutes so I can apologize."

That got his attention. "Apologize?"

She took his hand and led him to the couch, both of them sitting. "My . . . approach last night was . . . well, inexcusable. I was short and blunt and lacked the compassion that I should have had. For that I am sorry."

"Okay." His frown led her to decide she needed to explain the events of last night.

Stephanie sat on the edge of the couch, her hands fidgeting in front of her. "Christy had a rough night. Here in the parlor, a couple got a little too intense into an argument and she reacted."

His face instantly changed from guarded to sympathetic. "Oh, poor kid. I must have missed it when I was helping Joe set up the lounge. I was wondering if being in the midst of all those people would make her panic."

Stephanie was amazed. This kind, gentle man knew enough about children in crisis to sense that last night might have been a threat. And had trusted her enough to handle the situation by herself. Her appreciation of him increased.

Coming back to her point, she said, "Yes, well panic would be a mild word. I thought we were over it by the time I got her settled down to sleep but then a nightmare woke her and . . . it just sort of freaked me out."

"Freaked you out? Why?" Tyler seemed genuinely interested.

Could she tell him why? Did she really want to get into her horrible past and the fear and grief that were in her heart, reflected in Christy's eyes? No, it was too pitiful. She was an adult that should be over it, singularly focused on the children put in her care.

Seeing that Tyler was waiting for an answer, she lied. "I had hoped that we were a little past the extreme response to stimuli. I know, too much to ask of a little girl, but still."

Tyler shook his head. "And it prompted you to seek me out and tell me you weren't interested in me? I'm sorry, I just don't understand."

"Christy needs me, Tyler. After her there'll be another child that needs me, and after that another. It's my purpose in life to help as many as I can. I can't let anything distract me from that, can't you see that?"

He didn't speak for a moment, his eyes pinning her. "Why is it your purpose, Stephanie Singer?" Her heart froze at the question. "Why is it your mission to save every abused child in the world?"

After swallowing hard, she said, "That's a stupid question, Tyler. And one I can't believe you're asking. You told me yourself that you wished you'd had an advocate like me working for you when you were a baby. Can't you see I'm needed?"

He studied her for another minute. "Okay. I understand. Is there anything else?"

She hated the coldness of his voice. This wasn't the Tyler Buchanan that she knew. Her heart hurt for the absence of their friendship.

That's what was lacking. Friendship.

"Yes, there is." She sat up straight and bravely looked him in the eye. "Just because we can't be romantically involved doesn't mean that I don't like and respect you very much. And it doesn't mean that I don't want us to be friends."

He just watched her, unmoving. It was unnerving to her.

"Tyler, you may not realize this but I . . . need you. I need your camaraderie, your insight, and your help. You're important to me." Unwanted tears filled her eyes at the prospect of not having him in her life. "Won't you say we can be friends? Please?"

A tear escaped her eye and Tyler's finger went to catch it. His other arm went around her shoulders. "Of course we can be friends."

She leaned her head against his shoulders and sniffed back tears, enjoying the strong feel of his body next to hers. Thank God, was all she could think. It hadn't be as evident to her until now what his friendship meant to her. The idea of him not in her life was unthinkable.

Getting her composure back, she straightened and chuckled nervously. "Okay. Okay." She wiped her eyes, making sure no other tears were forthcoming. She blew out a breath. "I'll get back to the kitchen now to help Mary. When I left her, Christy was making biscuits for tonight. She was so excited."

Tyler smiled warmly. "That's good."

"Okay," she repeated and stood. "We're . . . okay?"

"We're okay, Stephanie."

She returned the smile and backed up, banging the backs of her knees into the large wooden coffee table.

Tyler jumped up and took her arm. "You all right?"

"Ouch." Rubbing the backs of her legs, she said, "Fine. See you at dinner," and hurried away, her heart thumping in her chest the whole way to the kitchen.

The sight that greeted her there had her calming down and smiling. Christy was sitting on Mary's lap as she held a cold compress to the little girl's damaged eye. She was speaking in soft tones but Stephanie could pick up a little of the conversation—something about the time Bradley had gotten a black eye when a stray ball hit him on the school playground. Christy sat still listening, giggling at the funny parts of the story. Stephanie's smile widened.

"What's going on here?" She walked further into the room that smelled of a creamy, buttery sauce warming on the stove and homemade biscuits baking in the oven.

Mary looked up. "Oh, I hope you don't mind. I remember putting ice on Bradley when his eye got hurt last spring. Christy was rubbing it so I thought the coolness might take away any pain there."

So thoughtful. Even though she could scold herself for not paying attention to Christy's injury, she was more thankful for Mary's sensitivity. God bless the woman. "No, no, it's quite all right. I'm glad you noticed her unease." Stephanie sat next to them and bent to face Christy. "Is your eye hurting you, honey?"

"Not now. It feels g-good."

"Only like a snowball, right, sweetheart?" Mary smiled at her and she nodded.

Stephanie patted Christy's knee. "Glad to hear it." She bent to study the eye closer. "It's looking better." The shining expression on Christy's face lightened her spirit. With the exception to the understandable occurrence last night, she really was doing so much better. "You be sure to tell me if it hurts again, okay?" Christy nodded. "Mary, what else can I do to help?"

"Oh, my. You, Tyler, and Christy have been such a help I think we're all set for tonight. Why don't you sit and take a little break with Christy and me before dinner?"

She deserved it, didn't she, gently letting Tyler down when everything in her wanted to hold on to him, feeling his arm around her, his strong shoulder supporting her. But she'd made her decision and it had been the right one. As she looked at the little girl in Mary's lap she reaffirmed what she knew.

These children were her destiny in life. Not an adorable, brown-haired gentle man.

After more snow angels and a walk around the property, Natasha and Franklin were ready to retreat to the inn for a brief rehearsal. Franklin had determined that Natasha would have fun while she was here in Vermont and he considered it his responsibility to see to it. He had a whole list of things for them to do.

"I had another idea about the 'Jiggly Bells.' How does this sound?" Natasha launched into a jaunty version of the song, adding peaks and valleys before launching into a speedy race to the end of the song. Franklin laughed as he tried to catch up to her, playing a simple background. When they both finished, they collapsed into peals of laughter.

"That was delightful, my dear. It must be worked into our routine." He blew out a breath. "Although I think I can only play it one time through a day."

"You are not up to it?" Her brow arched playfully at him.

"I didn't say that. I just . . . okay, possibly I'm not up to it."

She giggled, her eyes sparkling. Did she know how beautiful she was when she was happy?

It was entrancing and he could have simply looked at her all day.

Her laughter stopped as her eyes focused on him. For a moment everything stilled in the room and he wanted to kiss her more than breathe. He stood and took a step closer as she watched him, her eyes sharpening with interest. His heart thudded, now knowing the taste of her lips, the sweetness he would find there. He swallowed and took another step, his hand caressing her arm. He moved closer, closer until . . .

Her phone rang a familiar tone that sent dread to his heart. He immediately saw it on her face. She started to reach into her pocket but he stilled her hand. "Don't answer it," he said softly.

"He will not be happy."

"It's time you were happy."

Her breathing came in shallow huffs. "He . . . has the power to take away all happiness."

Franklin held her hands in his, keeping her from answering. "How? What does he have over you?"

Big golden eyes blinked at him. "He controls the money. He is manager. If I do not follow his orders I will go back to Russia." The ringing stopped and he saw her wince. "He plans to send me back after Christmas."

His heart plummeted. "But he can't do that. You're an adult, a talented musician with many connections here in the states. Surely you can stay." Her head shook the entire time he spoke.

"My contracts with the symphony are through him. He can cancel them at his discretion.

I do not want to live on street, I do not want to be poor."

Something familiar and distasteful formed inside of him, so heavy and binding that it threatened to squeeze the life out of him. His eyes clouded as his thoughts traveled back to his childhood, the sights, the sounds, the smells. He thought he would be sick. Although he'd had hot chocolate outside and a light lunch afterward, his stomach knotted and tightened, as if in a silent plea to find some sustenance.

"You cannot understand."

His eyes cleared and he gazed at Natasha, her eyes watering. His voice was rough, low when he said, "I understand better than you think."

This apparently caught her attention as her eyes sharpened. "Tell me. Tell me about Franklin Murray. Tell me why your voice changes. Tell me where you are from."

His tongue lay heavy in his mouth. Did he trust her to reveal his secrets or should he acknowledge that this momentary interlude in his life would end soon enough and wherever Natasha went—back to the symphony or, God forbid, back to Russia—she'd know his secret, something he'd never told anyone. Something that had the power to tear apart his reputation. He tried to lighten the moment by putting on his best British accent and saying, "Didn't I mention it, darling?"

The honest interest he saw in her eyes hypnotized him, making him want to throw off the pretense he sometimes found so burdening and share the truth with her. Maybe he should, maybe it would be a good thing—

"Hey, you two. Dinner's on and Mary's been baking her famous biscuits." They turned to see Eldon's head peering around the doorway. "If you want any, you better not be late." Then he was gone, obviously heeding his own advice.

"Ah, dinner." Franklin held out his arm for Natasha to take. "I happen to be an admirer of a good biscuit."

When she gave a slight smile, nodded, and took his arm, he breathed a sigh of relief, grateful he'd been given a retrieve from possibly making a big mistake.

Chapter Eighteen

After dinner, Tricia and Darren sat with Christy in the parlor helping her with a puzzle of Santa Claus. Her thin little finger gently touched the puzzle and said, "Santa."

Tricia wrapped her arms around her. "That's right, Christy. Santa. Have you told Santa what you want for Christmas this year?"

Her eyes went to the doorway just as Sam and Eldon entered, she pointed and called out "Santa!"

"No, honey. That's Sam."

"I talked to him. He's g-going to get me what I want for C-Christmas."

Neither wanted to belabor the point about Sam so they concentrated on the puzzle instead.

"Oh, look, Christy. See the pretty kitten? She looks like one of ours. Do you like kittens?" Christy nodded, continuing to work on the puzzle while Tricia frowned. "I miss Lucy and Ricky. Do you think I should check on them?"

"Sure. Go ahead and call Vera, make sure they're okay."

Tricia pulled out her phone and made the call. Darren watched her, seeing the concern, the relief, and the joy as she listened to the report of their two cats. Putting her phone away, Tricia said, "They're fine. Enjoying their Christmas presents."

"Yeah, it was a good idea to have an early Christmas with them."

Darren saw that Christy was watching their conversation and thought he should explain. "We gave gifts to our cats before we left. They got a ball with a bell in it and a new cat tree to climb on."

"Oh, but do you know what Vera said they're playing with the most?" Tricia laughed. "That pink squeaky mouse we got at the last minute." Christy smiled and Darren chuckled.

Natasha and Franklin came into the parlor and began their warm up for the evening. Darren noticed that it was just the inn's guests tonight, along with a few close friends of Angela's. He was thankful. No way did any of them want a repeat of last night. His thoughts drifted to their argument in the lounge and making up this morning. Something Sam had said to him in the barn replayed in his head.

"Honey, I was thinking. When we're back home would you like to go with me sometime out to Alan's practice and help with the animals?"

He was surprised to see her face brighten. Her eyes fairly glowed and her smile beamed. "I'd love to."

"If you've wanted to before, why didn't you say anything?"

"I don't know. I guess I thought it was your way to relax, to blow off steam. I didn't think you'd want me along."

Had he somehow communicated that to her? "I never thought you'd be interested."

"Darren, don't you know me at all? Don't you know how much I love animals? I participate in the animal shelter's fundraisers, I volunteer when they need extra hands, I go over several times a month to help walk dogs. How could you not have known I'd love to help at Alan's practice?"

"I'm not a mind reader, Tricia. If you want to do something you should let me know."

She frowned at him. "Seems that when I do that, you tell me I'm obsessing and I should give you a break because you're sick of hearing about it." She gave a quick glance to Christy who thankfully wasn't paying attention. Still she lowered her voice to reply. "I can't help it if I get excited about something and want to talk about it. But while we're on the subject, I don't understand how you don't get excited when we find the answer to our problems."

"I didn't know we had any problems. I was frankly enjoying my marriage and my life. Besides, I already gave you what you wanted. You can't still possibly be mad at me."

"Darren, it's not a question of you caving to me and giving me what we want. It's about what we both want. It's about completing our family, making our marriage better."

"Is it so bad, Tricia? Really, is being married to me so bad that you need something else to make you happy?" Their voices had begun to raise, both eager to present his or her own side.

The blood drained from Tricia's face when she said, "She's gone! Christy?" Her head jerked around, surveying the parlor. "Darren, where did she go?"

He'd been so involved in their argument, he hadn't noticed the little girl leaving. "I'm sure she's not far."

But Tricia didn't hear him. She was frantically looking through the room. Watching her, Darren was also a bit alarmed. Not that the little girl had walked away from them.

But that his wife already had.

Tyler had been deep in thought all day. Sam had intimated to him that Stephanie might have a very good reason for not wanting a relationship with him. Later when speaking with her, he'd seen a shadow cross her eyes as she spoke of Christy's distress. He was sure that she'd been thinking about her own past.

She'd asked him to be her friend, just as Sam had said she needed. So, he'd put aside his love and be what she needed him to be—just a friend.

His hands were deep in a sink full of soapy water scrubbing a pot as Stephanie brought in the last of the dinner dishes. They'd urged Joe and Mary to take the evening off, especially after all the work they'd had cleaning the lounge and parlor, and let them take care of the kitchen. After Angela agreed, they'd gone upstairs to rest and spend some time with Bradley.

Her hair pushed back with combs, her face flushed from exertion, she still was the prettiest thing he'd ever seen and again he clamped down his desires to touch and hold her in order to be what she needed. "You got everything?"

"Yes. The dining room's all clean, ready to go for tomorrow." She glanced at the clean pots and pans draining on the counter. "Looks like you've been busy. I'll help." She got a clean towel and began drying.

"I'm so glad we could help out Joe and Mary this way. They looked beat."

"Yeah. Between the normal routine of running this place, plus the wolf, and the drama of last night, I don't know how they were standing this evening."

"It must get pretty busy at the orphanage."

Tyler smiled. "Sometimes. I can truthfully say there's never a dull moment." He began to regale her with stories from his many years at the orphanage—some crazy, a few sad, but many hilarious. Before long they were both laughing out loud at the humorous stories.

"Oh, thank you, Tyler. I really needed a good laugh."

"You're welcome." It was quiet for a moment before he said, "Christy doing okay today?"

"Seems to be. She's spent most of the day with the Matthews."

"They thinking about adopting her?"

Stephanie stopped drying and glanced at him. "I . . . can't reveal what's going on with one of my kids."

"Understood." He went back to washing dishes. "They seem like nice people anyway." Shaking his head he added, "Christy needs a break."

"Yeah." Her voice was low, her actions slow, and her eyes focused far away.

"I know I didn't have the best childhood, being abandoned as a baby and all, but at least I wasn't abused. I can't imagine what that's like."

Her hands stopped for a second, and started again more vigorously. Her eyes filled and she blinked continuously to keep the tears away.

Tyler's heart went out to her, hating that she was keeping so much inside. Softly, as if approaching a hurt animal, he said, "It must have been terrible for you."

She sighed. "You learn to live with it." Her head jerked toward him, evidently realizing what she'd just said. "I mean, she'll learn to live with it."

He took the pot and towel from her hands and set them aside, gently taking her hands in his. "We're friends, right? Tell me why you were so freaked out by Christy's reaction last night. It mirrored yours, didn't it?"

Her big blue eyes implored his, tears starting to spill out. He knew she was calculating whether to trust him or not. He hoped she would.

With a sobbing hiccup, she nodded. Now his heart clenched, wanting desperately to ease her pain. He guided her to the table and when they sat, he pulled his chair close so he could put his arm around her shoulders. "Tell me."

Her voice was quiet but raw, a piece of silk pulled over a sandpaper. "My parents never wanted me. They always blamed me for their problems." Tyler rubbed her shoulder, his heart breaking for her. "The money was tight because I needed to go to the doctor or I needed childcare so they could work. The . . . hitting didn't start until my father lost his job and started drinking." Tyler swallowed hard, not sure if he was ready for what was to come.

"I was the classic case. I wore long sleeves year round so no one saw the bruises. I was taught to say I was clumsy if anyone noticed. It was the way my life was until I entered middle school."

"What happened then?" His heart accelerated watching her eyes dilate as if going back to that time.

"He'd had enough. He left. And it was just my mother and me." She was quiet for so long, he wondered if she'd go on. Carefully, he rubbed her shoulder, a gesture of comfort and encouragement.

"She took up where he left off." Tyler squeezed his eyes shut. "Although she was more inventive. She liked to use a hot iron."

"No, Stephanie." No matter that they were only friends, he pulled her into a tight hug, just as much for himself as for her, rubbing her back, feeling the tension she was holding in.

"She got into drugs along with her drinking. When I was seventeen I came home from school one day and found her dead in her vomit. Overdose."

"I'm sorry."

"I was close to finishing high school, almost eighteen, so child services let me finish out the year living with an elderly couple across the street." She huffed out a chuckle. "They couldn't hear, could barely see. But at least they didn't hit me. I thought I'd died and gone to heaven."

"Oh, honey. You never ever should have had to endure that. I wish I could have been there to stop it." He felt a trickle of moisture on his shirt, the result of her tears. "It explains why you're so good at your job. It explains your beautiful heart for these children. I . . . I think you're the bravest woman I've ever known."

The moisture grew and she began to shake. Her hands went around to his back, holding tightly. Her sobs grew louder and his heart cried with her.

He held her, wondering if she'd ever shared her brutal story with anyone. If she'd been sent to the orphanage as a child, they'd have made sure she spoke with a counselor. It was still a good idea and one he'd mention to her at some point.

As her tears fell, he murmured encouragement, stroking her back and dropping kisses on her tearstained cheeks. They sat like that a long time until she finally relaxed against him. When she sniffed, he pulled out a handkerchief for her.

"Thanks." She wiped her nose and sat up. "I didn't mean to blubber all over you. I don't do that sort of thing."

Which made it more significant that she had done it with him.

"It's okay. That's what friends are for." He smiled warmly at her, pushing a strand of hair out of her eyes.

The swinging door from the dining room flew open and Christy ran in, her face pale as she quickly scanned the room.

"Christy? What's wrong?"

When the little girl saw Stephanie, she ran to her and threw her arms around her, starting to cry. Stephanie pulled her closely, whispering that everything would be all right.

Watching the two, Tyler was amazed at the skill with which Stephanie handled Christy, instantly changing from grieving her own past to focusing completely on the child in her arms. She knew the right words, the right touches, everything to calm the hurting child's soul. He was not only mesmerized, awed, but deeply in love with this woman. He scooted his chair closer and wrapped his arm around the two.

The door again opened and Darren and Tricia stood searching the room. "Oh, thank God," Tricia said, running to Christy.

She knelt next to Stephanie's chair. "Honey, what happened? You didn't need to run. Darren and I were just having a discussion. We didn't mean to frighten you."

Stephanie looked up and Tyler was shocked to see a fire come into her eyes. "Mrs. Matthews. I believe I should have a talk with you and your husband."

"All right." Tricia's subdued tone revealed her concern.

"Tyler, after I get Christy to bed this evening could you watch her while I speak with the Matthews?"

"Sure."

He was only glad that this angry Stephanie would be directing her emotions toward Darren and Tricia and not him.

Chapter Nineteen

Angela was beginning to worry.

It was only a couple of days until Christmas and anxiety had seemed to settle around the inn.

Stephanie had apparently had a tense evening meeting with the Matthews over their behavior in front of Christy. Tyler and Stephanie had come to some kind of agreement but the emptiness in her eyes and the desire in his broke Angela's heart. Natasha and Franklin's relationship seemed to be moving forward, although he was still speaking with that transparent accent of his. She knew there were still things they needed to discuss.

And she was still worried about the wolf. In the dead of the night she'd heard a howl in the forest behind the inn, just a short one, but one that somehow seemed taunting, warning. She shuddered.

After sharing her concerns with Sam, she poured him another cup of coffee. "But I know everything will work out. What did William Shakespeare say? 'All's well that end's well.' I'm expecting the same at the Sleep In Heavenly Peace Inn."

The dining room was quiet this time of the morning, as everyone had scattered. Darren had gone skiing while Tricia was resting. Stephanie and Christy had gone with Mary and Bradley to Stowe Village to look at the Christmas decorations. Franklin and Natasha were visiting the barn.

Joe and Tyler were looking for tracks in the woods behind the inn.

"True. But I think our biggest concern is Christy. How in the world are we going to help her get her Christmas wish? That little girl deserves a wonderful Christmas but I'm afraid she's going to be devastated when she doesn't get what she really wants."

Angela sipped her coffee, her mind whirling. "You already told me what she wants. Joe and Mary got the baby doll and bottle and the Candyland game. The Matthews bought the family of Barbies. Oh, and I found her the cutest little plush dog. Looks just like Frederica."

Sam paused. "You mean she hasn't mentioned to you what she really wants?"

"There's something else?" Sam winced. "Well, I'm all ears. What is it?"

"Perhaps Christy should tell you herself."

"All right. I'll ask—oh, Mr. Murray, did you need something?" The musician stepped into the room, appearing uncharacteristically shy.

"I was just wondering where Mrs. Puletti was."

"She's in the village shopping, dear. Can I help you?"

"I . . . was just wondering if maybe I could arrange something for tonight. You know Natasha and I aren't performing so I thought . . . an after dinner treat in the backyard patio. The weather is mild enough. It's supposed to be a clear night."

Angela could feel his eagerness. A smile curved her lips thinking at least this couple was making progress. "Of course. I think I understand what you'd like. How about a couple of Mary's homemade éclairs and a lovely wine to go with them. Oh, and soft music and candlelight. Just leave everything to me." She winked at him.

He returned the smile. "Yes. Thank you. Thank you, Angela."

"Ah, Angela. Joe might not think that's a good idea—being outside at night?" She knew Sam was trying to remind her about the wolf threat.

"I'm sure the patio behind the inn would be safe but I'll check to make sure with Joe when he comes back." She turned back to Franklin. "You just leave everything to me."

Once Franklin left the room, Angela said, "There, you see? Everything is going to fall into place, I just know it."

"Hmm." Sam shook his head and took another sip. "I don't want to be the negative Nellie here but I'd like to remind you of another saying."

"Which is?"

He pinned her with his stare. "It's always darkest before the dawn."

A premonition shuttered through her knowing that Sam was exactly right. She settled herself quickly. “And we’ll get through the dark, just like we always do.”

The door from the kitchen swung open and two children ran in followed by Mary’s admonition, “Bradley, Christy, don’t run in the inn.”

Sam caught Bradley around the waist, both of them laughing. “Did you have a good time in town, sport?”

“Sure did, Sam. The streets were covered in lights. And every store had a big Christmas tree that was decorated with stuff from that store.”

Angela held out her hand for Christy, who went to her and sat on her lap. “What about you, little angel. Did you have fun?”

She nodded, her smile a mile long.

“That’s good.” Angela lowered her voice to Christy and said, “I hear that you have a special Christmas wish.” The girl nodded. “I’d like to hear it, if you’d like to tell me.”

Christy first glanced at Bradley, who gave her an affirmative nod, his eyes serious and intent. She put her little hand to her mouth and leaned to Angela’s ear, whispering.

Angela swallowed hard, her eyes going to Sam. He lifted both eyebrows as if to say, “What did I tell you.”

She exhaled, completely speechless. When Christy reached her arms around Angela and hugged her tightly, her throat clogged with emotion and the desire to help this precious little girl.

Somehow she would figure out how to help her. Just as soon as her power of speech returned.

Natasha took extra time with her appearance, opting to skip dinner. Franklin had asked to meet with her for dessert and wine later and she wanted to look her best. No, that wasn't quite right. She wanted to look how she felt—hopeful, peaceful, for the first time in a long time . . . happy.

All because of Franklin. He'd been so kind with her, showing her how much fun the holiday season could be. Today he'd taken her to the barn. Amidst the sights and sounds of the enthusiastic animals, there was a kind of music flowing through the barn. Franklin had said it was nature's own symphony. She'd liked the sound of that.

She was finding out so many interesting things about the man, things she would never have thought. Things that fascinated her. Although he was a brilliant pianist, knowledgeable about a wide array of music, he also knew how to entertain the animals in a barn. His skilled fingers stroked each animal, speaking to them in calming tones. She envied them.

He had amazing insight—from tossing snowballs, making snow angels, and listening to nature's music—that made her relax. She hadn't thought of her uncle since ignoring his call.

He hadn't called again. She wasn't sure if that was a good thing or a bad thing.

She ran her brush through her long, dark locks, deciding to leave it down for their dessert. The large comfy, scarlet red sweater she'd bought on a whim in New York would be perfect to wear with her jeans. She giggled with glee at being able to wear something so "unprofessional" but comfortable.

When she went out the back door, she gasped. The patio was alit with strands of tiny white lights strung overhead. In the middle a small table was set with a white tablecloth and three golden candlesticks, flickering with light. Franklin stood next to the table, tall and handsome, dressed in jeans, gray turtleneck, and navy jacket. When the edges of his lips lifted, she felt herself melting on the spot.

"You left your hair down."

Her hand went to her hair, feeling self-conscious, which was silly. She was a professional, a self-assured woman.

Who was currently fighting a crush on the dreamy pianist in front of her.

"Yes." She took a step closer and he held out a chair for her to sit. "Thank you." Classical music played softly in the background. Patio heaters warmed the area. Still she shivered.

"Would you like coffee instead of wine?"

"No." He couldn't know her chill wasn't from the weather. She smiled when he handed her a glass.

It was quiet as they clinked their glasses and both took bites of their éclairs. "Mmm. Mary is an absolute treasure in the kitchen. Don't you agree?"

"Yes." Could she speak in more than one syllable words? She swallowed hard and tried. "This is very nice, Franklin. Thank you."

"I believe we were due for an enjoyable evening with no performances. I love to perform but it's nice to relax."

"Yes. Is good to rest fingers, no?"

He chuckled. "It is."

They continued with dessert, their conversation drifting to the inn, the people, and the season. When Franklin spoke of the New York Symphony, she felt herself tense. He apparently did also, as he said, "What's wrong?"

Natasha sat back, fighting a wave of sadness. "I do not know if I will return. My uncle . . . he may . . ." Her eyes met his. "I may not have a place when I return to city."

Franklin put his napkin down and also sat back, studying her, which made her squirm in her seat. "I've been thinking about your problem, Natasha."

"You have?"

"I have. And I believe I have an answer for you." Her heart quickened. Could he possibly have a solution that she hadn't thought about?

He lifted his glass and said, "You can fight." He saluted and took a sip.

Irritation bubbled up in the pit of her stomach and her pulse accelerated. "What is that you say? You tell me to fight? Just fight as if so simple. You do not know what you say. To go against my uncle will mean the end of all hope of freedom. There is no fighting him, he is powerful."

Her voice lowered a bit. "I am not coward. If I thought I had chance I would give everything I had to be free of him." She fought back the emotion causing her eyes to fill.

Franklin reached across the table for her hand and again his accent slipped. "I didn't mean to make you unhappy. And I didn't mean to suggest that it would be an easy or comfortable process."

She pulled her hand back. "You know nothing. You have always had your freedom, have gone where you wanted, when you wanted. You have not had to fight for basic rights you enjoy. You cannot know how I feel." A tear slipped down her cheek and she angrily pushed it away.

His hands in front of him, Franklin looked down and took a deep breath. She hadn't meant to be so sharp with him, especially since he'd arranged such a nice treat for her. "I am sorry," she whispered. "I have ruined your evening."

She stood to leave but Franklin quietly said, "Sit down, Natasha. Please."

There was no hint of an accent in his voice and she sat back down and waited. After a long moment, his eyes came up, weary and sad. "There are all kinds of bondage. In a way I think everyone has one to deal with, a time in one's life when he must decide if he truly wants to be free."

"And what was yours, Franklin Murray?"

Another extended moment. She wondered if he was actually going to answer her. When he did, his voice was gravelly, deep. Heartbreakingly raw. "I was born Francis Lorenzo Moretti, in a small two-bedroom walk-up in the Bronx. Second born son of Luca and Maria." Her mind swirled to catch up with everything he was saying.

"There were eight of us kids, living in the two-bedroom walk-up in the Bronx. It was all we could afford."

"I see." His expression was so solemn, she desperately wanted to lighten the moment. "I was right. You are American."

"Ding ding. Give the lady a prize." She frowned, not knowing what that meant. "Why pretend to be British?"

"Because, darling, I made a few enemies in my days as Frankie Moretti. Things were bad, financially. I found that if I wanted anything, like maybe an extra piece of bread, I had to find my own way about getting it. Sometimes my answers weren't so . . . legal."

"Oh." What could she say to that?

"I won't bore you with the details. Suffice it to say that by the time I entered high school I was on my way to also entering a jail cell. Until a teacher introduced me to the piano." Franklin shook his head. "Something clicked inside me. It was like I had been waiting my whole life to find that missing piece. For the first time in my life I felt a desire for other than food or drink. Music opened my eyes to other things in life—beauty, joy." His eyes pinned her. "Freedom." She could understand all those things when she played her violin.

"You see, Natasha, I know what it's like to not be free. I was bound by poverty. So many times I looked at my parents, my brothers and sisters and wondered why they didn't see it as well as I did. They seemed okay with their meager existence. But I never was. I wanted to be free of that life more than I wanted to take a breath. I wanted to be able to live the life I wanted to live without fear that I wouldn't have food to eat the next day."

His eyes seemed to glow. "It didn't come easy but I was determined. I decided to fight for my freedom. And that's exactly what I did, every day from that first piano lesson until I was able to change my name and go to Europe to study." She frowned and seeming to comprehend her unspoken question, he said, "I wanted a fresh start, a new life." He reached across the table and took her hands. "Maybe that's what you need."

Her eyes widened. "I should change name and speak . . . differently?"

Franklin chuckled. "Not at all." He rubbed his thumbs over the backs of her hands, a comforting, relaxing touch that almost brought a purr from her lips. His next words erased all soothing feelings. "You should stand up to your uncle."

Her stomach tightened and sweat formed on her neck as she shook her head. "I do not know."

"How about if I help you?"

She studied the man in front of her, confused again by the compassion he showed. "Why? Why would you do this for me?"

"Because . . . well, I . . ."

She might have been offended that he couldn't find a good reason to help her but something in his eyes and voice told her it wasn't the case. And was his face blushing slightly? This was new.

"'Well, I' what?"

"I like you, Natasha. No, that's not right. I mean, it is right, but it's more. I care about you. I want to see you happy, I want . . ."

Warmth filled her at his faltering words. He liked her? A smile blossomed on her face as happiness filled her soul. "You want . . ."

"Just that you . . . that I . . ." He cursed under his breath and leaned over the table taking her face in his hands and kissing her hard. The kiss softened and Natasha couldn't hold back a dreamy sigh.

The kiss went on and on and she wanted so much to take it deeper when she heard a sound in the distance.

"The wolf?" Christy asked as she sat in Mary's lap.

Mary stopped reading "The Night Before Christmas" and tried to think of comforting words. "I don't know, honey." She looked over to Stephanie for help.

"I'm sure it's nothing, Christy." Stephanie gently rubbed the little girl's arm.

"Course it is. It's the wolf," Bradley, who was sitting on the other side of his mother, added, prompting Mary to give him a frown. Getting the message, he said, "But he's probably just out for a walk, that's all."

Joe walked into the parlor and finding Mary, gave her a nod. Then abruptly turned to leave.

Sam, who'd been sitting nearby reading, said, "I'll go with you, Joe."

Christy jumped to her feet and ran to Sam, throwing her arms around his legs. "Don't go, Santa!"

Obviously a little embarrassed, Sam reached down and lifted Christy. "I'm just going to make sure the animals are safe."

Her arms went around his neck and held tightly. "I don't want to lose you, too."

No one spoke, as all the air seemed to be sucked out of the room. Mary could feel tears burning in her eyes. The festive Christmas lights and decorations of the room seem to mock the sadness of the moment.

Since no one appeared to know what to say, Mary took the initiative. She went to Sam and Christy and gently rubbed the girl's back. "Honey, Sam will be right back. In fact, he'll come in the parlor and give you a goodnight kiss, okay?"

Christy turned to Mary and nodded. Mary took that opportunity to take her into her arms and gave Sam a sad smile, which he returned before leaving with Joe.

Angela who had been watching everything unfold stood and went to Mary, softly brushing the child's hair. "He'll be fine, honey." A hand went to her throat. "Oh, good gracious. Natasha and Franklin!" She hurried through the inn to the back door.

Mary sighed. So much for the couple's romantic evening.

Chapter Twenty

"Now you go and enjoy the party. Bradley, let's you and I go take a spin." Stephanie smiled at Mary's excitement, heightening her own. Christy held her hand, bouncing on her toes, also filled with anticipation.

She knew Angela, Mary, and Joe had debated back and forth whether or not to have the annual ice skating party scheduled for the day before Christmas Eve. In the end, the decision was made to have the party. It was a special occasion that the people of Stowe along with frequent visitors always looked forward to and Angela couldn't bring herself to cancel. But in concession, Joe would spend the party watching the area, along with others from animal control and local authorities to keep everyone safe.

They pulled on skates, Stephanie making sure Christy's were tight enough. "Okay, kiddo, let's see how you do."

Even though she was tiny, Christy's grip was painfully tight on Stephanie's hand. She tried to soothe her, pointing out different things as they started for the ice. "Have you ever skated before?" Christy shook her head. "Well, you are going to have so much fun. The trick is to keep your ankles straight. And just glide." She nodded.

They tentatively stepped onto the ice and started the trek around the pond. Christy's expression was determined, something Stephanie appreciated about the girl. And recognized in herself. They shuffled for a while, as Christy got more accustomed to the feeling of gliding. Stephanie relaxed a little, enjoying the coolness of the breeze on her face, the feel of her feet moving smoothly over the ice, hearing the giggles and chuckles of people having a good time. It was a happy day.

Until she saw Tyler.

Ever since she'd told him about her past, she'd been relieved. Now he could understand her mission in life and the fact that it couldn't include him. So she should have been happy to see him skating with another woman.

But she wasn't.

Who was she? She seemed a little young for him. And a little too happy to be holding his hand taking a turn around the pond. Did she just trip on purpose? Her smile as Tyler steadied her irritated Stephanie. Boy, was that a ploy if she'd ever seen one. Obviously the girl could skate, moving effortlessly over the ice. She probably just wanted Tyler to hold her. The irritation rose.

Did he know that she was faking her inexperience? Men were so clueless about things.

"Step-anie? Like this?"

Her attention jerked back to the little girl speaking. "Yes, sweetheart. You're doing great, just great. I knew you'd pick it up quickly." She sped up a bit. "How about we go . . . ah, this way." She eased closer to Tyler and his "date" hoping to catch what the girl was loudly giggling about.

Unfortunately, she got a little too close and when they turned, the girl ran smack dab into Stephanie, causing her to lose her balance and tumble to the hard ice, with Christy on top of her.

"Stephanie! Christy! Are you two okay?" Tyler reached down, first lifting Christy as if she weighed nothing and setting her on her feet. Then pulling Stephanie up next. Her hands couldn't resist holding to his strong biceps, indulging herself in a little internal appreciation.

"We're fine. Thank you." Stephanie pushed her hair out of her eyes and tried to put a smile on her face. "Hello," she directed to the girl next to Tyler.

"Oh, I'm sorry. Stephanie, this is Cammie Young. Her aunt is Jessica that owns the local spa. Cammie, Stephanie Singer. She's a children's social worker from Burlington." Tyler smiled widely as he lifted Christy up in his arms. "And this is Christy. She's coming to live with us at the orphanage in Newport."

Stephanie wondered if Cammie thought the "us" referred to her and Tyler.

"Oh, what a sweet little girl. How are you? Tyler, she is adorable." From her tone she clearly wasn't thinking of Stephanie and Tyler together. And why did that irk her even more?

"Yes, she is. So, you learning to ice skate?" Christy gave a nod. "That's great, sweetheart." He kissed her cheek and set her down, keeping his hand on her shoulder. "It's a nice party, isn't it?"

Stephanie was about to answer when Cammie said, "It really is. Angela does this every year and it's a highlight of the season." *He was talking to me. Probably. Maybe.*

"Santa!" Christy's face brightened and her little arms stretched out.

"Who?"

Christy held back the urge to roll her eyes at Cammie when Sam skated to them.

"Hi Christy. Stephanie, Tyler. Cammie. How's your mother doing? I heard her arthritis had flared again."

"Fine, Sam. I'll tell her you were asking."

"You do that." Sam lowered his voice and leaned toward her. "Did she send you with her famous coconut cake?"

Cammie giggled, a light-hearted sound that Stephanie knew just had to be fake.

"She did. She and I made it this morning. It's on the refreshment table."

"That's just fine. How about you skating with an old man and having a piece with me?"

She hesitated, clearly not wanting to leave Tyler's side. Stephanie held her breath until Cammie said, "Sure. Tyler, I want another skate with you this afternoon."

Tyler grinned. "Of course. And be sure and save me a piece of that coconut cake. That's my favorite." *Since when did he become so confident around women?*

"Why don't you let me get Christy a couple of cookies while we're at it?" Sam asked. "We'll find you when we're finished." Stephanie was thankful for the excited look Christy was giving her. And a little apprehensive to know that she'd be alone with Tyler. Well, as alone as she could with the whole town surrounding them.

"Fine. But no more than two cookies, please."

Happy as can be, Christy skated off holding Sam's and Cammie's hands.

Stephanie couldn't think of a single thing to say.

The music abruptly changed to a slower song, "The Christmas Waltz" and she felt as shy as a freshman at her first prom.

"Well, I guess unless we want to get run over, we'd better skate." Tyler motioned ahead of him and she was a bit disappointed that he didn't take her hand. But she only had herself to blame. This was what she'd asked for—friends, nothing else.

"Cammie seems . . . nice."

"She is. She's lived in Stowe all her life. Except when she went to college in New Hampshire. She's an accountant for the ski resort and helps her aunt at the spa."

"Wow. Sounds like you've gotten to know her pretty well for just having met today." She didn't mean to sound so catty.

"Huh? Yeah, we enjoyed talking. She's real sweet."

Eldon's slightly grumpy voice came through the sound system. "Couples dance, everyone. Couples dance. Guys, if you're on the ice, take hold of the girl next to you and skate together. Otherwise, get off the ice!"

Tyler laughed. "I think Eldon could use a few tips on emceeing a holiday event." He easily took Stephanie's hand and she cursed the giddy butterflies it released inside of her. His calloused hand fit so nicely around hers, she hoped the song lasted as long as a five-movement symphony.

Just then, Tyler waved at Cammie, standing next to the pond. Stephanie's blood heated. "So, Cammie. Nice girl. Pretty. Jessica said she teaches Sunday school. She sounds perfect for you."

"Perfect for what?"

"Of course, it's a long way from Newport to Stowe, unless she's ready to move up there. I'm sure she could get a job as an accountant anywhere, right?"

"Stephanie, what are you talking about?"

"But as long as the van is broken down I guess you can get to know her here. That's convenient, don't you think."

Tyler shook his head in confusion. "Not sure what you mean but you did remind me. Harv is here, the mechanic? Says the parts should be in this afternoon. We can leave tomorrow and be in Newport by noon. Maggie at the orphanage already has a ride for you with Caitlyn, a social services worker in Newport with family in

Burlington. She's leaving tomorrow afternoon so you can be home for Christmas. Great, right?"

"Yeah. Great." Her heart felt like a lead stone. Just what she wanted, to be alone in her apartment for Christmas. Of course, it had been what she'd planned all along but since they'd been stranded at the inn, she'd had glimpses of a different life. Unfortunately, a life she didn't feel she could ever have.

"If you don't mind, Tyler, I think I'll sit out the rest of the song."

They stopped skating and his hand gently touched her arm. "Is everything okay?"

The tenderness in his brown eyes, his soft voice made her heart melt a little more for him. Why couldn't she just admit she was in love with him and wanted a relationship with him?

Their eyes connected and for a moment she saw hunger, desire, everything that she felt mirrored in his eyes. She longed to confide in him, tell him everything that was on her heart, but the words wouldn't come. She couldn't. Some things were more important than her wishes.

"Everything's okay, Tyler. Christy and I will be ready to go tomorrow."

She skated away from him and just before stepping off the ice, turned for another look at him. Just as she thought, had hoped really, he was still watching her. She gave him a sad smile and turned away. But as her foot moved onto the snow, she lost her balance and went down, knocking into the sound system table. The music jumped ahead onto a Christmas hip-hop song, then a country two-step, finally settling into a bluesy jazz version of "White Christmas."

Eldon's voice blared on the sound system. "Okay, obviously the couple's skate is over. Skate however you want. But be careful!"

Stephanie felt her face flame just before Eldon looked over the table. "Hey, you want to watch where you walk? You're lousing up the music."

With the remaining shred of dignity she possessed, she stood, brushed herself off, and walked to the refreshment table. Where she would *not* be having coconut cake.

Darren and Tricia skated slowly to "White Christmas."

"You're really quiet."

Darren knew that was so. After they'd argued in front of Christy, sending her running, he couldn't stop thinking over the situation.

He tried to smile, holding her hand tighter. "A lot on my mind. But let's forget everything else and just enjoy the moment." She leaned into him, letting her head rest against his shoulder as they glided around the pond, Christmas music playing softly. This was what he wanted, time with his wife, the woman he loved, just being happy together.

"Hi, you two."

The greeting had them both looking over to see Sam skating with Christy. "Hey, Sam." Darren smiled and said, "Hello, there, muchkin." He couldn't imagine what the child thought of them.

Her hesitant glance told him she probably didn't know what to think also.

"Christy, you're skating so well. Good for you." Tricia's overly cheerful voice was grating. She dropped his hand and held it out to the girl. "You could probably teach us how to do it. Why don't you come skate with us for this song?"

She glanced at Sam. "Go ahead, honey. Give ole Sam a chance to rest."

Without speaking, Christy took Tricia's hand and settled between the two. They settled into an easy pace. Darren could almost feel the excitement vibrating in Tricia. And his contented existence was gone.

He wondered why that was. After all, he wanted a child as much as Tricia. Well, probably not as much. No one wanted a baby as much as Tricia. It seemed to be the most important thing in her life, supplanting even him.

And maybe that was the crux of his discontent.

He watched her chat and chuckle with Christy, her attention solely focused on the child. He wondered if he was even needed.

Normally he wasn't a selfish man, nor was he a needy one. But ever since Tricia had gotten on this kick to have a child, his life hadn't been the same and not in a good way.

As she continued to ignore him, he wondered if this was to be the norm of his life from now on? He glanced around at the happy families skating, the smiling couples. Why couldn't that be them? Instead he was miserable. And his wife didn't seem to care.

Enough about him. He'd try to adjust. After all, Tricia wanted this so much.

"Is this your first time skating, Christy?"

Tricia shot him a glare. "Of course, it's not. Can't you see how well she skates?"

Now what had he said to incur her displeasure. Clearly the little girl was a beginner, was it so bad to point that out?

"Darren wasn't being mean, honey. Sometimes he just doesn't know how to talk to little girls."

For some reason that didn't sit well with him. "I guess I'm not used to it. Just like you."

Tricia slowly turned her head to face him. "What's that supposed to mean?"

"Your baby voice. Christy isn't an infant. I highly doubt she enjoys being spoken to that way."

"Of course she does. Everyone likes to be spoken to in a sweet, caring tone. Even you."

"How would I know? No one ever speaks to me in a sweet, caring tone anymore."

Nor could he see her speaking to him that way for a long time, if her pinched expression meant anything.

"How's everything going?" Mary skated by, holding on to Sam's arm. Before the Matthews could respond, she said, "Christy needs a scarf." She pulled a knitted, bright pink scarf out of her coat pocket. "Angela brought this out for her. Isn't it beautiful?" Mary stooped down and smiling, wrapped it around Christy's neck. "Do you like it, sweetheart?"

She nodded. "I like pink."

"Thanks, Mary. We have so little experience we wouldn't have known that Christy needed a scarf. Glad you were here." From the corner of his eye, Darren saw the heated look of his wife. Good. In fact, he had a few other things to inform her.

"In fact, I think we could both do with scarves ourselves. You mind skating with Christy while we fetch ours?"

"No, of course not. Come on, Christy. Let's show everyone how it's done." The little girl grinned and nodded as they skated off.

Darren didn't notice Sam's eyes going back and forth between him and Tricia. He vaguely heard him say, "I think I'll go . . . ah, help Eldon with the music."

A tension filled moment passed and Darren said, "I think we should talk." It was passed time to talk but so be it.

"That is a good idea," Tricia replied coldly as the music changed to the song "Grandma Got Run Over By a Reindeer."

They walked away from the pond and Darren blurted out, "I don't want a child, Tricia. At least not right now."

Whatever she'd prepared herself to say evidently blanked from her mind as she stood staring at him. It probably hadn't been his best approach, but he was tired of this game they seemed to be playing.

He blew out a sigh. "I mean, yes I'd love a baby if we ever got pregnant, or adopt a child if the timing was right, but I'm not . . . fanatical about having one. I'm really happy the way our lives are right now."

That loosened her tongue. "How can you say that? We're alone, we're not complete. It's just the two of us."

"I like the two of us."

As if choosing her words carefully, she said, "So do I. You know I love you, but I feel . . . incomplete. Worthless. I want to be a family."

He frowned. "Tricia, we are a family, we've always been a family. Adding a kid isn't going to make us one."

"You just don't understand." She shook her head, frustrated.

"I understand that you're worried you're missing out. I understand you somehow feel you need a purpose. I understand that . . . for some reason you've decided that I'm not enough for you."

He let that sink in for a minute. It was what he'd been feeling for too long.

She wouldn't look at him as she said, "What about Christy? That sweet little girl needs a home."

"Yes, she does and she deserves a home that is ready to receive her and provide the love and stability she needs. But it's not us."

"You're opposed to adopting?"

He thought for a moment. "No, not really." The unease crept back inside, what he'd been purposely ignoring to make Tricia happy. "Honey, I don't feel right about this. Christy is a special little girl and I'm fond of her but . . . I just don't feel we're the right parents for her."

Tricia's outburst was sudden, knocking him back on his feet. "You're wrong! We are exactly what she needs. And you're wrong when you say this is about you're not being enough for me. This has nothing to do with us, it's something that I want for my life. For our lives. And it's something I'm going to have."

Darren felt a chill skid down his spine. The tone in her voice was strange, hard, unbending. His body tense, he said, "What do you mean?"

She turned, her eyes looking directly into his. "I'm going to have children with or without you. We have an opportunity with Christy. If your answer is no then you leave me no choice."

He held his breath waiting. "And what's that."

"I think we should split up."

Chapter Twenty-One

"I'm exhausted. I haven't skated so much since my kids were little ones." Sam wiped the sweat from his brow and stared at Angela. "Looks like we've got a perfect record for the day—all failures."

Angela's eyes found Natasha and Franklin, standing next to each other watching the skaters on the pond. "Let's see if we can't change that, gentlemen. Eldon, get ready with a quiet, romantic song." The man exhaled loudly and looked through the list of songs on his playlist.

Wasting no time, Angela walked over to the duo and said, "How come you two aren't out there?"

"I'm not much of a skater," Franklin replied.

"I am not one also." Natasha gave a shy smile.

"All the reason for you to take the chance to improve your skill now." Angela herded them over to where the extra skates were kept. "I think we have a pair here for the both of you. Let's see." She dug through the box and pulled out skates. "How about trying these on?"

Franklin glanced at the size and frowned. "How did you—"

"Now hurry. You don't want to miss your chance." She winked at Franklin, who helped Natasha over to the chairs.

"These fit perfectly." Natasha held her feet up in front of her. "Like glove."

"Yes." Franklin glanced down at his own skates. "Amazing how she'd know our sizes." He decided to forget the mystery that was Angela and concentrate on the here and now. "Well, shall we?" With a grin he offered his hand to Natasha and the two stepped gingerly over to the ice.

"I am not sure about this." Her voice was small, jittery.

"It's fine, honey," he said without accent. "I'll be right beside you. You'll be fine."

Her answering smile warmed him more than his coat and gloves. Even though he was probably as unsure as she was, he wrapped her hand around his arm and carefully moved onto the ice. The music suddenly changed to a soft, slow ballad. Perfect.

They stumbled together, neither speaking, her body close to his. This was so much better than the simple politeness they'd had since their romantic evening on the patio. It hadn't turned out the way he'd wanted. He'd never expected to confide his secrets to her. He hadn't planned on giving her a motivational speech or volunteering to be her coach in living life to the fullest.

And to confess that he "liked her" like a silly schoolboy. Yeesh! He was amazed she still wanted to spend any time with him. But then their kiss . . .

If only that wolf hadn't interrupted them, as well as Angela urging them inside.

Now the politeness. He hated it. Well, time to rise to the occasion and get them through this awkwardness.

"You didn't skate much in Russia?"

She shook her head. "I never had time. How about you? New York has ice skating does it not?"

He grinned. "Yeah. A few times I managed to snag some skates, don't ask, and try it out." With a shrug he said, "It seemed like a lot of work to go nowhere." His eyes met hers. "I suppose it was because I didn't have a partner with me."

Her eyes flickered and briefly went to his lips. "Yes. I can see that would make difference."

Her body relaxed into his and he suddenly felt ten feet tall as they glided to the music. She sighed and leaned her head against his and his heart almost burst. He wanted to explore this attraction they had for each other, now and past their time in Vermont.

He knew he didn't deserve her. He'd lied and cheated his way to the life he'd had. Not that he didn't have talent as a musician but he well knew there were hundreds probably just as talented as he and yet he was living the high life.

And now there was Natasha. There was no doubt that he was falling in love with her and the thought, which should have terrified, even amused, him only added to the warmth he felt, that he wanted to share with her.

He couldn't wait.

"Natasha." Her lovely eyes went to his and he almost forgot what he was going to say." Still he murmured, "You are so beautiful. You take my breath away."

"Franklin," she whispered.

"Don't go back to Russia. I'll figure out a way. Stay, I . . . don't want to lose you."

Tears filled her eyes. "Oh, Franklin. There is nothing I would like more. I'm not sure . . ."

"We'll find a way. Believe me, I've learned in my life that there's always a way for what you really want. Just say the word and I'll move heaven and earth to make it happen."

For a moment her face brightened, overtaking the sun. Her eyes were sparkling gold nuggets, giving him a hope that he could have even more than he'd ever dreamed to wish for in life.

Just as quickly her face drained of all color. Those golden eyes became terrified as she stared ahead. Franklin tightened his hold on her. "Natasha? What is it?" He followed her gaze and saw three men standing on the edge of the frozen pond, watching them. Two of them were like football linebackers, tall, huge shoulders, arms at sides with hands in fists. He couldn't see their eyes that were hidden behind sunglasses but he was sure they were glaring.

The man in the middle was shorter, slighter of build. Even from that distance Franklin could see the man wore a designer suit, impeccably tailored. The sunglasses he wore were no doubt expensive. His lips were curved into a knowing grin. Franklin felt Natasha shiver next to him.

"Your uncle?" She nodded. Her body trembled and he immediately hated the man.

Franklin stopped on the ice and turned her to him, and taking her arms in his hands bent slightly so that he was in her direct field of vision. "I'm right here, Natasha. I'll go with you. We can face him together." She swallowed hard, her expression tight. "If you want freedom, you have to fight for it, remember? But you're not alone. I'll be with you."

She just stared at him for a long moment. As if the words finally made sense, she breathed in and out, and nodded.

He helped her to the side but kept his hand firmly around her, ready to meet the dreaded uncle.

The man in question, whose smug expression never changed, held out his arms and began speaking in Russian.

Franklin didn't release her. "This must be the uncle. I'm Franklin Murray. Natasha's . . . partner." He hoped the inflection on the word "partner" would convey his interest.

Finally the uncle deigned to grace Franklin with a glance, a perusal really. "Ah, yes. You have been accompanying Natasha on piano." Franklin didn't try to correct him by stating his own credentials as a musician. "Natasha will be returning with us now. You are free to go."

The abruptness of the announcement threw Franklin off. He was reduced to blink and say, "Excuse me?"

The man's eyes sharpened on Natasha. "I am afraid my niece took off without my knowledge. Since she is here in United States due to my sponsorship that was unfortunate mistake." His eyes narrowed. "I am sure you did not realize what you were doing, my sweet. It is time we go now."

"Mister . . . Safina, is it?" The man nodded. "As I am sure you have noticed, Natasha is of age to make her own choices. And she would like to stay and finish out her contract, before returning to New York."

His eyes showed only amusement. "Is that true, Tasha? You would rather stay in this country than return to land of your birth? Where you are treated like royalty? I cannot understand it." His expression showed otherwise.

Her body was still trembling. Franklin turned to her and saw the frightened look in her eyes. Holding her firmly, he said, "It's all right, honey. Tell him. Be strong."

"Uncle Vladimir." She swallowed hard and took a deep breath. "I will not be returning with you. I . . . would like to stay. Even if it means being on my own."

His expression never changed. "I see. And how will you live without my benevolent help?"

"I . . . I will work hard. I will find way."

He stared at her for a moment and chuckled. The chuckle became a laugh, and the laugh was loud and long. Franklin was enraged on behalf of her. "Glad you agree. Now if you'll excuse us, we have some skating to do."

Before he could stop him, the uncle grabbed Natasha's arm and pulled her away. "Enough of this foolishness. We are leaving." The other men flanked his side, ready to protect but they didn't stop Franklin, who lunged forward. One of the men gave an elbow to his gut, effectively knocking the air from his lungs.

"Franklin!"

Natasha's cry filled him with renewed strength. He pushed one of the unsuspecting guards away and jabbed the other in the stomach. Reaching the uncle, he yanked his hand off Natasha. "Hey, buddy. The lady does not want to go with you, take a hint."

The guards returned and Franklin readied himself to deal with them. His Bronx upbringing didn't fail him as he kicked one and punched the other in the eye, ignoring nearby observers' shrieks. He went after the uncle but one of the guards pulled him back and he was forced to return his attention to him, kicking out the man's feet, landing him on his back. The remaining guard jabbed Franklin's jaw before getting an uppercut to his and stumbling back.

The other returned and grabbed Franklin's arms behind him, lifting him, giving him just enough leverage to kick the other guard, now charging him, back across the snow, into a tree.

The uncle, eyes bulging, stepped to Franklin. "You are trying my patience."

"Uncle, let him go. Please." Franklin hated the pleading in her voice.

"What is going on here?" Angela and Sam came running over.

The uncle surveyed the avid interest of the crowd and lowered his voice. "I apologize for trouble. I only need to see who is in charge and then I will be on my way."

"That's me." Even though his swollen jaw throbbed, Franklin could hear the ice in Angela's tone. "I am the manager of the property and before we go on, you'd better release my guest before I press charges." The uncle glanced at the one holding Franklin and nodded. He released him and Natasha went to him instantly, rubbing his arms, giving him a sad smile.

"I am Vladimir Safina. My niece is under my protection while she is in your country. Also, my legal authority when dealing with her performances. She had no power to sign contract to play here, therefore agreement is null and void. However, not to inconvenience you, I am prepared to settle matter." He reached into his pocket, pulling out a fat money clip. "How much to compensate for Natasha's departure."

"I don't want your money, Mr. Safina."

He chuckled. "Of course you do, Ms. . . . I did not catch your name."

"The agreement was with Natasha, not you, so it will be resolved between us."

"But I just said—"

"I heard you." Her authoritative voice stunned Franklin, but even more surprising, it stopped the uncle. Angela turned to Natasha, taking her hand. "The choice is yours, honey. What would you like to do?"

Apparently the uncle had regained his voice because he cleared his throat and said, "I'm afraid is not question of what she wants. As her protector, I cannot allow her to perform with someone with criminal record."

There were gasps and murmurs through the crowd who had decided to watch the dramatic scene play out.

Franklin's body tensed, felt his stomach slowly slide down to his shoes, knowing all too well what was about to happen.

His perfect life was about to end.

"A person's past doesn't mean much to us here," Angela asserted.

"You mean fact that this man is not who he says he is, that is going by assumed name, that is from poor neighborhood in New York and not European man he pretends, that does not mean anything to you?"

"No. And don't even try to tell me more. I know his real name. I know his parents. They are fine people who work hard." Her eyes hardened. "They never had to intimidate to get what they want."

"And they live in poverty."

"They live in love. And contentment. Which is more than I can say for you."

Franklin felt he was outside of himself watching some movie play out before him. This couldn't be about him. Wait, did she say she knew his parents? That can't be. He'd only told one person of his background. How . . .

Blinding betrayal whirled through his body so fast he thought he might collapse. His eyes pinned Natasha. "You . . . told Angela? You told your uncle?"

"What? No, of course I would never do."

"Then how . . ." He couldn't form the words to accuse, his depression was so deep.

"Mr. Safina, you've disrupted our pleasant outing. I would like for you and your associates to leave. Now."

"Gladly. Natasha, collect your things and we will leave."

"Uncle. Please, no." Tears had started down her cheeks.

"Natasha," Angela said softly to her. "It's your decision. Whatever you want to do, dear."

The moment was packed with tension as Natasha's face tightened, her jaw clenched, but her eyes watered. He watched, somehow knowing that the last vestiges of what could be with Natasha were slowly fading into oblivion. He watched her turn to her uncle. The uncle gave her a hard look that Franklin couldn't decipher, causing Natasha's tearful eyes to widen.

And he knew. It was over.

Natasha cleared her throat. "I will play with Franklin tonight. Tomorrow I will leave with you."

Just as Angela was about to speak, yelling came from the distance and off in the woods a loud crack of gunfire echoed through the countryside.

The music stopped and everyone stilled, waiting.

A lone call of a wolf sounded, causing a panic among the crowd. Everyone hurried to throw off ice skates, grab their families, and race to their cars. Stephanie grabbed Christy and together with Tricia, ran for the inn. Angela wrapped an arm around Natasha and walked briskly, glancing around to see Mary and Bradley behind them. Sam encouraged the others to seek shelter, while Eldon dashed toward the barn.

The party was definitely over.

Chapter Twenty-Two

The next morning luggage littered the front hall. Everyone was planning to leave the inn today. Mary really couldn't blame them, although her heart was heavy.

The wolf was still at large and nearby, clearly getting braver by coming out in the daytime. Joe had issued a strict warning that no one should wander outside unless absolutely necessary and only accompanied by him.

No one spoke at breakfast. It was if a heavy dark cloud covered the dining room. There were no words to say. Even the fact that is was Christmas Eve didn't seem to matter.

Mary tried to lift everyone's spirits with hot banana nut bread, quiche Lorraine, and fruit salad. No one ate much.

She cleaned the kitchen, leaving them to their silent breakfast when Bradley came down the back staircase with heavy steps, sighing loudly. Not him, too.

Trying to sound cheerful, she said, "So, anything special you'd like to do today, honey?

Maybe after everyone has checked out at noon we could watch a Christmas movie together."

"Maybe." He slumped into a chair, his head resting in his hand. "Mom?"

She wiped her hands dry on the towel around her waist. "Yes, honey?"

"You think it's too late to ask Santa for something else?"

Mary's brows lifted and she joined him at the table. "It is kind of late. Something you want to tell me about?"

His brows knitted together, his mind so clearly deep in thought. She couldn't help pushing a strand of dark hair back from his eyes. The love she felt for her child swamped her in its intensity. She was so thankful for her son. Deep in her heart she . . . no, she wouldn't go there. Like the patient mother she tried to be, she waited.

"There's something I want really bad. But it's sorta private."

"Hmm. Maybe I can help."

His big brown eyes went to hers and he hesitated. "Christy wants a real home. With a mom and a dad."

Clearing her throat she said, "I'm sure she does."

"For Christmas. She wants it for Christmas. We, ah, asked Sam and Angela about it. Don't that count like asking Santa hisself?"

"I . . . don't know about that. What did they say?"

"That miracles take time." He frowned and asked, "Why, Mom? Why do miracles take time? Why don't God just go 'bam' and then it's done?"

Why indeed. And why did children seem to ask the most unanswerable questions known to mankind? She wrapped her arms around him and kissed the top of his head. "I'm not sure I can give you a good answer. I do know that we don't know everything involved. Sometimes things have to happen, things have to work together before a miracle can happen."

"Like when I ran away and you and Papa decided you loved each other?"

Her throat thickened, remembering that stressful time. "Like that. Although, your running away nearly killed me first, so please don't see that as the solution for any problem." She shuddered thinking of Bradley going into the woods now with the threat of the wolf.

"But I want this miracle for her."

Mary's heart softened at his concern for this little girl they had all come to love. Her little boy wasn't asking for a new toy or game but a miracle for Christy. Surely God in heaven would recognize that. She lowered her head to his. "I want this miracle for her, too. Tell you what. I'm going to believe and ask along with you, how's that? And we'll just see what happens."

Bradley wrapped his arms around her and squeezed as tears she hadn't known where there spilled onto her cheek.

The kitchen door swung open and Angela entered carrying a pile of dishes. "I think everyone's finished with breakfast."

She sniffed and turned. "Okay. I'll get right on that."

"Don't worry about it," Stephanie called from the door, her hands also filled with dishes. "We've got it." The young woman had a defeated air about her, as if the burdens of the world sat firmly on her shoulders. She was followed by Tricia and Natasha, each carrying bowls and dishes from the dining room. Mary gaped.

"You all don't need to help clean up."

"You have been so kind, Mary. Let us do this thing." Natasha, her hair pinned up, dressed in an elegant silk pants suit, gave a slight smile that came nowhere near her eyes.

"Yes, it's the least we can do." Tricia looked terrible, her eyes red, her posture slumped. "Before we all leave." Her voice choked on the last word.

Mary's heart went out to these women she had come to care for in such a short period of time. Not only was she sad to see them go, she hated that they left with such heavy spirits.

Christy came into the kitchen, carrying a small plate, looking alone and lost. Sad. Mary thought she was going to start bawling right there. She just wanted to wrap her up in her arms and hold on to her forever.

Angela intervened. "Mary, why don't you put on water for tea? We can sit here in the kitchen and have a cup." The slight nod and intensity of her eyes told Mary that Angela planned to impart a few words of wisdom with the ladies. Good. She felt like she could use a few of those herself.

Soon the women were settled at the table. Bradley had taken Christy into the parlor to play one last game before she left. Mary said a quick silent prayer as Angela glanced at the women in front of her.

"Well, it's been an . . . interesting holiday season. I hope all of you will take good thoughts about the Sleep In Heavenly Peace Inn with you." No one spoke.

"I'm sorry the wolf has marred your vacation. It's really been a most unusual few weeks."

"I don't understand it, Angela," Mary said. "We've never had anything like this happen before."

"No. Strange, a wolf, all alone traveling through the wilderness. I can't imagine what it must feel."

"Don't tell me you feel sorry for it."

"Well, it is one of God's creatures. Whatever the problem, something's wrong. It must feel disoriented or frightened, thinking it has no one." The women were quiet, all in their own thoughts. "It's probably scared. Living beings make bad decisions when they're scared." Silence.

She sighed. "Ah, well, I hope that each of you will have a wonderful Christmas." She paused for a moment and her voice lowered but held a strange intensity. "And I hope you have the courage to accept your true Christmas wish."

The women looked at Angela. Mary felt a shudder go through her. She wanted to ask her what she meant but decided to do that later.

"I must return to Russia," Natasha suddenly said. The others murmured their concern and hopes for her. "It is best that I do."

"But Natasha, if you want to stay here, surely there are those that will sponsor you. Certainly the symphony. If they won't, we will." The others agreed. Mary saw her comment had touched her.

"Thank you, but no. Is . . . best for everyone." Natasha took a sip of tea, effectively closing the offer.

Stephanie sighed loudly. "I suppose I'll be back in Burlington for Christmas."

"Do you have relatives there, dear?"

Mary smirked. If anyone knew Stephanie's background, it would be Angela.

When Stephanie shook her head, Mary said, "Well, for goodness sakes, why don't you spend Christmas with us? We'd love to have you."

The hopeful glint in Stephanie's eyes moved Mary. "I . . . really wouldn't want to put you out."

"Nonsense, dear," Angela asserted. "After you drop Christy off with the orphanage in Newport, come on back here."

"Do you really need to leave today with Christy and Tyler? Why can't the three of you just stay on for a few more days? If it's the cost, I'm sure we could work something out."

"Mary, I'm sure that Tyler is needed at the orphanage. And Christy needs to get acclimated to her new home as soon as possible."

A sob came from Tricia. "Sorry." She binked hard, followed by another sob. Mary went to the counter and brought over a box of tissues, grabbing one for herself and setting the box on the table for Tricia. "I . . . hate to see her go to the orphanage." All the women wiped their leaking eyes.

"We all do." Angela put her hand on Tricia's shoulder. "What that sweet little girl needs is a home."

Tricia grabbed another tissue, the sobbing continued. Mary wondered why the woman was so emotional. She knew she and Darren had been spending time with the little girl but—

"Darren and I are splitting up."

No one spoke. No one moved. The air in the room seemed to be gone as everyone absorbed the news.

"We . . . were thinking of adopting Christy." That was news to Mary. "But Darren says he's not interested in adoption at the moment, if ever. I . . . told him if he didn't change his mind, we should split up. He . . . hasn't changed his mind. In fact he hasn't spoken to me since."

They surrounded her as only women could do, stroking her, whispering words of encouragement. More tea was poured and Christmas cookies were brought out as the comfort continued.

Mary hoped the refreshments, consolation, and Angela's words would bring about the miracle each woman needed.

He heard the two children before he entered the room.

"Don't be sad, Christy. It's not Christmas yet," Bradley said, hoping to cheer her up as he moved his game piece. She didn't look at him but waited for her turn to roll the dice.

"Mom says sometimes a miracle takes time 'cause we don't know stuff." She sighed and took her turn.

When Sam walked into the room, Bradley nearly pounced on him. "Sam, what are we going to do? Nothing's happening."

He took a seat at their table. "I know it doesn't look like it, Bradley, but you never can tell."

"But that don't help Christy. She's gonna leave soon and go to the orphanage. And all our plans will go up in smoke!" Bradley's arms went up and down in a grand gesture. Sam hid a smile.

"It's Christmas. You're supposed to get what you want at Christmas, right? I mean, if you've been a good kid and Christy has been good." He turned to her. "Haven't you, Christy?" She nodded.

Sam scratched his beard. This was a tough one. "It may . . . take a while, kids. That's all I'm saying."

"Well, gosh, that just stinks!" Bradley's eyes grew big and he covered his mouth with his hands and muttered. "I hope Santa didn't hear me say that. I really want that . . ." He glanced around and seeing the coast was clear said, "D-o-g."

Sam couldn't hold back the grin. "I'm sure he knows that."

Christy hopped off her chair and walked to Sam, climbing up on his lap. Her damaged eye was now opened a bit, thanks to Mary's continual compresses. The other eye, filled with innocence and hope, stared at Sam. "I-it's okay, Santa. I'll wait." She wrapped her arms around him and Sam closed his eyes and held on tightly.

"Precious little Christy. You'll get your wish, I'm just sure of it. And you'll do wonderful things in your life. Just keep believing."

"I will." Sam swallowed the lump in his throat, wishing he could do more.

"You and Bradley deserve all the Christmas presents you want. You—wait." He lifted his head as a thought ran through. To himself he muttered, "Maybe. Just maybe it's worth a chance.

"Bradley. Don't you think Christy should have her Christmas presents before she goes?"

"Huh?"

Sam stood, his mind racing. "In fact, the inn has a few gifts to give all the guests before they leave. Let's get everyone in here." He hurried out of the room, calling over his shoulder, "Spread the word, kids! Get everyone in the parlor."

Sam ran to the barn all set to grab the presents for Christy that were hidden. He was not prepared to run into Tricia, who sat weeping while she rubbed Frederica and murmured to her.

"Oh, pardon me. I didn't mean to bother you. I just have to get a few things off the shelf." He moved to the area and pulled down a large blanket that hid Christy's presents. Turning he said, "You didn't come out here by yourself, did you?"

"No. Joe walked me out. He wanted to check the yard again."

"I see." He reached down to give the dog a soft pat. "This dog sure seems to like you and Darren. I can't understand how it keeps finding you wherever you are."

Tricia lowered her head to nuzzle the dog. "She's a sweetheart." The dog moaned, obviously loving the attention.

"You and Darren seem to love animals. I'm surprised you only have two cats."

She chuckled. "Yes. Our condo board frowns on a menagerie of animals in the complex. We'd talked at one time about buying property outside the city, having as many pets as we wanted."

"What happened?"

She shrugged a shoulder. "Life. Darren's father got ill and needed him at his practice, which is in the heart of Atlanta. I manage the business. Or did. We were a team." Her voice choked on her last word.

"So Darren gave up his dream for his dad."

"Yes. Darren is like that. I constantly wish he'd just tell me what he wants instead of asking me what I want."

"Maybe he's afraid you won't like his answer."

Tricia's hand on the dog stilled. "Maybe."

Obviously the woman was struggling in her marriage and he didn't want to pry. Exactly. Just help her to think a few things through.

Sam sat next to her. "I don't think it'll be long before Frederica gives birth." Tricia nodded. With a sigh, she said, "It must be amazing, to be part of creating life, creating a family. It must make a person feel . . . worthwhile, important." Her eyes watered.

"Hmm. I've always thought what told us we were important wasn't creating, but that we were created by a loving Creator."

He decided he'd leave her with that thought and stood. "How about coming with me into the parlor? Angela has a gift for you before you leave."

She sighed again and gave the dog a last rub. "I'll be there in a moment."

The door opened and Darren came in, stumbling when he glimpsed Tricia. "Oh. I can come back."

"No, come on in," Sam said. "Tricia and I were just checking on the animals as I'm sure you want to do as well. But when you're done, we're asking everyone to meet in the parlor. Angela has gifts for everyone."

"Okay, Sam," Darren said with little enthusiasm.

Darren was tongue-tied. He'd struggled all night with what to say to Tricia. The jest being that he wasn't going to be bullied into adopting, how insensitive to the child. But he loved his wife. She wasn't thinking clearly at the moment so what was he to do?

He walked to the dog and rubbed her. "She looks good."

"Yes. Breathing normal, heart rate normal."

"I'm impressed. You should have been a nurse."

She sniffed. "I don't think I'd like dealing with people. That's why I'm good at keeping your books."

"Yes, you are. I'd really hate to lose you." He hoped he conveyed with his tone that he wasn't merely speaking of her work in his practice.

"Darren . . . I . . . I can't really talk right now."

Although discouraged, he understood. She looked so fragile at the moment, he was afraid he could blow her over with a breath. "Okay. Maybe once we're back in Atlanta?" She nodded.

They both petted the dog and their hands bumped. The touch was like electricity, sending a surge of longing jolting through his system. His eyes met hers and a spark of hope lit inside him at the yearning he saw in her. That hope was quickly dashed when he realized it was probably yearning for a child and not him.

He stood. "Well, I think we should probably go to the parlor. Not keep everyone waiting." Leaning to give the dog one last pat, he said, "You hang in there, girl. Have courage."

His words reminded her of what Angela said. *"I hope you have the courage to accept your true Christmas wish."* What was her true Christmas wish? She would have automatically said it was to have a child but the idea of spending her life without Darren didn't sadden her, it totally devastated her.

But she still wanted that purpose of being a parent. So, where did that leave them?

She knew Sam was right. Could having that attitude help solve the problem?

Natasha was just finishing packing when she heard a knock on her door. "Come in."

Looking more handsome than he had a right, Franklin entered, his face serious and weary. "We need to talk." All pretenses of an English accent were gone.

"There is nothing to say. I am returning to Russia." She closed the top of her cosmetics case a little harder than necessary."

"Why? I don't understand. I thought you and I . . ." She stared at him waiting for him to finish the thought. "It's not what you want. You could stay, I'd help you."

"Is not possible. Too much is at stake."

"What?" He reached her in two steps and took her arms in his hands. "What are you not telling me, are you protecting him? You?"

Tears started down her cheek. "You! I'm protecting you!" She began to sob, lowering her head. He pulled her into his embrace, rubbing her back.

"It's all right, honey. Don't you know I don't need protecting? I'm a big boy."

She shook her head. "He will tell everyone." His hands stopped on her back. "He will stop at nothing to destroy your reputation if I stay." Her moist eyes looked into his. "I have seen him do it to others. He will not hesitate to do it to you. Franklin, everything you've worked for, everything you've created will be gone."

She saw a flicker of dread in his eyes for a second before he recovered and said, "But what about us? Natasha, I—"

She quickly put her hand over his mouth. "You cannot have feelings for me. The price is too high." Their eyes held for another moment until she couldn't stand there any longer. "I need air." She left the room hoping he wouldn't follow, stopping in the hall as the pain of her life came crashing down on top of her. How hard to love a man so much and be the worst thing for him. "I have courage, Angela," she murmured. "Unfortunately, I cannot have my true Christmas wish."

Outside, Tyler was loading the luggage into the repaired van. "Anything else?"

Stephanie shook her head. Glancing up, she realized he wasn't looking at her. "No. That's it."

He shut the back and turned, his hands on his waist surveying the inn. "I'm going to miss this place. Sure is great luck that we got stranded here."

"Yeah."

"Hey, I know you probably want to get back to Burlington, but you're welcome to have

Christmas with us. The orphanage always does it up big."

She tried to smile. "That must be nice. Like you have a large family to share the holidays with."

"One of the perks, I guess. I know Christy would love for you to stay. Might help her, you know, get used to the place."

She wouldn't get sucked into his big brown eyes again so she looked away and shook her head. "No, the quicker I leave, the quicker I can adjust. I mean, Christy can adjust."

Tyler frowned. "You said 'I.'"

"I meant Christy."

He studied her. "Are you having trouble letting Christy go? I know you wanted to find her a good home and all but . . . is something else going on here?"

She wanted to scream, "Yeah, you big dummy, it's you I don't want to leave," but instead shook her head. "Nothing else going on. All good. Well, as good as can be."

He narrowed his eyes at her. "Nope, I don't buy it. Something else. What?"

"Nothing!"

"Then why is your face red? Why are you defensive? Why are you yelling?"

"Just leave it be, Tyler!"

"I won't. You said you wanted to be friends, so we're friends. You can tell me anything, dump on me if you want to. But I hate to see you in pain."

"Really? Really! Well, maybe you should have thought about that before you decided to get a new girlfriend so soon after me. How do you think that makes me feel?"

"Huh?"

"You are so oblivious. Cammie likes you, don't you know that? She wants to get to know you and it's shredding my heart to pieces the way you . . . seem to like her." She couldn't stop the tears when they came. "It's like it's always been in my life, I can't trust anyone, I can't count on anyone. That's one reason I work so hard at my job, it's all I have."

She sniffed, deciding to just let all that was on her mind come out. "It never has been that I didn't want you, but Tyler, I spent the first seventeen years of my life cowering and hiding from those who were supposed to care for me. They didn't protect me, they hurt me. As much as I want you, how do I know that you won't turn around and do the same to me when I need you? I mean, already you have girls lining up to be in a relationship with you."

"Girls?"

"But you want to know the really sad thing about all this? It doesn't seem to matter at all about my past or what I want for the future. I have no earthly idea how to stop the fact that I love you!"

She watched, as Tyler seemed to freeze right in front of her, saying nothing.

Mortified and determined to make a dignified exit, she spun around, only her darn feet got twisted in the slushy ice and all her concentration went into keeping from falling over.

Gaining her balance, she stomped forward, only to confront a deep patch of snow. She trudged through that, getting wet up to the knees and barely keeping vertical.

No way she'd turn to see if Tyler was watching her. Of course he would be. Probably grateful he'd shed the crazy woman he'd been interested in.

She'd told him she loved him and he'd stood there, eyes wide, startled, as if a ghost had appeared in front of him. Just because she'd said, "I love you."

Oh, no! She'd said, "I love you." She squeezed her eyes together and carefully walked the steps of the inn, wanting to shrink into a tiny snowflake and just blow away.

Her eyes scanned the porch, the place Tyler had kissed her for the first time and the sweet moment flooded back to her mind. Well, bittersweet now. She'd just have to move on with her life's plan.

But how was she going to sit in a car with him for a couple of hours.

Her hands froze on the porch railing as the words of Angela came back to her. *Have the courage to accept your true Christmas wish.*

She hesitated and shook her head. It was never about what she wanted but what she had to do.

She didn't hear an elated Tyler mutter, "I love you, too."

Angela watched as the noise in the parlor picked up when everyone came in and sat at a couch or chair. “Thank you, everyone,” Angela began. “I always give a gift to our leaving guests and since you’re all leaving today, I thought I’d do it together.” Her brows furrowed. “Where’s Natasha?”

Everyone turned toward Franklin, who cleared his throat. “She, ah, needed some air.” His voice was low, barely audible.

“What?”

“She’s on the back porch,” Joe stated. “Said she’d join us in a few minutes.”

“All right.” Angela turned to Bradley. “In the meantime, Bradley why don’t you hand Christy the gift I have for her?”

He chose the correct one from the others under the tree and walked to Christy, who was holding Stephanie’s hand and sucking her thumb. “Here, Christy. I hope you like this. Merry Christmas.”

When she just stared at the present, Stephanie took it. “Isn’t that nice, honey? Thank you, Bradley. I’m sure she’ll love it.”

“Well go ahead, sweetheart. Open it up,” Joe said, smiling.

She pulled off the papers to reveal a brown box. Stephanie helped her open it and a smile started on her face as she pulled out a small plush dog that looked exactly like Frederica. “Oh, boy!” As everyone “Aahed” and cheered, she held it to her chest, loving the toy animal.

"It's a custom for us to give to each guest a special remembrance of their time here." She hesitated, wanting Natasha to join them. "I hope you all know how much we've enjoyed having you as guests; however, now we consider you family." She noticed Tricia flinching. "You're welcome back anytime." Her eyes took a moment to meet each person's, hoping she conveyed her love and comfort. No one spoke.

The sentimental mood of the room was instantly changed when Mary looked around and said, "Where's Christy?"

Her words were followed by a loud howl.

The closing of the back door sounded through the inn and Stephanie paled. "She's gone outside," she shrieked and ran, Tyler at her heels.

"Wait! I'll go!" But Joe was a few steps behind the two, followed by Franklin.

The others stood, concerned. Tricia walked to Darren. "What can we do?" The sound of a dog barking caused her to gasp and clutch Darren's hand. "Darren!"

"On my way." He ran out of the room, the others behind him.

"Christy! Where are you?" Joe yelled studying the backyard. He'd left Mary, Bradley, and Angela, reluctantly peering through the kitchen windows.

Natasha hadn't been on the porch and Franklin called out for her. In the back of his mind, Joe thought something was different about the man.

"Look there." Eldon pointed to the cross-country trail.

"What do you see?" Sam asked, running up next to him.

"Tracks. Several."

"Joe!" Darren caught up with him. "Frederica's out. Did she come this way?"

"Her and Christy. Looks like Natasha, too."

"What do you want us to do?" Tricia asked from behind Darren. Franklin followed her.

"What are you all doing here? Go back to the inn and wait. Or stay with the animals in the barn."

"Joe. Listen." Sam held his hand up and everyone was quiet. In the distance was a growl followed by a low howl.

"We'd better hurry," Franklin said, heading out, not waiting for Joe.

They made their way through the trail, coming to a clearing that opening up onto a wide meadow. They could see little Christy running after the dog, Natasha, urging her to stop. Tyler, Stephanie, and Franklin didn't hesitate but hurried through the snow.

Joe heard another growl and saw at the edge of the clearing, across the meadow from them, the dark eyes of the wolf, stalking his prey. "No!" His heart tripled in speed, as did his feet.

What happened next made his head spin.

Chapter Twenty-Three

The dog saw the wolf and stopped. She barked and when Christy caught up to her and Natasha put her arm around her, the dog stepped in front of them, to block the wolf as Frederica growled between barks. That in no way deterred the wild animal.

The wolf stepped out a few feet, judging the distance and then to Joe's horror, let out a howl, getting ready to pounce. Joe aimed his gun and fired hoping he'd scare the wolf.

"Be careful!" Darren said. "You could hit the girls or the dog."

The scenario grew worse when Stephanie reached them and pulled Christy into her arms, holding her tightly. Joe could almost see the wolf lick his chops.

The dog continued barking as Franklin ran past the girls, screaming and waving his arms, hoping to distract the wolf.

"What are you doing?" Natasha called out.

"Hey, I'm a kid from the Bronx, looking for a good fight." His body readied to defend as his eyes stayed on the wolf. "Bring it."

"You are crazy, Franklin Murray!" Her voice choked when she added, "Watch your hands."

The wolf seemed amused by the exchange and divided his time glancing first at the girls and dog, then at Franklin, probably deciding which would taste better.

It turned toward the girls and before it could approach, Tyler threw himself over them, covering them with his body. Confused by this new development, the wolf approached, tired of games and ready to attack. Franklin's taunts and Joe's series of gunshots did little to deter him as his steely eyes narrowed before launching himself.

Tyler's foot came up to smack the wolf on the jaw, effectively stunning him. This gave Joe enough time to get closer to take aim but at that moment, Frederica crept away, taking the wolf's attention. Apparently the dog was the best target so the wolf started toward her.

"Darren!" Tricia screamed.

"I see. Here Frederica, come here girl!" Darren put a finger in his mouth and whistled loudly. The dog turned to the noise and seemed to understand. She plunged through the snow, trying to make her way to them, her heavy body slowing her down.

Just enough for the wolf to get closer.

Darren took off at a dead run to get to the dog. The wolf reared preparing to jump and Darren wrapped his arms around the dog. The wolf dived, going airborne, aiming at dog and man but just as he ascended, Joe heard a "whop" sound behind him and the wolf landed in a heap a few feet away from Darren and the dog.

Joe turned and was stunned to see Sam holding a gun. "Tranquilizer. Animal control is on the way. Let's see how everyone is." Sam's businesslike attitude helped slow his pulse a bit as they walked over to his brave guests.

Meanwhile, Mary's pulse was hitting the danger point. They'd heard the howls, screams, and the barks. And the gunshots.

"Where are they, Mom? What's going on?"

"I don't know, honey." Her eyes went to Angela, pleading. "Is everyone all right?"

With a smile, Angela said, "Have faith, dear."

Mary wanted to scream, to rant her frustration but she bit her tongue. Angela walked to her and put her hand on Mary's arm. "They're coming now." The words sent a calming balm flowing through her body. She heard rustling through the back woods and turned to see the group returning.

Sam led the way, followed by Darren who was carrying the dog, and Tricia with one hand gently stroking the dog, the other arm around her husband. Tyler followed, both his arms around Stephanie, and finally Natasha and Franklin, their arms around each other.

Mary was getting worried again until she saw Joe carrying Christy tightly, her little face hidden against his chest. She blew out a huge breath of gratitude. “Bradley, go to the hall closet and pull out several blankets.”

“I’ll start a pot of coffee and cocoa,” Angela said.

With tears in her eyes, Mary ran out the back door, to Joe and crying, threw her arms around the two. As she rubbed Christy’s shaking body, she looked up to Joe, ready to tell her husband the deep desire she’d been hiding in her heart. “Joe—”

“We need to talk to Stephanie. About Christy.”

Through her tears, Mary nodded. “She belongs with us. Doesn’t she?”

Joe couldn’t speak but merely returned the nod.

Angela walked out the backdoor, watching the group in front of her. Tyler and Stephanie were embracing, Natasha and Franklin were kissing passionately. Angela blushed.

Darren and Tricia exchanged tender looks while caring for the dog, and Mary and Joe held Christy tightly. The way it was meant to be.

Angela breathed a sigh of relief. Things were going to work out for everyone.

“Where’s Eldon?”

“He’s waiting with the wolf for animal control.”

“All right. Let’s get everyone indoors so you can tell us what happened,” Angela said, ushering the group toward the inn.

Inside, the group returned to the comfort of the parlor and Sam got a warm fire going in the hearth. Blankets were distributed, along with coffee and hot chocolate.

The cozy room was filled with an atmosphere of relief, joy and yes, love. It gladdened Angela's heart. Everyone listened as Sam retold the story of what had happened in the meadow.

"Why did you go outside, Christy?" Angela asked.

The girl, cradled in Mary's arms, Joe and Bradley sitting close by, said, "I-I wanted to s-show Fur-ed-erico my new doggie. I-it looks like her. She was going i-in the woods."

"I saw little girl run off so I followed," Natasha said.

"My brave, sweet darling," Franklin murmured and kissed her.

Angela took a sip of coffee. "Seems you're not ignoring your heritage, Franklin. Your parents will be very proud."

Joe snapped his fingers. "That's it. The accent is gone."

Franklin smiled, his arm holding Natasha closely. "It is. And I'm okay with that. To be honest, even I was getting a little sick of it." Natasha giggled and rested her hand against his shoulder.

Darren and Tricia sat on the floor, a blanket around them, another around the brave dog they continually rubbed. "You should have seen Frederica. She's a real hero."

"Yes, she it." Angela glanced at Bradley and then at the Matthews. "No one has claimed her. It's obvious that she adores you two." She gave one more glance at Bradley and saw that he was softly talking to Christy, pretending the toy dog was talking to her.

"Why don't you . . . adopt the dog. We'll keep her until she gives birth, of course. As soon as she's allowed to travel, you can take her. We'll help you with any paperwork and shots needed."

Darren turned to Tricia, hopeful. She smiled and said, "Well, it wasn't exactly the adoption I'd expected but . . . somehow it feels right." Darren's face lit up brighter than the large Christmas tree. He leaned over and kissed her.

"Speaking of adoption," Joe began. "Stephanie, we'd like to speak with you."

She turned her dreamy gaze away from Tyler. "Yes?"

After a nod from Mary and a "Go ahead, Papa" from Bradley, he cleared his throat and said, "We'd like to adopt Christy."

The announcement surprised the room but didn't stop the cheers and good wishes from everyone. Angela sighed, looking heavenward with a thankful heart.

"I think that can be arranged," Stephanie said. "I'll speak with my supervisors." Her gaze returned to Tyler. "And I think I have some pull with the orphanage since I'm close to one of their most trusted staff members." Tyler didn't hesitate giving her a little kiss. The cheering continued.

With all the emotion in the room, no one noticed three men entering.

Angela flinched. One more crisis to deal with.

"Good day. Natasha, are you ready?"

The room grew eerily quiet. Natasha glanced at Franklin, who nodded, and turned to face her uncle. She visibly swallowed hard and stood. "I will not be going with you, uncle."

He seemed a bit amused by her words. "What?"

"I have decided to stay in United States. In New York. I will play my violin here."

The only sound in the room was the ticking of the regulator clock on the wall. And Natasha's heavy breaths.

"I see." The man folded his hands in front of him, appearing to be a voice of reason and concern. Angela knew neither was correct. "And how will you do that? The contract with New York Symphony is through me. You have no contacts, no agreements. Even apartment I allow you to live in is through me. Tasha, you cannot survive without me."

Franklin shot to his feet. "She doesn't need you, Vladimir. She is talented enough and smart enough to make it here without your help. In fact, she has the respect of everyone in the symphony and New York. She'll have no trouble finding plenty of work. But more importantly, she has friends. Friends that will make sure she'd not alone or in need of anything you might deign to dole out to her.

"In short, Vlad. She doesn't need you."

His eyes sharpened. "Nor does she need to be connected to poor boy from Bronx who spent more time in jail than he did school. Something I am sure you would not like spread among upper class of world you so desperately want to be part of."

Franklin straightened, fists clenched at his sides. "Go ahead. Tell the world everything, I no longer care."

Angela was proud of the fact that Franklin spoke in a clear, no nonsense tone. It wasn't British, it wasn't the Bronx. It was just Franklin.

"In fact, I've been a coward for too long and I'm done with that. I'm going to embrace my past, use it in my future. And thanks for that, by the way. Because of your intrusion I've decided to start a scholarship program for low income kids in the Bronx with a bent toward music. I'll probably even start teaching there myself." His lips curved in a grin. "You may be responsible for the next Chopin. Hey, maybe I'll even name a scholarship 'The Vladimir Safina Scholarship' after you. What do you think?"

Natasha giggled and Franklin put his arm around her, pulling her close. "You don't have to worry about Natasha, Vlad. She'll be fine."

Vladimir opened his mouth to speak but Angela shot him a look that she knew went straight to his heart. The man's eyes were glued to hers as she communicated silently that he was done here. His eyes widened and his mouth stayed open, nothing coming out.

Finally, he pressed his lips together, turned, and left with his two big goons. Cheers erupted again and Natasha and Franklin hugged.

Angela clapped her hands. "Well, now it doesn't look like there's a big hurry anymore for any of you to leave. Why don't we have Christmas Eve and Christmas Day together, huh?"

Everyone was getting ready for a big surprise that evening. Angela wouldn't tell anyone what was going on, but Natasha was suspicious. Franklin had a smug grin on his face as if he knew something.

Her hair fell long down her back and she giggled as she shook it back. Franklin handed her winter hat and scarf to her and helped her bundle up, her spirit light in anticipation of the evening.

"What're we going to do, what?" Bradley bounced in front of his mother, Christy at his side, imitating him. "Give me a hint." Natasha knew how he felt.

Everyone heard noises outside and Darren looked out the front window, smiling. "I think the surprise is here."

Tricia joined him, her hand coming to Darren's back. "Looks like fun."

The children ran to the door but halted when Mary said, "Hold it, you two." She knelt to make sure both were covered in enough layers for ten children. She smiled and gave each a kiss on the cheek.

Joe opened the door, his jacket covered with sprinkling of fresh snow. "All right, troops. We're ready to go."

"Where are we going?" Tyler asked, his hand in Stephanie's.

"Now that the wolf is taken care of, we're going for a hayride over the countryside to celebrate." Bradley cheered, echoed by Christy.

Everyone walked outside to see a large wagon filled with hay and decorated with colorful lights. The driver tipped his hat and turned to the horses.

Joe climbed up first and helped Mary, Angela, Bradley, and Christy. Darren helped Tricia up. "Honey, do you think it's okay to leave Frederica?"

Darren grinned. "We won't be gone that long." He gently pushed a strand of her hair back. "I love you, Tricia Matthews."

"Back at you, honey," she said softly, burrowing close to him on the bench seat, a blanket around them.

Stephanie and Tyler were next. His hand guided her to the ladder but as she stepped up, her foot completely missed the rung, probably because she was looking at Tyler, causing her to stumble backward, into his arms.

"Stephanie Singer, I love you, even though you're a mess. You'd better marry me so I can keep you safe. From snow drifts, flying garland, stray wolves."

She laughed and nodded. Throwing her arms around his neck, said, "I trust you, Tyler."

They smiled and kissed before he helped her into the wagon.

That left Franklin and Natasha. She turned her attention from the wagon to the contraption behind it. Franklin guided her over to stand in front of it and she gasped before letting loose a burst of joyful laughter. "Jiggly Bells!"

Franklin laughed. "I decided it was time you dashed through the snow in a one horse open sleigh."

Her eyes met his, becoming blurry with happy tears. "Jiggly Bells." She took his face in her hands and kissed him tenderly.

Once seated, Franklin took the reins to drive. "So, my dear. Tell me how freedom feels?"

Natasha's eyes went to the sky, watching a scattering of snowflakes drift about. "More wonderful than my heart could have imagined. Is like air of Vermont—refreshing, invigorating . . ." She caught a snowflake on her glove. "And filled with million amazing possibilities."

When everyone was settled, a shout went to the horses and they set off down the lane, o'er the fields, the group singing Christmas carols and laughing along the way.

Except for Natasha, who snuggled up with Franklin and discovered "what fun it was."

Christmas morning began before dawn with Bradley jumping on his parents' bed and declaring what day it was. He stopped by Christy's room to wake her before Mary could stop him and the two hurried down the stairs eager to open presents.

Mary had made sure that everything Christy had told Sam she wanted was wrapped and under the tree. She smiled to herself, thankful and hopeful that it was the first of many Christmases together. She blinked back the tears at the thought.

As she made coffee to wake herself and Joe, she said a quiet prayer of thanks. Thanks for receiving her deepest and most heartfelt Christmas wish. She sniffed before she cried aloud.

The back door opened and Tricia hurried in. "Mary! Have you got any more towels that we can use for Frederica?"

"What?" She glanced out the window. "What's going on?"

"She's having the puppies. Now."

"Oh, good Lord!" Mary quickly went to her old towel box in the mudroom and put them in the dryer to warm up. She was so full of questions, she didn't know what to start with.

Bradley and Christy came in to see what was taking so long and when they heard the news, both began asking questions.

"We woke up about four. I . . . just had a feeling. When we went to the barn, we heard her moaning. Darren took one look and knew the puppies were coming. She just entered the second stage of labor. It won't be long now."

"Wow! Their birthday is Christmas Day!"

"Seems appropriate, wouldn't you say?" Mary added. She pulled out the warm towels and handed them to Tricia. "Bradley, get your Papa. Tell him what's going on."

"Should I get Sam and Eldon?"

She hesitated. "Um, they had to leave yesterday. I'm afraid we're on our own."

A few hours and a couple of pots of coffee later, everyone sat quietly in the barn. Even the other animals sensed the imminence of new life and respectfully kept the noise down.

The final count was five puppies—three boys and two girls. As the group cooed and held the dogs, Mary said, "What are we going to do with these little ones?"

Joe lifted a shoulder. "I suppose since Frederica belongs to the Matthews, they should have a say."

"I'm open to suggestions," Darren said, softly rubbing the tired mama.

Joe and Mary shared a look and turned to Bradley. "Son, why don't you pick one out?"

His eyes grew big, his mouth gaped. "I . . . it's what I really wanted for Christmas!"

Joe hid a grin and winked at Mary. "Imagine that. I guess you're going to get your wish, then."

"This one!" Bradley lowered his head to the pup he held in his arms. The animal licked his face making him giggle. "Wait, it is a boy puppy, isn't it?" He leaned toward Christy. "Don't want to make that mistake again."

Darren checked and said, "Yep. It's a male."

"Whew!" Everyone chuckled at Bradley's exclamation.

"Well, looks like everyone got what they wanted for Christmas," Bradley announced. "I got a dog and Christy got to live here with us."

"Wait, that was her Christmas wish?" Mary asked. "The one she shared with Sam and Angela?"

Angela smiled, her eyes going to Mary. "Merry Christmas, dear."

Mary's voice choked on tears. "Merry Christmas, Angela."

"Oh, I think I hear the phone. I'll get it." Before anyone could say anything, she hurried out of the barn to the inn's kitchen. "Good morning, Sam. Everything go well last night?"

His chuckle was loud and long. "Smooth as silk. Just calling for the rundown on everyone this morning."

"We've had a bit of excitement. Frederica went into labor. She just delivered five puppies."

"Ho, ho! I'm so sorry I missed that! What an amazing Christmas."

"One of our best yet." The silence on the other end caused her to sigh. "I suppose you want to know what's next."

"Of course."

"Franklin will gift a girl pup to Natasha, which they'll take back to the city."

"Won't that be hard seeing as they'll probably be traveling with their jobs?"

"No worries. Franklin has a big family who'll love to babysit. And who'll become Natasha's new family. Especially after she and Franklin marry next year."

"Ah, I'm so glad. Weren't sure about them at the beginning. So much animosity between them."

"So many times animosity covers deep fear."

"And what about young Stephanie and Tyler?"

Angela sighed. "She just needed to see that she could trust someone again and she certainly can trust that young man. He adores her. They'll find out that together they are stronger, more competent, and can accomplish much more than they ever could apart."

"But they live so far apart."

"Yes, but with Stephanie's stellar record, she'll have no trouble transferring to Newport and adding to the orphanages pool of resources. In fact, they're taking a puppy to the orphanage to become a sort of mascot."

"The children there are going to be very blessed to have those two."

"I agree. Tyler and Stephanie will be surrogate parents to all of them."

"Which makes me think of Darren and Tricia. Seems they've settled their disagreement."

"Absolutely in a way that I think neither expected. You see, certain people in the world have a special gift—a love and desire to protect God's creatures. These two have it but have been blocking that gift just in the living of daily life, but no more. They'll take Frederica and two puppies back with them."

"What about their condo?"

"Going on the market. They'll settle outside the city on a large piece of property where they'll have as many homeless and injured animals as they want."

"I can completely understand that." Sam chuckled, then grew serious. "But what about children?"

Angela paused. "I really don't know. Not anytime soon. They'll be too busy, moving to the country, selling their practice—"

"Selling their practice?"

"Darren's going back to school. To be a veterinarian, working with his brother."

"That's so good."

"Yes, it is. They understand their purpose now and not only have accepted it, they're thrilled about it. God will richly bless them."

"Of that, I have no doubt. And our beloved Puletti's? What about them?"

Angela's joy overflowed in her laughter. "We'll get a new addition. Permanently in a few months. Actually, two new additions. Bradley gets the last puppy."

"Oh, I'm so glad. He really wanted his own dog."

"Yes, but Fred?"

Sam laughed out loud and Angela could almost see his face beaming. "Oh, and I know that Christy will love her present from Santa—the Santa doll with the blonde little girl on his lap. Well done."

"What? Don't know what you're talking about."

Angela chuckled. "Have it your way. In any case, it's turned out to be a very blessed Christmas."

"Indeed. It's a shame the owner couldn't be a part of all this."

"How do you know he wasn't?"

There was silence before Sam said, "I knew it? He *was* around! Am I right?"

Angela chuckled. "Yep. Who do you think provided the wagon and sleigh last night." Her eyes twinkled, a glow over her face.

"And drove the wagon."

THE END

Other Sweet Romance Holiday Stories by Malinda Martin

Sleep In Heavenly Peace Inn

Three couples at the Sleep in Heavenly Peace Inn must deal with their tumultuous relationships. With the help of three children, a man with a white beard, the inn's mysterious manager, and a reindeer, maybe they can do just that.

Christmas Grace

It's the most wonderful time of the year for everyone in Charity except Grace Hudson. She associates Christmas with bad memories and is determined to be immune from the cheerful holiday. All she really wants is to sell the diner that she inherited and move far away. Award-winning photographer Stuart "Mac" McCrae needs to get that one perfect picture before heading south for the holidays. The only thing holding him back is the small, undecorated diner that sits in the middle of the beautiful main street of Charity.

Comfort And Joy

Joy Bisset never lives anywhere for long. However, Charity, Florida is slowly capturing her heart. And seeing Holly, Noel, and their lonely father Ross struggling, she can't help but lend a hand. Ross Jackson is swamped, running a business and raising his two children. So the lonely widower can't resist the offer from the petite new waitress at Hal's Place to help with the kids. Then when Joy needs help, Ross and his family come to her rescue. It doesn't have to be personal and he doesn't have to forget the vows he made to his late wife. And she doesn't have to lose her heart to the strong, handsome man. But Christmas is a season for miracles, especially in Charity.

Merry Mary

All your favorite Charity characters are back to enjoy the season in the charming small town that lives up to its name. Mary Swenson's vision of a quiet Christmas spent with her father is shattered when she's made the director of the Charity, Florida Christmas Eve Parade. Then her estranged mother, a successful events planner in New York, shows up with a sexy assistant to help plan the parade. Trevor Crane isn't exactly sure why he's in a small Florida town for the holidays. He only knows that his employer, the spirited Merrilyn Kennedy Swenson, needs him and if he's going to take over her business one day, he'll do her bidding. Even if it means ignoring her beautiful daughter.

Carol Of The Bells

It's Christmas in Charity, which means time for another sweet Christmas romance. Shy, kindergarten teacher Carol Baker is in love with the resident scientist slash professor. Problem is he doesn't know her. Dr. Bradley Moore is making a splash in the science world but finds himself distracted when the pretty teacher asks for his assistance with a project. With counsel and help (?) from Grace, Big Jed, Holly, and others in Charity, maybe this unlikely pair will get together. But not before they learn the true meaning of the words of the Christmas angel—"Fear not."

Christmas Dad

Bethany and Samuel Fitzgerald are tired of having no dad for the holidays. When they discover a friendly transient at the inner city help center where their mother volunteers, they devise a plan to hire him to be their "Christmas Dad."

Forgetting Christmas

Ali Benson wakes up from a car crash with the last six months of her life forgotten. Along with the fact that she's engaged to marry Michael Grayson, her handsome boss, on Christmas Day. Ali and Michael deal with the season in different ways as she tries to remember and he tries to forget. But this Christmas they'll both have to confront the truth. And hopefully find that sometimes remembering is the best part of Christmas.

Coming Next Month

The Midnight Kiss

There's an old legend concerning the males of the Farrell family. On a special New Year's Eve, each one will share a kiss with the love they are destined to marry.

. . . Whether they like it or not.

For a sneak preview, turn the page.

The Midnight Kiss

The only thing worse than being alone on New Year's Eve was being alone at a party on New Year's Eve. But if she hadn't accepted her attorney's invitation to attend the firm's annual bash she would have been spending the evening with her mother.

A close second to being alone at a party on New Year's Eve.

The room was filled with beautiful people. Beautiful, cultured, intelligent people who probably didn't have a thing in common with her. She glanced at the conservative attire, black and beige gowns and cocktail dresses, black tuxedos. Her eyes glimpsed her deep red dress with the flirty skirt. Her silver pumps practically glittered in the dim lights of the room, entirely out of place with this group. She took another sip of her champagne and sighed. Maybe she should just go home to mom.

Across the room she noticed a man standing amidst a group. Her eyes were drawn to something about him. He wore the standard black tux but his casual stance spoke of confidence. His eyes crinkled as he laughed at something said and even from across the room, she could tell they were a stunning shade of blue, unlike any she'd seen before. He spoke to the others in his group with an ease of being comfortable in his own skin, something she admired. She couldn't help wondering about him. Who was he and why was he more interesting to her than anyone else in the room?

She wouldn't approach him to find the answers for several reasons but the main one being the female that was with him, laughing loudly at the joke he must have told. The woman looked the perfect girlfriend for any lawyer. She was thin, dressed in an elegant, yet demure black sheath, brilliant white pearls glimmering around her neck. Her glossy blonde hair was pulled into a French twist, her makeup was understated but perfectly applied. She watched as the woman leaned into him, her hand caressing his arm, enjoying his attention. Could she blame her?

"Gabrielle, there you are. I've been looking for you."

She smiled. "Hi, Joyce. I haven't been here long. Thanks for inviting me."

Joyce Burns, ambitious law partner of Creighton, Banks, Tomlinson, and Burns took her arm and led her deeper into the room. The woman, short and compact, friendly face that hid a killer instinct, said, "I'm thrilled you're here. We love sharing New Year's with our favorite clients." She stopped and whispered, "And your Christmas gifts for me and my office definitely made you our favorite client. My husband wants to petition to make you a saint."

Gabrielle laughed. There were perks to owning a large, successful lingerie company, one being to share with others. It was a trait her mother possessed and had taught her—a positive trait to offset the glaring mistake her mother had made and the one Gabrielle feared repeating.

"Now, I want to introduce you around." Joyce took her arm and strolled. "Quite a few eligible bachelors here. Handsome, successful. Just let me know if one interests you."

Gabrielle tensed. "Thanks but no thanks." To Joyce's confused expression she said, "I'm so busy with my company, I'm afraid I just don't have the time." Or the inclination.

After a moment of Joyce's scrutiny, the woman sighed. "Such a waste. To be as young and beautiful as you and not be in love."

She shrugged. "I love my business."

"Yes, but will your business keep you warm on a cold night?"

"When I use my profits to buy flannel sheets, yes." They both chuckled and Gabrielle was relieved when Joyce turned the conversation to business.

"Before I forget, I wanted to mention that I'll be adding an associate to the team regarding your case."

Her face tightened. "Oh, does that mean that it's a bigger case than we expected?"

A former employee of "Lingerie By Gabby" had filed a suit, saying Gabrielle had stolen her designs when in fact, the employee had been fired for stealing from the company coffers.

Joyce patted her hand and said, "Not at all, but I do want another attorney with us. You know, my daughter is about to give birth in Connecticut.

If I have to leave, I want someone familiar with the case to assist."

The world of suits and cases, law and procedure was so foreign to her. She'd just have to trust Joyce, which she did. She nodded and said, "So, who's going to be helping?"

Joyce grinned and headed for Mr. Confident Blue Eyes. Her pulse raced and her breathing grew shallow. It couldn't be.

"Max? If you've got a moment?"

Yep. It was him.

"Joyce. Happy New Year." He reached over and gave Joyce a peck on the cheek, smiling. Gabrielle already liked him.

His eyes wandered to her and she felt she could have drowned in the depths of the blue. He gave her a smile that went through her body, warming her like a soft blanket on a cold night. She returned the smile.

Breaking the spell, Joyce said, "Same to you. I'd like to introduce you to someone." She turned and said, "Gabrielle, this is Maxwell Farrell, one of our most brilliant attorneys who I happen to be personally grooming to become the next partner of our illustrious company. Oh, Max, FYI, the partners are meeting in April. I'm hoping to present your name at that time."

"You're an angel, Joyce."

The woman chuckled and put her arm around Gabrielle. "Max, Gabrielle Bellini, president and owner of 'Lingerie by Gabby.' I told you about her case."

His eyes stayed on her, sparkling with warmth. “Yes, the one you want my assist with.” He stretched out his hand and said, “A pleasure to meet you.”

“Yes, you, too.”

After shaking, Max’s arm was yanked and he turned. “Oh, I’m sorry. Allow me to introduce Kay Woods.”

“How do you do?” Gabrielle said, shaking the hand of the man’s date.

“Very well, thank you. ‘Lingerie by Gabby.’ Isn’t that the little factory on the lower Eastside?” Her eyes were shrewd, as if sizing up the competition.

“No, actually. We’re on Fiftieth and Lexington. Feel free to come by sometime and I’ll give you a free sample, if you’d like.”

“You’re sweet,” Kay said, her expression implying the opposite. “Max, I think I saw Mr. Banks over by the bar. We really must say hello, you know he doesn’t usually attend parties.” She wrapped her arms around his arm and with one finger, caressed his bicep.

“Of course, in a minute.” Apparently unaware of the power play, Max said to Gabrielle, “I’ve been looking over your case, Ms. Bellini. I don’t think you have anything to worry about. Joyce has done an excellent job in preparing for court.”

Her eyes were momentarily blinded by the man’s smile. “Good. That’s . . . good.”

“Oh look, honey, Mr. Creighton just joined him.”

"You two go on ahead," Joyce said. As soon as they were out of earshot, she murmured, "Shrew."

"Excuse me?"

Joyce shook her head. "Nothing." Smiling, she said, "Come on and get in on this delicious buffet. By the way, great dress!"

As the clock neared the midnight hour, Max stood by large windows looking down on the madness of Times Square, grateful he wasn't there. The twentieth story ballroom afforded him the opportunity to view the large crystal ball as it descended, bringing in the new year, while staying out of the masses. Good deal.

He wondered if he could see his brothers. Anthony was down there somewhere with his girlfriend, and Charlie, a cop, was on duty. He hoped they were okay and . . . safe. Not from pickpockets or drunken partiers or even serial killers. He hoped they were safe from the Farrell folklore. He wondered how his father's talk, the one he'd been given tonight, had gone over with them. Surely they'd been as excited as he had with the same old spiel.

Glancing through the room, his eyes fell on the stunning woman Joyce had introduced him to. Gabrielle Bellini. Successful, savvy, generous. And exquisite. Her hair, a mass of dark brown with flecks of red, fell in curls around her bare shoulders reaching almost to her waist. Her dark eyes were big and yet made the most interesting oval. Quite exotic. And her small smile had literally knocked him back. If Kay hadn't been there, he'd have engaged her in conversation.

Max sighed thinking of Kay. Was he a cad for forgetting he had a date when a stunning female that had his heart pounding in his chest walks up? Obviously he should rethink his seeing Kay outside of the office.

He studied Gabrielle. The red dress she wore revealed a toned, curvy body. Being that she owned a lingerie company, he could only guess what finery she wore beneath. A waiter passed and he snagged a fresh glass of champagne.

She caught him staring and smiled. He saluted with a lift of his glass. Thinking this was the perfect time to get to know her—for her case, that is—he walked over, grabbing another glass from a tray as it passed.

"You looked thirsty." He offered the glass and their hands brushed. Hers was soft, delicate.

"Thank you." He watched her take a sip and lick a drip off her lips, a shade of red that matched her dress.

Music started in the room and couples took to the dance floor. She glanced in that direction and said, "It's a nice party, isn't it?"

"It is." He turned to the window. "Best view in the city."

They both gazed at the party occurring below them, comfortable with the silence. Finally, she said, "I've only been in that craziness once, when I was a senior in high school."

"What'd you think of it?"

She took a deep breath. "Great, if you like standing all day with a bunch of loud tourists determined to party and get drunk. Once was enough. What about you?"

"My mother talked my dad into taking us a couple of times when I was growing up. Even though it was a pain, she loved it. New Years in Times Square was special to her and she wanted to share it with us."

"That's a nice memory. You have brothers and sisters?"

"Two brothers. You?"

"Only child. I envy you."

He smirked. "Sometimes I wished for only child status." She giggled, a throaty sound unlike the delicate woman before him, and sent a spear of desire through his body. He took a sip and then said, "Actually I pitied my parents for having to raise us. We didn't make it easy. I mean, one of us turned out to be a lawyer."

Again the giggle. "What about the others?"

"Anthony's a contractor and Charlie's a cop."

"Your mother must be really proud."

Max couldn't help the lump that formed in his throat or the ache in his heart. "Ah, she passed away ten years ago."

Her smile faded. "Oh, I am so sorry."

"Thanks." His eyes went back to the crowds below. "Mom loved New Year's Eve. My dad kissed her for the first time there. She said they both knew then that they'd make a life together."

"What a sweet story."

Uncomfortable, Max cleared his throat determined to change the conversation. "I'd like to meet with you before the court date. Just in case I have to take Joyce's place. Would that be all right?"

"Sure. Just call my office and we'll set something up."

Before he could answer, the band played a loud fanfare and the leader said, "Get ready, everyone. Only a minute to go!"

Max and Gabrielle found themselves pushed against the windows as everyone rushed to watch the ball make its journey to the new year. As they bumped against each other, she said, "Sorry."

"No problem," Max replied, not bothered in the least to have her body slide against his.

The anticipation grew as everyone started to chant the time. "Ten-nine-eight."

Max looked around for Kay. Shouldn't your date be by your side when the clock struck midnight?

"Seven-six-five."

Maybe he'd walk around and try to find her. After he watched the ball fall.

"Four-three-two-one! Happy New Year!"

Cheers, whistles, noisemakers filled the air. All around him, couples were having that first kiss of the new year. Feeling a little left out, he again scanned the room for Kay.

Then he noticed Gabrielle. As she also watched all the kissing, she looked . . . lost, lonely. As if everyone there were part of a secret club that had no intention of admitting her. Had he ever felt that way? He remembered distinctly leaving the hospital after his mother died. Yeah, he'd felt that way.

Apparently, she sensed his gaze and turned to him, giving him a small smile that was like a punch to the solar plexus. In that moment he wanted desperately to make Gabrielle happy.

Taking a breath he said, "You know, I think it's probably bad luck to go against tradition."

"Huh?"

The edges of his lips quirked. "Midnight. New Years. I believe you're supposed to share a kiss. Do you mind?"

"Ah, okay. I am sorta superstitious." He took that as permission and stepped closer to her, still giving her the opportunity to refuse if she wanted.

Cautiously, he leaned in. "Happy new year, Ms. Bellini." Gently, he touched his lips to hers, his intention being a simple kiss, a mere meeting of the lips to fulfill tradition. And to hopefully get the lonely look out of her eyes.

Who knew he was to get the surprise of his life.

***The Midnight Kiss.* Coming next month.**
For updates, go to www.malindamartin.com.

Want more sweet romance? Claim your free book, *Tennessee Waltz*, at www.malindamartin.com.

Ben Malone is the sheriff of the small county he grew up in. Not his original plan for his life but he's adapted. When a storm blows in, bringing a young mother and her two children, he's determined to protect them. It's his job. Just because the woman has beautiful wheat-colored hair and a secret that makes her eyes haunted, it doesn't mean he'd interested.

Ellie Kent must make a new life for her and her son and daughter. Even though she's tired of traveling and the town of Ellerton, specifically the sheriff, has been kind, they've got to keep moving on so they don't bring trouble to the area.

Dear Reader,

Thank you so much for joining me in another Christmas at the Sleep In Heavenly Peace Inn. These characters have come to mean so much to me and I love to see the magic of the season change their lives for the better.

There's a lot in store for sweet romance readers in the new year with not only a new trilogy of books—The Midnight Kiss trilogy—but also re-releases of the first four Castle Clubhouse series, along with a prequel novella and the next story in the series. Next Christmas, we'll go back to Charity, Florida to check in with Grace, Mac, and the Jeds, among others.

If you haven't joined my email list for news and updates, please go to www.malindamartin.com and sign up. You'll receive a free book, *Tennessee Waltz*, just for signing up, along with the sequel, *Tennessee Shuffle*, next year.

As always, I so appreciate your support and encouragement. You can always reach me through my Facebook page or website, as well as info@malindamartin.com. If you would, please be sure to leave a comment on the *Sleep In Heavenly Peace Inn Two* book page. This helps the book sites to advertise to other sweet romance readers. Let's spread the word that there is a market for clean, inspirational romance!

May you and your family experience the true joy of Christmas this year, not only now, but through the coming year. “Glory to God in the highest. Peace on earth and goodwill to all men.”

Blessings and Merry Christmas,
M.M.